"You have a b**g corner of your** **the pad of her** **corner of his n**

"Did that get it?" Reese asked, his voice noticeably huskier than usual.

"No. Hmm." She leaned forward slowly, her gaze locking on his. "Guess I'll have to get it this way."

She closed the distance between them very slowly, giving him plenty of time to pull away. But he didn't. He sat perfectly still, unable to believe that this beautiful, fey creature was leaning in toward him, closer and closer.

Gently, so lightly he barely felt it, her mouth touched the corner of his. Her lips were soft and plump, and then—

Jesus, Mary and Joseph. That's her tongue.

She licked the corner of his mouth. It was a quick little flick with just the tip of her tongue against his skin, but there was no mistaking it. All of a sudden, there wasn't nearly enough oxygen in his living room. Either that or he was no-kidding hyperventilating.

"There," she whispered. "That's better."

* * *

**The Coltons of Kansas: Truth. Justice.
And secrets they can't hide.**

* * *

**If you're on Twitter, tell us what you
think of Harlequin Romantic Suspense!
#harlequinromsuspense**

Dear Reader,

Participating in one of the Colton continuities has always been a big deal for me. I love getting to play with a bunch of my esteemed fellow authors on what is usually a very lonely job. Plus, it's exciting to see the great things they come up with as we flesh out a new series together.

But I have to confess I was terrified when asked to write the final book in this installment of the Colton family saga. It's a big responsibility to give you, awesome reader, a satisfying story in its own right, but also to tie up all the loose ends of a whole family full of unfolding happy-ever-afters.

Thankfully, the authors who went before me in this latest collection gave me the most amazing cast of living, breathing characters to play with as I crafted my own story within the world of the Colton clan. Truly, they made my job easy, and for that I am extremely grateful. Almost as grateful as I am to you—for making it possible for me to tell these wonderful stories of love and family conquering every challenge set before them with laughter, grit and grace.

Without any further ado, I'd like to invite you to sit back, relax and enjoy this story. Happy reading until the next time we meet between the pages of a book!

Warmly,

Cindy

COLTON IN THE LINE OF FIRE

Cindy Dees

HARLEQUIN
ROMANTIC
SUSPENSE

Special thanks and acknowledgment are given to Cindy Dees for her contribution to The Coltons of Kansas miniseries.

Recycling programs
for this product may
not exist in your area.

ISBN-13: 978-1-335-62681-3

Colton in the Line of Fire

Copyright © 2020 by Harlequin Books S.A.

This edition published by arrangement with Harlequin Books S.A.

For questions and comments about the quality of this book, please contact us at CustomerService@Harlequin.com.

Harlequin Enterprises ULC
22 Adelaide St. West, 40th Floor
Toronto, Ontario M5H 4E3, Canada
www.Harlequin.com

Printed in U.S.A.

New York Times and *USA TODAY* bestselling author **Cindy Dees** is the author of more than fifty novels. She draws upon her experience as a US Air Force pilot to write romantic suspense. She's a two-time winner of the prestigious RITA® Award for romance fiction, a two-time winner of the RT Reviewers' Choice Best Book Award for Romantic Suspense and an *RT Book Reviews* Career Achievement Award nominee. She loves to hear from readers at www.cindydees.com.

Books by Cindy Dees

Harlequin Romantic Suspense

The Coltons of Kansas

Colton in the Line of Fire

Runaway Ranch

Navy SEAL's Deadly Secret

Mission Medusa

Special Forces: The Recruit
Special Forces: The Spy
Special Forces: The Operator

The Coltons of Roaring Springs

Colton Under Fire

Code: Warrior SEALs

Undercover with a SEAL
Her Secret Spy
Her Mission with a SEAL
Navy SEAL Cop

Visit Cindy's Author Profile page at Harlequin.com for more titles.

Chapter 1

Bedroom eyes.

Detective Reese Carpenter had no-kidding bedroom eyes.

And he was flashing them at her right now, leaning his elbows on the high counter at the front of her crime lab. How was a woman supposed to get any work done with a guy so flat-out sexy hanging around? It was all she could do not to stop, stand and stare at him. And maybe drool a little.

"Have you got anything for me?" he asked.

His hair was dark, his eyes bright, movie-star blue, brimming with sultry charm, sophisticated intelligence, wry humor and a hint of mischief. Totally made her think of sex—great sex and lots of it.

"Earth to Yvette Colton. Come in."

She blinked rapidly, clearing the image of her sister's

cop-partner naked and in her bed, taking her to the stars and back. Darn his bedroom eyes, anyway.

"What do you want, now?" she asked in an aggrieved tone. "Or are you finally going to give up telling me how to do my job and just take over the forensic lab yourself?"

As pretty as he might be, Reese Carpenter was also an almighty pain in the tuchus. A know-it-all who got all up in her business and was forever telling her how to do her job. This might be her first time running her own crime lab, but she'd trained with the best forensic scientists in the business, thank you very much.

"You gotta help me out, here," her unwanted visitor declared. "I need something concrete I can pin on Markus Dexter. Give me a smoking gun. I *know* he did it."

"It" being the double murder of a woman, Olivia Harrison, and a private investigator, Fenton Crane, twenty-six years ago. Their bodies had been hidden in the walls of the Crest View warehouse in Braxville, Kansas, and discovered during a renovation last summer. To complicate matters, the entire warehouse had been blown up by a saboteur last month.

"I can only process evidence so fast, Detective. And it's not like that's my only case. In fact, at the moment, I'm running tests for arsenic on the remains of the Crest View warehouse."

"Did you find any?" he asked.

"Not in this sample. It appears the arsenic-laced wood was used only for framing walls. The floor joists didn't contain arsenic, but their wood was sourced in North America. Only the batch of wood from China was contaminated."

"As we thought," he responded with a brisk nod.

She turned her attention back to the test tube in her hand, but he huffed audibly. She looked up once more, surprised that he was still hovering in her lab. He declared, "I *have* to find something to tie Dexter to the bodies in that warehouse."

"I thought your job was to be a dispassionate investigator and go where the facts lead you, and not go looking for facts to support your theories."

He huffed harder, turned on his heel and stomped out of her lab, his business-suit-clad physique entirely too tempting to be legal.

An hour later, Reese was back. "Anything?" he asked without preamble.

"No. And I won't find any answers if you keep interrupting me," she snapped at him and his bedroom eyes. This time he'd lost the coat and tie and wore only slacks and a white dress shirt that showed off shoulders in no need of padding to make them appear athletic. He wasn't a bulky guy, but he definitely was in great shape. Moreover, his sleeves were rolled up to reveal leanly muscled forearms still holding over a bit of tan from last summer.

A flash of irritated blue was all she glimpsed of his expression as he turned and stomped out…again. She totally knew the feeling.

Another hour passed. This time he merely poked his head in through the hallway door and called out, "How about now?"

"Go away, Carpenter!" she called back. At the moment, she was bent over a spectrometer trying to recalibrate the stupid thing so she could run the last batch of wood slivers from the Crest View warehouse explosion.

She added for good measure, "And don't come back until I call you or you've got a darned good reason for interrupting my work!"

* * *

Exactly one hour later, her lab door opened again.

She didn't even bother to look up. "Reese, I could set my watch off your visits down here. Are you setting an alarm for every hour on the hour to remind yourself to come to my lab and bug me?"

"Yeah, actually. I am."

That made her glance sidelong in his direction. "You do know that pestering me incessantly isn't doing a blessed thing to speed up my work, right? I'm handling all this evidence as quickly as I can, and you poking at me isn't going to make the work go any faster. It's only ticking me off."

He shrugged and grinned without a shred of remorse.

Man, his smile was nearly as lethal as his eyes. It was all boyish charm and manly sex appeal. She looked down at her workstation hastily, not seeing a thing on her computer screen. "At least turn your alarm off," she muttered. "You're driving me crazy."

"I can work with crazy," he purred. "I would only be worried if you didn't have any opinion at all about me."

That made her head snap up. New tactic from him, perhaps? If badgering her didn't yield the proof he needed to convict Dexter, was Reese going to try to seduce it out of her? Gulp.

Right now, she was dissolving mortar scraped off bricks at the Crest View crime scene into a solution she would run through the spectrometer. She was hoping to find the chemical composition of the explosive used to demolish the building, and while she was at it, look for arsenic that might have seeped into the walls from the contaminated wood that was used to frame the structure.

"Go. Away. And quit bugging me. You're a pest."

"Aww, come on. I'm not that bad. Let me help with something."

She pointed a long glass pipette at him like a magic wand, waving the pencil-thick stirring stick at him and intoning, "Begonus pain-in-the-assikus."

He laughed, and darned if that mischievous sparkle in his eyes didn't get even more pronounced. "Admit it. I'm a cute pain the ass, though."

Her gaze narrowed. "Toddlers are cute. But that doesn't mean I want one running around my lab wrecking everything in sight."

"Did you just call me a child?" he asked darkly.

"I might've," she replied defiantly. Dang it. Her and her big mouth. It was forever getting her into trouble. And now an intimidating cop was abruptly staring at her in cool challenge, his eyes as hard and cold as chips of sea ice.

"We'll see about that," he murmured. "I'll bet I can change your mind fast enough."

"Oh, yeah? How?" she blurted. Dumb, dumb, dumb. The first rule of dealing with alpha males was never, ever to throw down a dare in front of one.

Reese moved swiftly around the front counter and he loomed over her, six feet tall to her five feet, five inches on a good day. In socks. Thick ones.

All that crackling sex appeal was suddenly back, pouring off him in tangible waves. Dude. How did he do that? One minute he was a total pro—just the facts, ma'am—and the next he was this smoking-hot chick magnet, all come-hither looks and irresistible, masculine charm.

It was those cursed bedroom eyes of his.

One thing she knew for sure, this man was strictly off-limits. No way was she sleeping with a guy who could kiss and tell to her big—protective—sis. And given that Reese and Jordana spent hours and hours together every single day at work, Reese would surely end up spilling the beans.

Her sister was an excellent cop and talented interrogator. Jordana would pry every sordid detail out of her partner.

God, what she wouldn't give to be able to manage this infuriating man the way her sister did. As it was, he was a constant thorn in her side, continually commenting on her procedures, calling her out for every corner she dared to even think about cutting, watching her like a hawk, down to the most minute detail of her job.

It wasn't that she minded being held to a high standard or even to perfection. It was the insufferable way he did it that drove her around the bend. More than once in the past year, she'd seriously considered killing him. And she *did* know how to hide his body.

Honestly, she had no interest in dating any cop. Not only would it be it tricky at best to date someone she worked with, but cops were not her jam. They tended to be so confident. Assertive. Convinced of their rightness at all times.

Nope. Reese Carpenter could take his bedroom eyes and seductive smile and flash them both at some other poor soul who had no idea what an irritating man lurked behind them.

She took a step back and carefully released the deeply annoyed breath she realized she was holding. "Why are you here, Detective?"

"My name is Reese. Feel free to use it, dar—"

She interrupted his drawl. "Do *not* call me darling. Or honey, or anything pertaining to sugar. And if you call me little lady, I will have to shoot you."

He grinned. Lazy, sexy, *knowing*. What the heck did he think he knew about her that she didn't?

Nope, nope, nope. Not getting personal with this guy. She would not lob even a hint of encouragement in this supremely arrogant male's direction.

"How's the evidence processing coming from the bodies in the wall?" Reese asked in an abruptly impersonal, professional tone.

Whoa. Mental whiplash.

Something in her tummy fell in disappointment. Well, shoot. She wanted him to quit flirting, and now she was upset when he did? Yikes, she was a hot mess.

She cleared her throat, stood as tall as she could and tried to sound marginally like the expert in her field that she was. "Umm, I just got back the analysis of the insect carcasses found in the wall with the bodies."

"Are they twenty-six years old, too?" he asked dryly. "We already know Olivia and Fenton were killed that long ago because of when the building wall they were hidden in was built. I can't understand why you wasted department money sending out some dead bugs to tell us that."

"Because I'm good at my job," she replied tartly. "And because I noticed right away that the types of bugs found in the walls with each body were different. But I'm not a forensic entomologist, so I spent some of your precious police budget on having an expert examine them."

"And?"

"And, the insects found with the woman were primarily mosquitoes, flies, and interestingly, earwigs."

"What's so interesting about earwigs?" he asked.

"They're predominantly spring insects."

"So?"

"The insects with the male remains included spiders, fleas, and notably, stink bugs."

"Stink bugs."

She nodded. "Stink bugs. They're predominantly a fall insect. We can conjecture from the different species of insect remains that our bodies in the walls were murdered some months apart. Something like six months. Ms. Harrison was closed into the wall in the springtime. Mr. Crane's corpse wasn't entombed in the wall until the fall."

She waxed enthusiastic, as she usually did when her job yielded fascinating results. "If we assume the killer or killers hid the bodies quickly after time of death, we can conclude that they were murdered *months* apart." She finished in triumph, "We're looking at two distinct and separate homicides."

Reese groaned.

"What?" she blurted, startled. She'd expected him to be excited by her find.

"The department is stretched thin as it is investigating one murder. And now you want to double the workload?" he groused.

"I still think the two murders were committed by the same person. Both were struck in the back of the head by a person about six feet tall and right-handed, using similar force and similar blunt objects for each blow. You're still only hunting for a single killer. But two murder scenes. Two sets of motives."

"We'll never find the murder scenes. They were erased a quarter century ago. There won't even be trace evidence left by now."

A pang of grief stabbed her in the heart. Her best friend in middle school, Debbie Boyd, had been murdered almost fifteen years ago. Any evidence from her death was also likely degraded and long gone. Like her killer. Yvette's own frustration at having never solved Debbie's murder was the main reason she hadn't strangled Reese Carpenter already. She actually understood his burning drive to solve the Harrison-Crane murders.

"Speaking of murder scenes, how goes the processing of the materials we brought in from searching Markus Dexter's home?"

Dexter—one of the two main partners in Colton Construction, which built the Crest View warehouse—was the prime suspect in the cold case killings after he had mysteriously disappeared from Braxville shortly after the bodies were uncovered last summer.

She answered, "I'm digging through everything you brought in as quickly as I can, but I'm a one-woman lab, and it's going to take me some time to get through it all."

The number of evidence bags brought in from the home numbered in the hundreds, and some of the contents would require scientific processing. She was still entering a description of the contents of each one into a database along with the date, time and place it had been collected. She had yet to even begin examining the evidence inside the bags.

"Have you found anything to link Dexter to the murders?" Reese asked. She detected an underlying note of desperation in his voice that actually provoked answering sympathy in her gut.

"Not yet."

"But you'll keep looking? You gotta help me out, here, Yvette. I *need* a positive link between Dexter and the murders."

Lord, that man was pushy. "It's not as if the guy left a candlestick in his desk drawer with a card taped to it saying, 'Murder weapon used in the library by Professor Plum,' if that's what you're asking."

"Are you always so prickly?" he demanded.

"When people interfere in my work and prevent me from doing my job, always."

He threw up his hands. "Okay, okay. I can take a hint. I'll get out of here."

"Did you actually have a specific reason for coming down here this time? I did make that a pre-condition for you coming back to bother me, as I recall."

Her lab was in the basement of the new Braxville Police Department building. It was as snazzy a facility as she'd ever worked in, and the new lab that came with it was first-class. She just wished there was funding for a second forensics technician to go with all the fancy, state-of-the art equipment.

Although, truth be told, Braxville wasn't normally a hub of violent crime, or much crime at all. The suburb of Wichita was usually a quiet, pleasant little place. She'd thought this would be a nice, quiet job when she'd come home to take the position after cutting her teeth in forensics at the big FBI lab in Quantico for a couple of years.

Reese was speaking. "…on my way out when these boxes of files were messengered over from the Colton Construction firm."

Boxes, plural? She mentally groaned.

He continued, "Fitz Colton's assistant sent them over. Apparently, you asked for these?"

He stepped out into the hall and dragged in a handcart with four, three-foot-long cardboard boxes stacked on it. He hefted each one onto the counter between them. From the weight of them, she gathered the things were stuffed from end to end with all of Markus Dexter's office files from nearly thirty years with the firm.

She groaned aloud this time. There went her evenings for the next month. No social life for her, no matter what Jordana and Bridgette said about her needing to get out more. She'd even made a New Year's Resolution at her sisters' urging to expand her life beyond the lab, maybe even date a little, this year.

Admittedly, it was a half-bottle-of-wine-induced resolution. But her sisters were not wrong. They'd both taken a chance and found love recently. In fact, they bordered on downright annoying to be around in their mutual, delirious bliss.

She supposed it wasn't a bad ambition to find for herself a tiny sliver of the happy glow that clung to both women these days. Not that the dating pool in Braxville was anything to write home about. Even though the town was growing and gentrifying fast, it was still a small town at its core. There were still plenty of country music, pickup trucks and dirt roads to be had here.

Funny, but it had taken going to the other side of the country to finally appreciate her hometown. As a restless teen, though, she hadn't been able to get out fast enough. Hence, Washington, DC.

It hadn't just been the offer of heading up her own lab that lured her back. Although, very few twenty-five-year olds got an opportunity like this. Her original plan was to stay here no more than three or four years and then head for another large city and a high-powered crime lab as a senior investigator. Maybe Denver, or even New York City, next time.

But now that she was back, she was finding that Braxville wasn't half as bad as she'd made it out to be when it was the only place she'd ever been.

She wasn't sure where the future would take her, now. Advancing her career would still take her to a big city. But reconnecting with her family might just convince her to put down roots here. She was torn…and she didn't like being uncertain about anything.

Meanwhile, she'd been back here almost exactly a year and had yet to go on a single date. It wasn't that she was horrible in the looks or personality department. Granted, she was a known workaholic. But she liked to think the right man could coax her out of her lab and into a better work-life balance.

Although, at this point, any work-life balance would be an improvement. Her social life was completely nonexistent. Her gaze refocused regretfully on the huge, dusty boxes of files sitting on the counter in front of her. And it was about to stay that way for a while.

Apparently, her New Year's Resolution to get out more, or at least date a little, would go the way of most resolutions, scrapped within a week of its making. Ahh well. It had been a nice dream while it lasted.

"You need some help going through these boxes?" Reese surprised her by asking.

"Umm, no. That's okay. I'm sure you're plenty busy chasing down leads of your own and doing detective stuff."

A slight frown gathered between his perfect angel-wing brows. "You sure?" he asked quietly. "That's a lot of files."

Cripes. He had a bedroom voice to go with those blasted bedroom eyes of his. Her heart pitter-pattered at the low, sexy rasp. But to be honest, it was the hint of gentleness, concern even, in his voice that did her in.

Nobody ever worried about her. She was smart, collected, organized. Had her life together. She didn't need anyone to help her out with anything. At least, that was what they all saw when they looked at her.

None of them saw the lonely young woman who often felt like an outsider in her own family. The Coltons had big personalities—big lives, big loves, big fights, big laughter. She was the quiet one of the bunch. An afterthought baby—an accident after the arrival of the triplets. An afterthought child, growing up in the background as the triplets took the lion's share of care and attention from everyone else in the family. A too-young afterthought when social outings were planned for her older siblings. Mostly, just an afterthought.

"If you change your mind and want some help with these files, let me know, okay?"

"Fine. Whatever," she mumbled.

Reese turned and left the lab, his frame lean and athletic in the way of a tennis player, or a martial artist. He was one of those naturally graceful people. And she was… not. She could find a way to trip over a crack in a sidewalk. Heck, the shadow of a crack in a sidewalk. Klutz was her middle name.

She sighed and reached for the nearest box of files. Yep. Almost too heavy for her to move down to the floor without dropping it. Sheesh. How did Reese make lifting this onto the counter look so easy? The guy might not be bulked up, but he was stronger than his frame suggested at a glance. The stupid boxes were crammed to the gills with what must be thousands of pages of documents. And it was her job to look at every last one. Ugh.

Depressed, she sat down at her computer to log the boxes of files as evidence and start a trail of custody so they couldn't be altered or tampered with. She was nothing if not a stickler for proper handling of evidence. Her private nightmare was the ever-present specter of mishandling or contaminating a piece of evidence and a killer going free because of her mistake.

She spent the remainder of the afternoon cataloguing the hundreds of fingerprints lifted from the Dexter home search. Not surprisingly, most of them came from Dex. Yvette had to give his wife, Mary, credit for being a heck of a housekeeper, though. The woman had left only two full sets of prints behind in the entire house. Given the size of the Dexter mansion, that was impressive. Talk about being a thorough cleaner. Her kind of woman.

Quitting time for the nine-to-five employees in the police department came and went, and she heard the police shift change over her head with a half hour or so of scraping chairs, clumping footsteps and vague sounds of laughter and talking. But, by six o'clock, silence fell over the building.

Wednesday was half-price beer night down at Dusty Rusty's Pub, and a lot of the cops liked to meet up there after work. Ever since she'd come back to Braxville she'd had a standing invitation to join the crew at Rusty's. Apparently, a bunch of the force was going there tonight to toast surviving New Year's Eve—the worst working day of the year for police.

She might've considered going—chasing after her New Year's Resolution—except she was wearing an old shirt and a pair of jeans that had gotten too loose in the past few months as she'd clocked too many hours on the Harrison-Crane murders and forgotten too often to eat. Not to mention, she wasn't wearing a lick of makeup, and this morning, she'd twisted her wet hair up into a bun that would still be damp if she let it down, which meant it would hang in sad chestnut strings around her face.

Goodbye New Year's Resolution, hello long night at the office digging through dusty, dull construction contracts.

Might as well get comfortable. She turned off the bright, institutional overhead lights and turned on the lamp at her desk, an antique she'd brought in to lend a tiny touch of femininity and personality to the antiseptic lab. It had a printed silk shade with pink cottage roses on it and pretty crystal bead fringe all around its scalloped bottom.

After kicking off her shoes, she slipped on a thick pair of fuzzy socks, pulled up a streaming classical-music channel on her laptop and brewed herself a cup of hot tea while Chopin piano nocturnes played soothingly in the background. "Well, Earl Grey, you get to be my date tonight," she murmured. "Here's to us, your lordship."

She'd been at it for a couple of hours, long enough to know that these boxes of files were going to be pure, unadulterated misery to slog through, when the lab door opened without warning.

She looked up, startled.

"You again! What do you want?" she complained as Reese Carpenter poked his head in.

He stepped all the way inside, carrying a large, flat cardboard box balanced in his left hand, and a six-pack of beer in his right hand. "Figured I'd find you here. I saw Jordana and Clint at Rusty's, and they guessed you'd still be here slaving away."

"Yeah, well, I've got an annoying detective riding my back day and night, demanding that I magically process weeks' worth of evidence with a wave of my magic wand." She gave the pen she'd been taking notes with a swish and flick in his general direction.

"Man, I hate it when cops throw their weight around like that," he commented wryly.

"Hah!" she responded. "What are you doing here at this hour?"

"What are you still doing here?" he demanded. "Aren't you a nine-to-fiver?"

She shrugged. "I'm working. I really am up to my eyeballs in evidence to dig through."

"Right. Enter *moi* to save the day. Or the night as it were."

"Seriously. What do you want, Reese?"

"You and me. We're having a date. Pizza and beers over a pile of Markus Dexter's files."

Her jaw sagged.

What. On. Earth?

Chapter 2

Sheesh. Did she have to look quite that shocked at the notion of him being a datable male of the human species? He wasn't a complete troll. Multiple women had told him over the years he had a bad-boy vibe. Apparently, that was a huge turn-on for many women. Never mind that he was a cop and committed to protecting truth, justice and the American way at all times.

Reese stepped fully into the lab, relieved as hell that it didn't have the same reek of chemicals and death that always pervaded the morgue.

"Mood lighting? Soft music? Were you expecting somebody, Yvette?"

She abruptly yanked her cute fuzz-clad feet off her desk and sat up straight in her chair. "No! I would never—"

"Hey, it's okay," he interrupted. "If you want to bring your dates down here, go for it. I mean, it's a little kinky. Crime lab and all. But it's still no skin off my nose."

."What dates?" she muttered under her breath.

His eyebrows shot up. Yvette wasn't dating? At all? Color him shocked.

"Really? You're not in a steamy relationship with some smoking-hot guy?" he asked as he set the pizza and beer down on the high counter across the front of the lab and walked around it.

She rolled her eyes at him. "I'm not about to start discussing my personal life with you."

He shrugged. "You could if you wanted to. Tell me about your personal life, that is. I can keep a secret. I know all of your sister's dirty little secrets, for example."

"Oh, yeah? Like what?"

He grinned. "Nice try, but my lips are sealed."

"Can't blame a girl for testing an assertion like that."

"What are you up to so late?" he asked, scanning the piles of papers filling the entire surface of her normally pristine desk. As he'd suspected. She was elbow deep in files from the ginormous boxes he'd brought her this afternoon.

She looked up at him with those huge, meltingly dark eyes of hers and he felt his knees go a little wobbly. "You didn't answer my question, Reese. Why are you here?"

Her skin was like literal velvet, pale and perfect, dewy looking. And he wasn't a guy who thought about skin being *dewy*, like ever. But hers was. She was so damned beautiful. He couldn't understand why every unmarried guy in the department wasn't down here sniffing around, but it was their loss if they didn't see her. He bloody well did.

He pulled over a chair from the conference table and sat down at a right angle to her at her desk before he answered her question. "I'm here because I thought you might need sustenance. And another pair of hands and eyes."

"But…why?" she asked blankly.

"Why not? Doesn't anyone ever help you just for the hell of it? Because you could use a little assistance?"

"No. Not really."

"Then, kid, your luck has changed."

A smile started slowly on that lush, kissable mouth of hers. Her chin ducked a little, and she glanced up at him sidelong, shy pleasure glinting in her gaze.

Good grief, how didn't every guy in town see how sexy she was? Not that he was complaining. Their loss. Less competition for him…

Whoa, whoa, whoa. He wasn't in the market for a relationship, and certainly not with his partner's baby sister. Down that path lay nothing but drama and misery. No way was he going to get himself trapped between two of the Colton sisters.

"What's your system?" he asked briskly.

"System?" Yvette looked up at him blankly.

"Surely you're not planning to study each and every piece of paper in this giant pile one by one, are you?" he asked incredulously.

She leaned back, looking mightily irritated. "How would you do my job? By all means. Enlighten me."

"Well," he said, scanning the folders on the table between them. "I assume most of the papers in there are construction related. Sales receipts. Contracts. Drawings. Permits. That kind of stuff."

"That has been the case so far," she said frostily.

"None of that is likely to have a damned thing to do with murder. I'd make one stack of files that have nothing but dull, boring construction junk in them. Then, the ones with correspondence, complaints, personal stuff—I'd make another pile of those. That one I'd take a closer look at, first. Then, if any clients jump out of that pile, I'd track down the construction files pertaining to them out of the bigger pile."

She looked annoyed, but shrugged in acquiescence. "That might be slightly faster," she allowed.

Slightly? It would shave days…weeks…off the process. But he was prepared to win gracefully. "How about you take a preliminary peek at the contents of each folder and then pass each mundane one to me? I'll alphabetize them by client name."

"Sort them by year first and then alphabetize within each year," she directed him.

He shrugged. "Fine. Let's rock and roll. We should be able to blast through these suckers in a few hours."

She squared her slender shoulders and reached for the nearest stack of files. "I've already looked at these. Nothing interesting in them. You can start organizing those while I get started on the next batch."

They fell into a rhythm, eating while they worked, her pulling fistfuls of folders out of the cardboard packing boxes, and then passing them to him one by one to put back in the boxes, sorted by date and name. They actually made a decent team. They were both focused and disciplined when it came to work.

After about an hour, though, he called a halt. "Break time. Do you need another piece of pizza or a beer?"

"Pizza," she said promptly.

He passed her a slice of Torrentino's finest with extra pepperoni.

"What does it say about me that I went to elementary school with Gus Torrentino?" she asked. "I'm feeling old all of a sudden."

"His older sister Mia was in a couple of my classes in high school. Nice girl."

"Her brother was a jerk. Used to pull my ponytail."

"Did you deck him?" he asked humorously. Gus had been a big kid and was a big man now. He rather relished the mental image of tiny Yvette standing up to the guy.

"As I recall, I kicked him in the shins. I didn't know yet to aim higher."

"Violent child, were you?" he asked dryly.

She scowled. "People had—still have—this annoying tendency to pat me on the head and treat me as if I'm some helpless little thing."

He twisted the top off a second beer and took an appreciative swig from it. "Duly noted. The lady is not helpless."

She made a face in his general direction. "Thanks for not trying to convince me that Gus liked me because he pulled my hair."

He frowned. "Bullying is bullying. Any boy worth getting to know would've treated you better than that. Been nice to you. Not tried to yank your hair out by the roots. My mama taught me to act like a gentleman around girls whether I liked them or not. My daddy taught me that the whole 'boys will be boys' excuse is just that. An excuse for bad behavior."

"I like your parents," Yvette declared.

"Have you ever met my parents?"

"No. But I already like them. They raised you right, or at least they tried. I'm now going to have to try to figure out where you went off the rails so badly."

He grinned at her, unfazed by her insults. Cops teased each other all the time, and his two younger brothers had made it their mission in life to try to get a rise out of him when they were kids. They'd rarely succeeded.

Shock of shocks, she smiled back. It was an intimate moment, made more so by the cozy lighting and pretty piano music playing softly. Glancing around the dim lab, he commented, "Who knew this place could actually be romantic?"

She shrugged. "It's the people in a space who create romance. Not the place itself."

"What's your idea of perfect romance?" he asked, his voice unaccountably rough. Weird. He didn't have a crush on this woman…right? "Let me guess. An expensive restaurant, a bottle of wine, candles and sparkly gifts."

She seemed startled that he'd pegged her. As if it was any challenge. Not. She'd hightailed it out of Braxville to the East Coast and a big urban center the day she'd graduated from high school.

"What about you?" she asked. "What's your idea of romance?"

"I like to be outdoors. I like mountains and beaches and campfires in any combination."

She laughed a little. "Then why on earth do you still live in Kansas? We have neither mountains nor beaches, here. Just mile after mile of pastures full of cows or fields full of crops."

"Eastern Kansas is a little hilly," he said defensively.

"Emphasis on little," she retorted, grinning.

"Yeah, but it's home. Family and friends are way more important than having a beach or a ski resort nearby. I can take a vacation to see those. But I like to be able to visit my loved ones easily and often."

He caught the frown that twitched across her brow. She didn't think family was the most important thing? Okay, that surprised him. She came from a big, loud, warm family. He'd have thought that, as a Colton, being close to family would have been something she identified strongly with.

"What's wrong with your family?" he asked curiously.

She looked startled at that abrupt question. "Nothing's

wrong with them," she answered defensively. "They're fine."

What wasn't she saying about her family? He sensed a mystery. And it wasn't as if he'd *ever* walked away from one of those.

She reached for another stack of files at the same time he did, and their hands bumped. A jolt of…something… passed through him. Hyperawareness of her and of how close they were sitting, their shoulders practically rubbing, and their knees bumping into each other from time to time as one of them turned in their seat.

She spoke briskly, with what sounded like false energy. "We'd better get back to work."

Trying to distract him, perhaps? Or maybe hiding something. Which seemed out of character for her. She didn't strike him as the least bit secretive. Was she more shy than she let on? He had a hard time buying that explanation. She came across as supremely self-assured. But then, he'd only ever talked with her about forensics stuff before.

He leaned back, stretching his shoulders. "What do you like to do when you're not here and chained to your desk?"

She looked up, a startled expression on her face. "Umm, I like to garden."

Made sense. Her white cottage, with its wide porch and gabled roof, was neat as a pin and flanked by beautiful landscaping full of bright flowers. No matter what time of year he drove past her place, it looked like a postcard.

"What else do you like to do?" he demanded.

"Not much."

His radar for evasiveness fired off hard. "Nothing else?" Dammit, the interrogatory was out of his mouth before he could stop it.

Her gaze slid off to one side. "Well, I, uhh, play some computer games to wind down after a hard day at work."

"Get out! Which ones?"

She named a couple of the popular ones that millions of players congregated on, but not the overtly violent ones. No surprise. Like him, she saw the results of violence often enough in her work not to find it entertaining.

"We'll have to get online together sometime and adventure," he declared.

She blinked, looking downright stunned. "You play computer games?"

"They're good for my reflexes and the dopamine dump of defeating bad guys helps me deal with stress from the job. Next time I'm online, I'll text you."

"That would be fun," she responded doubtfully.

"I guess we have a second date lined up, then." Color him possibly more surprised than she looked. She was so not his type. He was a flannel-shirts-and-fishing kind of guy. She was a big-city woman all the way, sleek and polished...way out of his league.

He reached for the file folders she held out to him and glanced up at her in time to catch her staring at him. She looked away fast, and rosy pink climbed her cheeks. She was blushing? For him? Well, well, well. Not completely immune to his charms, after all, was she? Glad to know he hadn't completely lost his touch with the ladies. He'd been starting to wonder after her continuous cold-shoulder treatment.

After another hour or so of slogging through files, he called for another break, and this time didn't ask her what she wanted. He merely opened a bottle of beer and passed it to her. She sipped daintily at it, which made him grin.

"You're supposed to just tip it up and slug it down," he commented.

"If you're a sweaty from working outside on a hot day,

maybe. I drink for the taste of it, not to get plastered, thank you very much."

"Let me guess. You're a wine-cooler type," he said dryly.

"Actually, I like a good single-malt scotch." She added, "To sip. And to savor."

"Okay then. Good to know. I gotta say, I'm surprised."

"I grew up in the Colton house. It was what the adults drank and what my older siblings snuck into when the adults weren't looking." She shrugged. "I used to ask to try it when I was a kid. Developed a taste for it over time."

"Your mother drinks whiskey neat?" he blurted. He'd met Lilly Colton, and she didn't strike him as a hard-liquor, hard-drinking woman. For one thing, she was a nurse. For another, she seemed the type to put kale in her smoothies and work out five days a week. For a woman with six grown children, she was fine looking and in great shape. Yvette reminded him a lot of Lilly, in fact. Yvette had her mother's auburn hair and porcelain skin. But where Yvette's dark brown eyes had come from was a good question. Both Fitz and Lilly Colton had blue eyes.

"When my mother drinks, which isn't often and takes something or someone literally driving her to drink, she has been known to toss back a shot of scotch."

"I'll be damned. You Colton women never fail to surprise me."

Their gazes met and that…something…passed between them again. A spark. Awareness.

Cripes. Who'd have thought he would find anything at all in common with this sophisticated, classy, intellectual woman, so unlike down-to-earth him?

That pretty pink color was climbing her cheeks again. He smiled a little at her and damned if she didn't smile back. Her gaze dropped to where their hands nearly touched on the file folders. Sonofagun. Yvette Colton not only knew how to flirt but was doing it with him. Well, go goose a moose.

She put aside her half-full beer and went back to work. "One last box," she announced. "With both of us working, we can kill it off tonight."

He had more paper cuts than he cared to count, and his eyes were crossing before she finally passed him the last folder, more like three hours later than two.

"Whew!" he exclaimed. "That was a bitch. How many folders did we pull out with personal information in them?"

"Only about thirty," she answered. "A far cry from the five hundred or so we started with."

He held out his closed fist and she stared at it in obvious confusion. "Fist bump?" he suggested.

"Oh." She shook herself a little. "Right." She reached out with her delicate, girly fist and touched her knuckles lightly to his big, callused ones.

"I hope you don't punch with a fist like that," he commented teasingly. "Didn't one of your brothers ever teach you not to stick your thumb inside your curled fingers?"

"They didn't teach me much of anything. The triplets were always more interested in each other, and my oldest brother, Tyler, was much older than me. I was mostly a nuisance to be tolerated by him."

He reached out and uncurled her fingers, guided her thumb to one side and recurled her fingers gently. "There. Now you're ready to properly punch someone."

"Good to know?"

He smiled lightly. "You never know when you'll need to haul off and defend your honor."

"This is Braxville. It's not exactly the wild, wild West."

"Take it from me. It has its dark underbelly. I would know."

She met his smirk with one of her own. "In case you forgot, I work for the same police department you do. I'm as aware as you are of the crimes that take place in this town."

So prickly, she was. Like a cute little kitten with its claws out.

"I didn't forget that you work for the department. It's just that you don't get out of this dungeon much. You don't roam the mean streets like I do."

She laughed, and the sound was rich and warm. It welcomed him to join in with her, in sharp contrast to her usual cool, distant demeanor. He tilted his head to one side, studying her as her humor faded.

"What?" she demanded.

"I'm curious about you."

"Nothing to be curious about," she retorted quickly.

"See? That right there. You don't want people getting to know you. When someone makes an overture, you push them away immediately. Why is that?"

"I do not!"

"Honey, I've been coming down here with evidence for the past year, and I don't know one, single personal thing about you. Not one."

"I told you not to call me honey," she mumbled.

"Fine. I don't know one damned thing about you, Miz Colton."

"My mother is Miz Colton. Not me."

"Can I call you Yvie, like your sister does?"

"No!"

She was working so hard to distract him—which was informative in its own right. She really didn't want anyone to get close to her. But he wasn't a detective for nothing. He wasn't an easy man to distract from his main objective, once he had one. And right now, he wanted to know more about her. "All right, Yvette. Tell me something no one in the department knows about you."

"This is work. It's not like I'm going spew every detail of my life to my colleagues. That would be wildly unprofessional."

"I get that. But we're not in the FBI, and this isn't Quantico. It's Braxville. Everyone knows everybody else. It's a tight community. And here in the department, we're family. But you hold yourself separate from the rest of us. Do you think we're not good enough for you?"

"Of course not. That's absurd!"

"Then what's the problem?" he persisted. Why he felt compelled to poke at this particular bear, he had no idea. But she'd bugged him ever since she'd come to work here. She was a mystery surrounded by a riddle wrapped in an enigma. Maybe it just went against his detective's soul not to understand what made her tick.

"I've got no problem. I think the problem may be yours, Reese. Perhaps you're just nosy."

He laughed easily. "Of course, I'm nosy. I'm a detective. It's in the job description."

"Well, I haven't committed any crimes and I'm not under investigation, so you can just take your nose and poke it somewhere else. In fact, you should go home. I didn't realize how late it was."

"We can look through the thirty files—"

"Go on. Get out of here. Scram."

Huh. This was a novel sensation. It wasn't often a woman kicked him out of anywhere. He stood up, collecting the remaining pizza. "You want the leftovers?" he asked gruffly, holding the box out to her.

"No, thank you."

"Cool. I'll have it for breakfast in the morning."

"Yuck," she muttered under her breath. "Bachelor food."

"I suppose you have eggs benedict, toast points and fresh-squeezed orange juice every morning?"

She snorted. "Hardly. I'm lucky to remember to drink a cup of coffee sometime before midafternoon most days. I'm so busy with these two cases that I barely have time to eat or sleep, let alone cook."

"I know the feeling," he responded fervently. The whole department had been working overtime to try to solve the baffling mystery of two dead bodies hidden in the walls of a building decades ago and to investigate the arsenic poisoning of a half-dozen Colton Construction employees.

He headed for the door and was almost through it before she called out softly, "Thanks for the help with the files. And thanks for the suggestion on how to sort them."

Wow. He didn't expect her to be civil after she gave him the toss like that. Strange creature, Yvette Colton. Cross between a fuzzy bunny and a prickly porcupine. Which he supposed made her a hedgehog. Good thing he liked hedgehogs.

Chapter 3

Yvette rolled out of bed Thursday morning feeling inordinately cheerful. What was up with that? It was a cold, gray day outside—that raw in-between of not quite cold enough to snow, but miserably cold and wet. Felt like a storm was coming. And the forecast on her phone bore that out. Temperatures were supposed to fall through the day and snow should roll in, tonight. But she still bounced out of bed full of energy and excited to get to the office.

Weird. Since when was she jonesing to dive back into the overwhelming workload piled up everywhere she looked? As she finished putting her hair up into a loose, attractive style, French braided in big chunks on the sides and ending in a messy bun at the nape of her neck, she reached for makeup and froze, staring at herself in the mirror. What was she doing? She never gooped up for work. Yet here she was, primping as if she was getting ready for a hot date.

Reese. This was all his fault. Him and his bedroom eyes.

What was wrong with her? Since when did one tiny scrap of attention from a man send her into orbit like this, crushing like a fourteen-year-old? He wasn't even a man she would have chosen, left to her own devices. More often than not, he was insufferable and infuriating, forever telling her how to do her job and not minding his own business. A wannabe cowboy, for crying out loud. He was basically everything that drove her crazy in males of the species.

Although, to be fair, he was also a walking advertisement for procreation. The kind of man who would give a woman beautiful children…

Whoa. Full stop. She was only twenty-five years old. She had *years* to go before her biological alarm clock started jangling warnings to get busy making babies. She didn't even want a serious relationship right now, let alone a permanent one. Her New Year's Resolution had been to get out. Go on a few dates. Not go looking for true love and forever after.

But it would be nice to feel this sense of excited anticipation a little more often. To look forward to trying new restaurants, checking out local hangouts, having the occasional adventure. Her life since she'd gotten back to Braxville had settled in a routine of pure drudgery. Work, sleep and more work. When had she gotten so boring?

When she'd lived in Washington, DC, she'd done something fun pretty much every weekend. She'd visited museums, gone to the theater, hiked, biked, hung out with friends…and she'd had tons of friends in DC. Here, she had her family. Her sisters. And both of them were head over heels in love and too involved in their own relationships these days to spend more than the rare free moment with her. Not that she blamed them or even begrudged them their delirious happiness. But she'd come home and more or less turned into a hermit.

She opted to wear a simple white Oxford shirt and a pair of khaki slacks today, lest she look like she was trying entirely too hard. Stomping into a pair of fleece boots, she grabbed her puffy down jacket. A certain chill that her furnace couldn't quite knock out of the air in her house announced that the cold front was already here.

She'd spent so long fussing in the bathroom that she had no time to stop for even a cup of coffee this morning on her way to work. Ugh. She was going to be stuck drinking the acidic sludge the beat cops brewed up and euphemistically called coffee.

The morning briefing was just breaking up when she arrived at the police department, and officers milled around being social before they headed off to their various assignments.

"Yvie!" her sister called out from across the jumble of desks in the squad room.

She made her way over to Jordana's desk, which butted up against Reese's, so the two faced each other. Her affectionate and outgoing sister, so unlike her, gave her a hug. "You look fantastic, sis. Any reason for getting all shined up?"

She frowned. Count on Jordana to call way too much attention to her. "Can't I put on a little makeup without getting the third degree around here?"

"Okay, okay." Jordana threw up her hands. "Never mind."

Reese arrived at his desk and set down a steaming mug of coffee. "Hey, Yvette."

She started to smile at him but stopped herself in alarm

when she remembered her nosy-as-heck sister was standing there observing the two of them.

On cue, Jordana looked back and forth between them shrewdly. "How'd your date go last night?"

Yvette stared. "How on earth do you know about that?"

"Oh, I'm the one Reese lost the bet to."

"What bet?" she asked ominously. She started around the end of the desk to confront Reese. Surely, this bet thing had been his idea.

Jordana chirped behind her, "I bet Reese that I could beat him at darts. Loser had to come back here and help you dig through files last night."

She reached Reese and glared up at him. "You lost a bet? *That's* why you helped me last night?" Hurt and betrayal swirled in her gut. It had nothing to do with liking her? Or flirting with her? Or just being decent? It was some stupid bet?

And here she was, painted up like a clown for him because she'd thought he actually liked her. Might even be interested in her. But no. She was a freaking pity case! Humiliation roared through her.

He shrugged down at her. "What does it matter? We got a lot done."

Self-control had never been her strong suit in life. In fact, she was downright impulsive by nature. Maybe that was why she cocked back her fist, hauled off and punched him in the stomach as hard as she could. Which wasn't actually all that hard because she was puny, and his abs turned out to be made of tempered steel. Her fist basically bounced off his stomach.

But pain still exploded in her metacarpal bones all along the back of her hand, a sharp reality check in the face of having done something colossally stupid. She stared up at Reese in horror as he stared down at her in shock.

More furious at herself than at him, she ground out, "Thanks for teaching me how to make a proper fist. Jerk."

She spun and marched out of the squad room, her face on fire. Silence had fallen all around her, and her face heated up with every step as she crossed the broad space amid stares from everyone.

Reese stared after Yvette thoughtfully. Normally, he would not take the least bit kindly to anyone up and slugging him. But he'd seen something in her eyes just before she'd hauled off and hit him.

Hurt.

She'd thought he brought pizza and offered to help her because he liked her. And she was hurt to think he'd only done it because he lost a bet. And as she'd turned away, he'd seen something else. A glint of shame in her dark eyes as they'd brimmed with sudden moisture.

Aww, hell. Tears were his personal kryptonite when it came to women. Now he felt bad. She was right. He'd been a thoughtless jerk. The second his partner brought up the bet, he should have made it clear immediately that he'd enjoyed working with her last night. But he'd been so startled by the violence of her reaction and the quickness of it that it didn't occur to him to correct her impression until just now.

Dumb, dumb, dumb.

Truth was he *had* only helped her because of that bet. But he'd had a nice time with her. Enjoyed getting to know her a little. He'd definitely enjoyed slipping past that cool-and-distant exterior of hers.

A low, angry sound like a threatening cat might make in the back of its throat made him look up sharply. His partner had moved over to stand exactly where Yvette had just been. Damned if Jordana's hand wasn't curled into a fist, too. Cautiously, he kept his abs flexed. She snarled, "What did you do to my baby sister?"

"Whoa, there, Jordana. Slow down. Nothing happened between us. I didn't lay a finger on her. I only came over here and helped Yvette sort through Markus Dexter's work files. I swear. You can go down and look at the boxes we went through."

His partner's threatening stance eased slightly, but her fisted hands still didn't fall down to her sides.

Lord, these Colton women were firecrackers.

"Go ask her if you don't believe me," he added desperately, eyeing Jordana's clenched fists cautiously. "Nothing happened."

She stared at him a moment longer and then nodded once, tersely. He stepped back quickly and changed the subject. "So. Where are we with tracking Dexter? Any hits on his credit cards?"

She sighed, and praise the Lord, shifted into cop mode, as well. "No hits at all. He's gone completely off the grid."

"Which is suspicious as hell," he commented.

"Oh, yeah. I seriously want to sit down with him and have a long conversation."

He'd bet. The man's gun had been used to shoot her brother, and Jordana was nothing if not protective of her family. Dexter's wife claimed the weapon must have been stolen by the shooter, and no doubt Markus would corroborate that story.

Frustration rolled through his gut. The police were missing something. A link, a bit of evidence, to prove that Markus Dexter had killed the young woman found hidden in the wall, Olivia Harrison, and the older man beside her, Fenton Crane.

The police guessed the private investigator, Crane, had come to Braxville looking for the murdered woman, and that was what had gotten him killed. But they had yet to find a solid motive for her murder. Reese's working theory was that Dexter and the woman had been having an affair.

Jordana interrupted his train of thought with, "I talked with another one of Mary Dexter's friends from her church, yesterday."

"Did this one also know about the rumors that Dex fooled around on his wife a lot?"

"Sure did."

"Did she give up any names?"

"No," Jordana answered in exasperation that matched his. "Dexter was careful. It's purely rumors and hearsay that he was having affairs all over the place. Apparently, everyone but Mary suspected he was stepping out on her."

"How does a woman miss years' worth of cheating? She struck me as a reasonably intelligent and aware woman."

Jordana shrugged. "Maybe she stayed with him for the money. Or maybe she knew about the other women and was relieved she didn't have to sleep with him. Maybe Dexter's epically lousy in the sack."

"Possible." It was as valid a theory as anything else they had to go on, right now. "How do we prove he was sleeping with Olivia Harrison when she died?" he asked.

"No idea. Did Yvette have anything new for us any of the forty-two times you've gone down to the lab to ask her this week?"

She'd noticed that, had she? In light of last night's date and this morning's disastrous aftermath, he should probably lay off forensic lab visits for a while. Jordana was a formidable woman and not one whose bad side he cared to be on.

"Your sister got the insect results back from the burial sites. It appears the Harrison woman was killed in the spring and Crane in the fall."

Jordana nodded. "That tracks with our theory that Crane came looking for Olivia after she'd been missing for a while and that he found her killer."

"We just need that one piece of conclusive evidence to identify the killer," he declared.

"Or a confession. If we can find Dexter and bring him in, I'm sure we can get him to spill his guts. He's no hero."

"Not fond of your daddy's partner, are you?" he asked.

"Dex is the one who first thought it would be a good idea to use arsenic-laced wood from China. I think he's a cheat and coward who took off as soon as the consequences of his crimes caught up with him," she replied sharply.

"Your father gonna testify against Dexter in the arsenic case?" he asked. He already knew the answer to the question, but it was a secret that he'd been involved in the plea negotiations, so Reese pretended ignorance.

She nodded. "His lawyer has nearly finished up the paperwork on a plea deal."

"Is Fitz gonna get any jail time?"

"Not the way I hear it. He's going to testify against Markus, and the DA is going to agree to let him sell his company and turn over all the proceeds to the victims of the arsenic poisoning and their families by way of a fine."

"Ouch. That's a big hit."

She shrugged. "My parents have plenty of money without the company. They own a bunch of land and real estate. And with Braxville growing the way it is, the value of all that is skyrocketing." She added, "If we can't nail Dexter for murder, we can at least charge him with illegally using arsenic-laced construction materials."

"If Dexter knows what's good for him, he's halfway to Tahiti by now," he commented.

She shrugged. "Here's hoping Dex doesn't know what's good for him."

Reese sank into his desk chair thoughtfully. He also knew what wasn't good for him, and that was messing around with Jordana Colton's baby sister. His partner had flared up like a mama bear at the mere idea of him hooking up with Yvette.

Too bad. Yvette was one of the most fascinating women he'd met in a long time. He never could resist a good puzzle, and she was definitely more puzzling than most women.

Chapter 4

Yvette literally ran for her solitary lab in the basement of the police building to hide from the indignity of what she'd just done. Cripes. She'd just slugged a cop in a room full of cops. As soon as the police chief, Roger Hilton, heard about it, she had no doubt he would summon her for a well-deserved chewing out.

Dumb, dumb, dumb! She knew better than to let her emotions run away with her like that! She'd gotten away with stupid stunts like that as a kid, but she was an adult, now. Allegedly a professional.

Kicking herself mentally, she opened a random box of evidence seized from the Dexter home in a recent search of it. Peering inside, she spied a pile of datebooks, each with a year embossed on the cover.

She picked one up and opened it. The pages were starting to yellow with age and the handwriting was in Markus Dexter's messy scrawl, which she knew well, now, after having stared at thousands of pages of his personal documents last night. She turned the book over. In faded gold, the year was stamped on the cover. She glanced through it and noticed right away that all of Dexter's appointments and meetings were identified only with initials. Never a name. She thumbed through a few more of the annual planners, and the same thing was true of all of them. The man *never* used names in his datebook.

Odd. Secretive.

Out of curiosity, she pulled out a random file from the year group that Reese had so carefully organized last night. What a jerk…

Focus, Yvette. Don't let some jackass man distract you from catching a murderer.

This particular file was paperwork associated with an apartment complex Colton Construction had built. She riffled through it until she found Dex's notes from a meeting in April. The date and time were noted at the top of the paper. Perfect.

Noting the client's name, Randall Pardo, she opened Dexter's planner to April. Huh. On that particular date and time, the notation was for O.Q. Did Dexter actually use a *code* in his own planner?

Paranoid much?

She sat down at her desk and fooled around with how to get from R.P. to O.Q. It didn't take her long to figure out that if she reversed the initials to last name first and then first name, she got P.R. Then, she backed up one letter in the alphabet—*P* went to *O*, and *R* went to *Q*.

She checked a few more appointments in that year and the code held true. She poked around and found the datebook for the year they thought the murders had happened and tried the same code on a few construction appointments. But it didn't work. She tried all the other datebooks, and that particular replacement code only worked in a single year.

He changed his code every year? Holy cow. What was the man hiding, indeed? This was the sort of behavior indicative of someone living a double life. *What's your other life, Markus Dexter?*

She did note that, particularly in the oldest calendars, many of the "appointments" took place at night, some late at night. The year after the Harrison-Crane murders, however, even the times for appointments began to be coded also, and she couldn't tell anymore if he was setting up late-night assignations.

She picked up her phone and dialed her sister. "Hey, Jordana."

"Hey, Yvette. Are you okay? What on earth happened between you and—"

She cut her sister off sharply. "This is a work phone call. I found Markus Dexter's appointment calendars, and I thought you'd like to know he never used names, just initials. Furthermore, he used codes to record even the initials. And, he appeared to use a new code each year to refer to whomever he was supposed to meet and when. I'll try to work out the codes if I can."

"Wild. Give me a shout-out if you need help deciphering them."

"Will do. Also, were you on the team that searched the Dexter house?"

"No, but Reese was in charge of the search. Why?"

"I'm curious if any secret hiding places were discovered. Secret compartments, false bottoms in drawers, hollows under floorboards, that sort of thing."

"I have no idea. I'll ask Reese and have him get back to you."

"Or you can just relay his answer to me."

"What on God's green earth happened between you two last night?" Jordana demanded.

"Nothing. Absolutely nothing. He showed up with pizza and beer, and he alphabetized files while I separated them into useless files versus files of interest."

"He didn't come on to you? Make any advances?"

As mad as she was at Reese and at herself, she certainly wasn't going to throw him under the bus by claiming he'd been anything other than a perfect gentleman. "No, Jordana. Nothing like that. At all."

"Then why did you punch—"

"I'm up to my elbows in alligators down here. I really don't have time to gossip."

"Fine. Look. While I've got you on the phone, would you like to go to Dusty Rusty's tomorrow night with me and a bunch of the gang from the department? Lou Hovitz is having his retirement party."

"No way—"

"Before you say no," Jordana interrupted, "You kind of owe it to Reese to go. After that stunt you pulled this morning, you need to be seen in public making nice with him. And *not* punching him."

Making nice with Reese Carpenter was the *last* thing she wanted to do. But darned if Jordana wasn't right.

She huffed. "Fine. I'll go to your stupid party at Rusty's."

"Great! I'll tell Reese."

"Jor—"

Her sister disconnected the call before she could stop her from telling her partner. She honestly couldn't tell if Jordana was merely trying to patch things up in the police department or trying to throw her and Reese together to see for herself what kind of chemistry they had.

Good luck with that, sis. She and Reese weren't even oil and water. They were fire and dynamite.

At least Reese's harassment campaign of hourly visits ceased today. She was vastly relieved for the first few hours of undisturbed, tomb-like silence in her lab. But as the worst of her embarrassment wore off, she actually found herself glancing up every hour and waiting for the hallway door to open.

The day passed, hour by endless, agonizing hour, with no sign of Reese. Her shame morphed into disgust at herself for actually missing the supremely irritating detective. She missed insulting him and throwing him out of her lab, and she missed his teasing and constant suggestions on how to do her job. And darn it, she missed his bedroom eyes.

She spent the afternoon digging through Dexter's home evidence, looking for any notations by the search team of secret hiding places they'd found. Nothing of the like was indicated anywhere. Which led her to believe the search party had missed something. Any man who created a whole new code every year for writing down his appointments, many of which happened at night, well after work hours, had secrets and lots of them.

The interview with his wife, Mary, had indicated she knew nothing of his extracurricular activities with the ladies. Which meant Mary was lying or else he was hiding a major part of his life from her. At a minimum, he must have a hiding spot in his home where he left his wedding ring when he went out. Maybe cash or dedicated credit cards he used to finance his dating habits. A man as careful as Dexter surely wouldn't charge anything to a credit card whose bill his wife might see.

She was startled to realize it was nearly ten o'clock when she finally pushed back from her desk to call it a night. She'd broken the code on a few of the most recent appointment books—they'd been relatively simple substitution codes. But a quarter century ago, in the time frame of the murders, he'd been more cautious with his codes. More to hide, perhaps?

Was it ageist of her to expect that a man in his late thirties might fool around more than a man in his sixties? Either that, or Mary Dexter might have been more suspicious back then. If only she knew more about the couple's relationship.

In the meantime, her suspicion that the search of the Dexter home could have missed something important intensified. Of course, it wasn't as if Reese would listen to her if she told him he'd messed up. After all, he not only thought he knew how to do his own job, but also hers.

She would really love to put that man in his place for once. How awesome would it be to tell him how to do his job for a change? Even better, to show him up at being a detective.

In fact...

She grabbed her purse and coat eagerly. How cool would it be to shove his superiority in his face by finding a secret hidey-hole in the Dexter house that he'd missed? Excited at the prospect, she went up to the evidence locker to find out if Mary Dexter had given the police a key to her home so the police could check it while she was out of town. The police had apparently asked her not to return to the home until her husband was apprehended. Whether that was because they thought Marcus was a threat to his wife or they thought Mary might aid and abet him in fleeing the country, Yvette had no idea.

Indeed, the department did have a key to the Dexter house. She signed it out and hurried out to her car.

It was a frigid night and the wind was bitter as she

crossed the parking lot. Snow scudded across the beams of light her car cast into the darkness, and the roads were treacherous with patches of black ice. The forecast storm had definitely arrived. The police were no doubt going to spend all night pulling cars out of ditches. She certainly didn't need to be one of them. Driving carefully, she guided her little car across town to the predictably ostentatious Dexter home and parked in the circular drive.

A surveillance detail had been set up to keep an eye on the house in case Markus Dexter came back, but no police SUV was parked out front. The unit assigned to the job must have been called out on some kind of emergency. No surprise with the roads as bad as they were. The Braxville PD was not a big outfit, and didn't always have the spare manpower to dedicate to this surveillance detail.

She hustled to the front porch, unlocked the door and slipped inside. Where to look for Markus's hidey-hole? The obvious place to start was a space he would consider his. An office or man cave.

His office was just to the right of the foyer behind a pair of French doors. The space was undeniably masculine, with dark paneling and heavy leather furniture. She took her time searching the furniture—desk, tables, cabinets—and then the room itself—bookshelves, walls, even the floor and ceiling. Nothing resembled a secret hiding place.

She walked through the rest of the ground floor and found no other room that stood out as a place Markus would consider his. She headed upstairs and found a billiard room, which she searched thoroughly. Nothing. She headed for the master bedroom. It was a shared space, but there would be dressers, maybe a closet, dedicated to his stuff. Still nothing.

Darn it. What if she was wrong? Relief took root in her belly that she'd gone on this wild goose chase alone, late at night, without telling anyone about it. She would hate to give Reese Carpenter even more fodder to tease her with.

She stopped in the middle of the master bathroom to think. What was she missing?

What about spaces in the house that weren't used often, like an attic or basement? The latter weren't common in this part of the world. The clay soil tended to heave and have terrible drainage, both of which made a slab foundation more practical than a full basement. Which she knew, compliments of growing up with a contractor father.

An attic, then. The house had a steep roof that surely had space under it for one. It took her a few minutes of searching to find a door tucked at the end of a hallway. She opened it and there was a narrow stairway leading up into blackness. Cold poured out of the unheated space. *Yes.*

She felt around for a light switch on the wall but didn't find one. Fishing in her purse, she pulled out the fist-sized titanium flashlight she always carried. That was her. Little Miss Preparedness. More like Miss Afraid-of-Catastrophes. Ever since Debbie's murder, she'd always carried something hard and heavy that she could improvise with as a weapon. In some ways, she was still that kid, terrified that the boogeyman would come for her, too.

She pointed her light at the wooden treads beneath her boots, and spied a layer of dust on them. Several sets of footsteps had recently disturbed it. No doubt those came from the police who'd searched the place.

She pulled the door shut behind her and started up the stairs.

With each step it grew colder, and a couple of the stair treads squeaked noisily, just like in a bad horror movie. She emerged into the cavernous space under the eaves. It had a finished floor, but the eaves were exposed. Shelving was installed in the area in front of her, stacked with plastic bins neatly labeled: Christmas decorations, door wreaths, seasonal decor, summer clothing. One whole side of this area was filled with hanging-clothing racks full of garment bags.

The half of the attic behind the stairs was a jumbled mess of cardboard boxes, broken lamps, old furniture and general junk that looked straight off the set of a stalker movie. All the area lacked was a creepy doll staring back at her, or maybe a dude in a mask holding a chain saw.

A chill shuddered down her spine and she clutched her coat more tightly around her throat. The good news was this was exactly the kind of space she would expect Markus Dexter to hide something in.

The organized section of the attic smacked of Mary Dexter's highly structured home management. Which meant Markus would likely not have hidden anything in the bins.

Gingerly, she made her way into the pile of junk. The dust was thick back here. Thick enough that she doubted the search party had even gone through any of this stuff. Of course, maybe they'd taken one look at the thick layer of undisturbed dust on the floor and decided no one had been up here for so long that it wasn't worth their time to search it.

Not that she blamed them. It was painstaking work, going through the mess one object at a time, feeling each item, peering underneath it for something taped to the bottom, examining everything for secret spaces. She shoved her hands into the seams of chairs, lifted cushions, opened drawers and boxes and generally hunted for a needle in a haystack.

She'd been at it for long enough that her nose was numb and her fingers ached from cold when she thought she heard something downstairs. She paused, listening. If the furnace fan had been off, she would have put the hollow bump down to the heat turning on. But it had been running continuously since she came into the house. Maybe the police returning to their surveillance post? They'd probably seen her car and were coming in to say hello.

She opened her mouth to call out a greeting but a chill of foreboding across the back of her neck stopped her. Or maybe it was just the general creep factor up here that silenced her.

She made her way over to one of the dormer windows to peer out at the front of the house. That was weird. A sedan was parked at the curb, but no police cruiser was parked in the driveway behind her little car. Maybe they'd gone around back. Which made sense. It made the police less conspicuous in the upscale neighborhood and maybe they would catch Dexter unawares. She picked her way through the clutter to a window facing the back of the sprawling property. Only snow stretched away below her, pale and undisturbed in the darkness. No police cruiser.

Then who was downstairs?

A door closed somewhere below her feet.

Okay. There was definitely someone in the house. And it didn't appear to be the police.

Her heart exploded into panic mode, sending blood surging into her ears, roaring a warning at her to run. Now.

A door opened nearby. *Was that the attic door?*

A surge of adrenaline made her entire body feel light and fast, desperate to move.

She heard a creak. That was a stair tread! Someone was coming up here.

Oh God, oh God, oh God.

She looked left and right. There was only the one exit from the attic. No way to creep out of here stealthily, then.

A hiding place. She needed to hide.

Frantically, she hunted for a spot shrouded in darkness, large enough to hold her but small enough to avoid detection. Tiptoeing, she eased back into the corner of the eaves where the roof angled down close to the floor and wedged herself behind a rusty metal rack with outdated seventies and eighties clothing stuffed on it. She turned off her flashlight and crouched in the darkness.

Quickly, she pulled out her cell phone, shielding the glow with her body. She texted 9-1-1.

This is Yvette Colton. Am inside Dexter home with intruder. If cops, tell them to identify themselves. If not, send backup ASAP.

If it was police in the house, the emergency dispatcher would contact them and tell them to call out.

Another stair tread squeaked loudly, this one practically at the top of the staircase. She peered around the end of the clothes fearfully. *Please, God, be a uniformed police officer.* She was breathing so fast she was starting to feel lightheaded as a bulky figure cleared the stairwell.

That was a dark wool overcoat. Not a cop. The figure turned away from her and turned on a flashlight. She suppressed an urge to cringe away from the light. Human eyes were much better at catching movement than making out still shapes, so her only hope to remain undetected was to stay perfectly still and hope she'd picked an adequate hiding place.

The sounds of boxes shuffling and something heavy sliding across the floor interrupted the cold and dark.

She measured the distance from herself to the stairs. Nope, she couldn't make a run for it unseen. The flashlight was hard and warm in her fist, and she gripped it so tightly her fingers ached. The shadow across from her in the dark was large. Undoubtedly male. She had basic self-defense training, but she didn't relish a hand-to-hand fight against that much bigger an opponent. Especially alone, in the dark, with no one nearby to help.

Whatever the intruder was looking for was taking him a while to find. The occasional grunt and muttered curse were audible as the scraping and shuffling of junk continued. What on earth was he looking for? She hadn't searched that side of the attic yet, which was both good and bad news. The good news was her footprints and handprints weren't all over the stuff over there. The bad news was she hadn't found whatever this guy was searching for so diligently.

Her nose tickled. An urge to sneeze built in her sinuses. No, no, no! She eased her hand up to her face and pinched her nose tightly, praying for the sneeze to go away. She held her breath for interminable seconds of terror until finally, blessedly, the urge to sneeze faded.

Something fell over loudly across the attic, and she jumped at the abrupt crash.

"Dammit," the intruder bit out in a deep, gruff voice.

Was this Markus Dexter? In the flesh? Or maybe a friend he'd sent in to find something? Or was this a simple thief?

The sound of a vehicle's engine outside interrupted the deep silence of the night. She saw the bent-over shadow straighten sharply and freeze. No doubt listening as hard as she was. Was that a police car pulling up? Normally, they would come in with sirens screaming in a situation like this to scare off an intruder without harming the civilian caught inside the house.

The shadow threw open a trunk lid and tossed out the contents behind him with thuds and clangs. He scooped up something and turned, picking his way fast toward the stairs.

Drat! He appeared to have found what he was looking for and was now going to flee with it. Whatever that thing was, she desperately wanted to see what he'd come for. What if it was the exact hidden thing she'd been searching for? She couldn't let this guy just waltz out of here with it. And she had no idea who'd pulled up out front. It could as easily be this burglar's accomplice as a police officer.

The guy cleared the pile of junk and raced for the stairs. He was getting away! Panic and urgent need to stop him spurred her to her feet.

She stepped out of her hiding place and turned on her military-grade flashlight, yelling, "Halt! Police!"

The man lurched violently and threw one arm up, shading his eyes and casting a deep shadow over his face, which totally obscured his features.

"Hands up! Lock your fingers behind your neck!" she shouted, moving quickly through the junk pile. What she wouldn't give to be carrying a firearm right now. As it was, she scooped up a long candlestick in her off hand as she passed where it sat on top of a cardboard box.

But the intruder had other ideas. As she approached, still shining the light in his face and hopefully obscuring hers—so he wouldn't see how young and small she was— the figure backed away from her.

She moved to block his access to the staircase, but he charged forward holding something square and bulky in front of him. He slammed into her, knocking her down hard on her back. Her head hit the floor hard enough to daze her and she dropped both her flashlight and the candlestick.

As he kept on going, more or less charging right over her, she grabbed at his ankle, hooking her left arm around it. He stumbled, forced to stop. Kicking violently, he freed his leg but dropped the object he was holding.

A voice shouted from somewhere below. "Yvette! Where are you?"

The intruder, who'd started to turn around to grab whatever he'd dropped, jolted. For an instant, he hesitated. Then, he abandoned whatever he'd dropped and raced down the attic stairs, taking the steps three at a time. She pushed up to her hands and knees but her head swam with dizziness and nausea rolled through her gut. No way could she stand, let alone give chase.

"Up here!" she called weakly.

And then she did throw up. Blessedly, her stomach was empty due to her failure to eat pretty much anything all day, and only dry-heaved.

She heard running footsteps. Doors slamming. A car motor revving behind the house. And then silence fell once more. She lay with her cheek pressed to the cold floor, her head spinning, and failure roiling in her gut.

The intruder had gotten away from her. She should've been strong enough, fast enough, to stop him. But he'd run right over her. She *hated* being weak and small and vulnerable. It was all of her worst fears come true, save the part where she was murdered like Debbie. Panic still roared through her and realization that she'd just come very close to dying made her hyperventilate.

"Yvette! Where the hell are you?"

"Attic," she managed to call back.

Light spilled into the stairwell from below, and running footsteps approached her. She braced automatically for another attack.

"Yvette?"

Well, fudge. She recognized that voice. *Reese.*

She exhaled a wobbly breath, and all of a sudden, tears

were leaking out of the corners of her eyes. She'd lived. For a few minutes, there, she'd been pretty sure she was going to die.

Big, gentle hands rolled her over. Sat her up. She surprised herself almost as much as she seemed to surprise Reese when she flung herself forward into his arms and let the tears flow. She clung tightly to his waist, absorbing his warmth and strength gratefully, inhaling the crisp scent of his aftershave as snowflakes on his coat melted against her cheek. It wasn't that she liked him for a second. It was just that…he was…well, safe.

"I've got you. The intruder's gone," Reese murmured into her hair. Then, "What the hell happened?"

"I… He… Ran… Fell…" she was gasping too hard to talk and her chest was being squeezed so tightly she couldn't breathe. And just like that, she was sobbing and shaking. No words at all came then. Just total relief that help, any help darn it, was here and that she hadn't died.

"Aftershock. Panic attack. Got it," Reese murmured. His arms tightened around her and he waited patiently for her to calm down.

He really was being half decent. But she still hated his guts.

Eventually, he tried again. "Tell me what happened up here. Did he hurt you? I need you to use your words."

Slowly, her terror receded in the shelter of his embrace. She shook her head.

"Can you talk, now?" he tried again.

She finally nodded against his chest.

Words. Right. She could do this.

She pushed back from his chest, and his arms fell away from her. The air was cold and unfriendly where his arms and chest had just been. She tried unsuccessfully to stand up, but Reese grabbed her shoulders lightly to hold her down.

"Let's take it slow. Where does it hurt?"

"My head."

Fingers passed over her scalp and neck carefully. "Jeez, short stuff. That's a nice bump you've got going, there. Did he hit you?"

She blinked, and it was her turn to stare into the blinding glare of a flashlight. "Could you get that light out of my face? My head already is killing me without having to look at it."

"Sorry." The beam tilted up toward the ceiling, and for the first time since he'd arrived, she made out his features. They were tight with concern. "Glad you're talking, again. Walk me through what happened, okay?"

"An intruder. Heard him downstairs. Then he came up here. I called for backup, but they—you—hadn't gotten here yet. He found something and started to leave with it. I had to stop him, but he slammed into me, and he—" She broke off, not only because she was babbling, but also because a terrible thought had just occurred to her.

"Did he take it with him?" she asked urgently. It hurt like heck to move her head, let alone focus her gaze to look around for whatever he'd been clutching to his chest when he'd charged her.

"Take what?"

"A box, or something big and hard about the size of a bread box."

"You mean this? It looks like a wooden jewelry box." Reese straightened from his crouch beside her and moved to an overturned box on the floor beside the top of the stairs.

"Yes. I'm pretty sure that's what the intruder was here to find."

"Who was the intruder? Did you get a good look at him?"

"No. I never saw his face. It was too dark and he hid it from me when I shone my light at him."

"What happened to you?"

"He charged me. Knocked me down. That's when I hit my head. I grabbed his leg, though. He dropped the box. Then he kicked free and bolted. Did you see him?"

"No. I came up the front staircase, but he must've taken the back staircase and run out through the kitchen. By the time I figured out he'd gone around me and I got back downstairs, I only saw taillights retreating in the distance. I didn't even get a model and make of vehicle, let alone a license plate," he said in disgust.

Another wave of nausea rolled over her, and she slapped her hand over her mouth. No way was she barfing in front of Reese Carpenter.

"You don't look so hot, Yvie."

"Don't feel so hot," she mumbled.

"Let's get you out of here. Can you walk?"

She honestly didn't know if she could stand. Reese reached down to her and lifted her by her armpits, then set her on her feet. She swayed as angry little men with jackhammers went to work trying to escape from her skull. She must have groaned, for Reese moved quickly to her side and looped his arm around her waist.

"Can you put your arm across my shoulder?" he murmured.

"You're hilarious. In case you hadn't noticed, I'm a wee bit height challenged."

He chuckled and shifted his arm to grip her shoulders, instead. "There. Now you can put your arm around my waist."

"What? Are you that desperate to have me put my hands

on—" She broke off. *Do not initiate banter with the hot detective when you're in no shape to make it down these stairs yourself.*

His waist was hard and narrow beneath her forearm. She'd always been a sucker for a fit guy, darn it. She was a runner, herself. Although, the weather had been so bad the past few weeks and the workload at the lab so massive she hadn't even been out for a jog since Christmas.

"Easy does it," he murmured as he guided her down the steps. "Take your time. And let me know if you need to stop and rest."

She had to give him credit. For once, he wasn't being a total jerk. Gently, he all but carried her down to the second floor and guided her to a love seat in a reading nook. "Will you be okay here by yourself if I go get you a glass of water?"

She started to nod, but her head throbbed at even the slightest movement. "Yes," she sighed.

He moved away from her swiftly, and the panic from before surged forward again. She was alone. Vulnerable. And this big, empty house was creepy as heck. She was relieved when he approached her swiftly carrying a glass brimming with water.

"Here you go. Sip it slowly." She took the glass he held out of her and did as he ordered. While she worked on getting down the cold water, he pulled out his cell phone and asked for a patrol car to be dispatched to the Dexter home immediately. He told the dispatcher he would stay in the house until it arrived.

But given the weather and condition of the roads, "immediately" turned out to be more like a half hour. Long enough for her to start feeling a tiny bit more human and for her stomach to settle sufficiently for her to contemplate walking out of here under her own power. She listened as

Reese ordered the uniforms to lock up the house, post no-entry tape and let nobody inside until he could get back here in the morning with a crime-scene kit.

And then he was back, standing in front of her, the jewelry box from before tucked under his left arm. She noticed for the first time that he was wearing jeans and a Kansas State University hoodie that made him look younger and infinitely less intimidating than the dark, severe suits he wore to work.

"Can you walk, or do you need me to carry you out of here?" he asked.

She looked up at him to see if he was making fun of her, but she saw nothing in his eyes to indicate that he was joking. Only worry shone in his baby blues. "I can make it on my own, thanks."

But, as soon as she stood up, a wave of dizziness washed over her and she swayed a little. On cue, he stepped close and wrapped his free arm around her waist.

"I said I can walk."

"I heard you. But I really don't want you falling down the stairs and hitting your head again."

"I can do it—"

He cut her off. "Yvette. I'm sure you can do it all by yourself. But let me help you, okay?"

"But—"

"Humor me. It'll make me feel better to steady you. I'm gonna feel like a complete jerk if you tumble down the stairs and break your neck when I could've lent you a hand."

How was a woman supposed to say no to that?

"Truce, okay? Just for tonight. You can go back to slugging me in the gut for no reason tomorrow."

She opened her mouth to declare that she had a reason for punching him, but then he would ask what it was, and she wasn't about to confess that she had a crush on him and was upset that he hadn't thought of their evening in the lab together as a date.

Seriously. How lame was that? When she thought the words through, she sounded like a total stalker.

She closed her mouth, kept her silence and let him guide her down the long hallway, down the stairs and out the front door. But when he guided her toward his pickup truck and not toward her car, she protested, "I can drive myself home!"

"I feel you trembling. You can barely walk. No way am I letting you drive. Besides, the roads are treacherous. My truck can handle the ice and snow worlds better than that shoebox on wheels you drive."

She opened her mouth to argue, but he pinned her with a look of concern that made the words die on her tongue, unspoken. Well okay, then. She let him open the passenger door of the truck, set the box inside, then put his hands around her waist and bodily lift her into the vehicle. The ease with which he hoisted her into the truck was a little shocking. He was *so* much stronger than he looked—and he looked pretty darned fit.

He went around to the driver's side, and the glow of the dashboard illuminated his profile. "How did *you* end up here at the Dexter house, tonight?" she finally got around to figuring out to ask.

"Dispatcher called me. I live about ten minutes away and all the other units were out on calls."

"Lucky for me."

"I'm sorry I didn't get there before the intruder hurt you."

"You got there in time to scare him off and make him drop whatever this is." She touched the wooden box sitting on the seat of the truck between them.

"Any idea what's inside it?" he asked.

"None. I'm eager to take a close look at it and its contents."

"First, I'm taking a close look at you."

Her gaze snapped up to his face, but he was staring out at the road and his expression gave away nothing. What on earth did he mean by that?

Chapter 5

Reese pulled into the attached garage beside his tidy little log cabin on the edge of town. He loved this place. Had bought the land raw and built this place with his own two hands. It took nearly three years to complete, and privately he was damned proud of it.

He came around to let Yvette out of the truck. She looked tiny and lost in that oversized fluffy coat, tucked inside his big heavy-duty truck. He'd about had a heart attack when he'd charged up those stairs to find her lying on the floor of the Dexter attic. She was lucky the intruder hadn't shoved her down the stairs or killed her outright.

He reached for her waist to help her down from the high truck seat, and she was slender even through her thick coat, but she recoiled.

"Truce, remember?" he murmured.

She nodded and let him lift her down from the high cab to the concrete floor.

"This way," he murmured, leading her around his truck and into the kitchen of his rustic home.

His sister-in-law called his taste *mountain-lodge-bachelor decor*. Whatever. It was comfortable and made him feel at home.

"Wow. This is nice," Yvette commented, looking around the open living-dining-kitchen area. "Did it come like this or did you remodel?"

"I built the place," he mumbled. It had been a labor of love, and he was proud of the end result.

"From scratch? All by yourself? Impressive."

"I bought this piece of land when I joined the Braxville Police Department and worked on it bit by bit as I had the time and money."

"Wow. How did you get those giant ceiling beams up there?"

She was staring up at the vaulted ceiling and huge log rafters that supported the roof.

"Took a whole keg of beer to bribe enough guys from the department to come out one weekend and help me hoist all those big logs up there."

"I had no idea you were the DIY type."

He shrugged. "I like to make things, work with my hands. But I don't get much time for it in my current job."

"Especially not with a murderer running around on the loose," she murmured.

"Exactly." He reached for her shoulders. "Let me take your coat. Why don't you go sit by the fireplace and I'll make you something hot to drink. Tea, isn't it?"

She looked up at him in surprise. "That's right. How did you know?"

"You've been bringing a cup of hot tea to staff meetings for a year. I'd be a pretty terrible detective if I hadn't noticed that by now."

"Fair."

He filled a kettle and put it on the stove to heat while he rummaged in his cupboards for tea bags. He had a box buried somewhere in the back of one. Bingo. He pulled out the semicrushed cardboard box and prayed that tea didn't go stale fast. No telling how long this stuff had been in his kitchen. He thought his mom had brought it over sometime last summer.

"Mind if I build a fire?" Yvette asked from across the large living space.

"I'll do it. Gimme a sec to get your drink pulled together."

"I can do it, for crying out loud."

He rolled his eyes as he put two tall mugs, sugar and creamer on a tray. He poured the hot water, plunked in a couple of tea bags and carried the whole affair over to the coffee table in front of the fireplace. This was about as fancy as he got in his house.

Yvette sat on the raised stone hearth beside the big fireplace, leaning down and blowing on a small fire she was nursing to life.

"Why don't you use the bellows?" he asked, reaching for the tool and passing it to her from where it hung on a hook beside the mantel.

She rolled her eyes and commenced squeezing the bellows, sending puffs of air into her little fire.

He sat down on the sofa to watch her play pyromaniac. "Tell me something, Yvie. Why don't you want anyone to help you with anything?"

"I let people help me with stuff."

He snorted. "You were barely conscious and didn't want me to help you stand up, let alone walk out of that house. And just now. You wouldn't let me help with the fire."

She frowned in his general direction but didn't make eye contact.

"I have a theory on it," he announced.

"Do tell."

"You're the baby of the Colton family, right?"

"I hate that term."

"Exactly! I'll bet everyone in the clan treated you as if you weren't capable of doing anything by yourself."

She looked up at him, her eyes wide and startled. "How do know that?"

"Hello. Detective, here. Student of human behavior."

She shook her head. "Doesn't it get exhausting having to know everything about everyone and everything all the time?"

"What do you mean?"

"Do you ever sit and oh, read a book or watch a movie—or do anything—without analyzing it to death?"

"When I'm off duty."

"Oh." The syllable came out as a soft sigh of breath as she turned her back on him to stare into the fire, which was starting to lick up around the medium-size sticks nicely. It would be ready for a small log in another minute or two.

He frowned at the back of her head. What had he done wrong to make her disengage all of a sudden? For as surely as he was sitting here, he'd managed to hurt her feelings. Was it because she thought he'd gone off duty to bring her to his—

Oh.

She'd hoped him bringing her here was a sign of personal interest and concern.

God, he was an idiot when it came to women. He'd totally missed that one.

"So, here's the thing," he said. "I need to ask you a few questions about earlier and do the whole cop thing for about five minutes. Then, I'd love to hang up my badge for the night to just chill and hang with you. Is that okay?"

"Umm, sure." She gifted him with one of those sexy-as-all-get-out sidelong looks of hers that made her eyes look even more exotic than they already were.

Whew. *Nice recovery, my dude.* Close call, there, with being a total ass.

"Okay. How about you start at the beginning and tell me everything that happened tonight."

He listened with interest to her theory that Markus Dexter was secretive enough to have hidden things in his home. Made sense. He was less thrilled when she got to the part about deciding to go have a look for herself in Dexter's house to see if she could find something he and his search team had missed.

He bit back a sarcastic comment about her trying to do his job for him. *Truce, man. Remember? You declared it. Even if she is a bossy little thing.*

Well, hell. Is that how he came across to her whenever he tried to give her suggestions about how to run her lab? He was just trying to help. He knew this was her first gig running her own crime lab, and he had a master's degree in forensics, which meant he'd spent some time in crime labs while he was in school. He'd picked up a few things here and there that might be helpful—

He broke off his train of thought, yet again.

Was he actually the know-it-all she accused him of being? When had *that* happened? He'd always hated bossy bosses who got all up in his business.

"Are you okay?" Yvette asked, startling him.

"Yeah, sure. Why do you ask?"

"You tuned out on me, there, for a second."

He sighed. "I was having an epiphany that you might have been right all along."

"About what?"

"That I've turned into my old man."

"Meaning what?"

"He's a dyed-in-the-wool know-it-all. Always butting in with advice and suggestions."

"Ahh."

"What does that mean?" he demanded.

"Nothing. Just ahh."

He had to give her credit for winning benevolently. She could've rubbed his nose in what a giant idiot he was, but she seemed willing to let it go without any gloating or I told you so's. For which he was immensely grateful.

He mentally gave himself a shake. "Okay. So you went to the Dexter home and started searching it."

"Right. But I didn't find any false walls or hidden compartments anywhere on the first two floors. So, I headed up to the attic. I was poking around when I heard someone enter the house."

"Did you call out?"

"No. I checked outside through the attic windows and didn't see any police cars, so I concluded there might be an intruder."

"Is that when you called 9-1-1?" he asked.

"Technically, I texted 9-1-1. And yes, I asked for backup."

"Then what?" he prompted when she fell silent.

"The intruder came up into the attic," she paused, then confessed in a rush, "and I hid."

"Good call."

"Really?" she asked in a small voice.

"Absolutely. You had no way of knowing if the intruder was armed, violent or homicidal. I assume you weren't carrying a weapon of your own?"

"I may be an employee of the Braxville Police Department, but I'm a forensic scientist, not a gunslinger."

One corner of his mouth turned up. "Go on."

"While I waited for help to arrive, I watched him poke around as if he was looking for something specific. When he found that box, he immediately headed for the stairs, and I panicked. I was worried he was going to get away with whatever I'd gone there to find."

"So, you thought it would be a good idea to confront this stranger…and do what? Demand that he hand over his prize?"

"I didn't get that far. I yelled for him to freeze and identified myself as police."

"You're not technically a police officer—" he started.

"I know that," she interrupted. "But he was about to leave. I had to stop him somehow."

"But instead of stopping, he rushed you, knocked you over and fled," Reese supplied. "How did you get him to drop the box, again?"

"I grabbed his leg as he ran past me. He stumbled and dropped it then. That was right when you yelled my name. He'd started to turn to pick up the box, but when he heard you calling out, he bolted."

"What are the odds the intruder was Markus Dexter?" he asked.

"I never saw his face. The man was about six feet tall and wore a long wool coat. It was bulky, as if he had layers of clothing under it. He had on a black knit hat, and gloves. He could be anyone. It's entirely possible Markus hired someone to come to the house and fetch that jewelry box. It would explain why the intruder took a while to find it."

"Dang it all," Reese muttered under his breath.

"I know you're jonesing to pin something on Dex, but I can't give you an ID I didn't make."

"Of course not," he agreed firmly. "We'll get him fair and square, eventually. Are you feeling up to looking with me at the box he dropped? I'm curious to see what all the fuss was about."

"We ought to take it back to my lab."

He glanced up at the windows. "Weather's getting worse. Roads are going to be nigh impassable soon. I say we have a look at it, here."

"Stubborn man," she mumbled under her breath.

"Practical man," he replied dryly.

"You weren't supposed to hear that."

"Sorry. Good hearing."

Her eyes narrowed. "Duly noted. Have you got a tool set with a small screwdriver, a magnifying glass and tweezers? Maybe a bright lamp? Oh, and a fingerprint kit?"

"Affirmative to all of the above. I'll assemble them at the kitchen table."

"I'll go get my cell phone," she replied.

"Why?"

"Pictures. Have to take them to enter the box properly into evidence. Assuming you plan to actually open it tonight," she added wryly.

"Oh, yeah. I definitely want to see what all the fuss is about. Bastard better not have hurt you over nothing."

"I'm not hurt."

"But you could've been. A few steps closer to the stairs and you could have taken a bad fall." The way his gut clenched at the idea of her lying broken and in pain—or even dead—at the bottom of that narrow staircase was shocking. He'd learned a long time ago how to distance his emotions from his work, but that skill seemed to have abruptly deserted him.

She seemed startled at the vehemence in his voice. Did she really have no idea that he thought of her as—his train of thought crashed off the end of the rails and plunged into a mental abyss.

How did he think of her? She was certainly more than a colleague. A friend? A challenge? A potential love interest? Darned if he knew.

They reconvened at Reese's wood-plank kitchen table. It was a single slab out of what must have been a massive tree when it was alive. She ran her palm over the satin-smooth surface. "Seems a shame to kill a tree this magnificent just so you can have a kitchen table."

Reese smiled a little. "This table's been in my family over a hundred years. And my great-granddaddy planted some of the first trees in the Kansas prairie. Trust me. The Carpenter family has helped many more trees grow than we ever cut down. You can put away your environmental outrage."

She rolled her eyes at him while he clamped a bright work lamp with a telescoping arm to the edge of the table.

He turned on the light and Yvette's whole demeanor changed. He was fascinated to watch her focus her entire attention on the damaged wooden box. Did she do that with her lovers, too? Concentrate all of her attention like that? It was sexy as hell.

One corner of the inlaid mahogany box was crushed, no doubt where it had hit the floor, and she took several pictures of that.

She photographed it from every conceivable angle, including having him turn it upside down. When she was satisfied with the lighting and the shots she'd taken, she finally nodded to him. "You can open it, now."

Except the lid was locked tight. He tugged on it to no avail.

"Can you pick the lock?" she asked, "Or do you need me to?"

"I can, but I don't think this is a regular locking box. It looks like a puzzle box to me," he answered.

"How's that?" she asked quickly.

"See this piece in the lid? It slides slightly to one side in these tracks." She leaned in closer to stare at where he was pointing, and he smelled the sophisticated warmth of her perfume. Or maybe that was her hair. Either way, she smelled like old money. Class. Way out of his league, for darned sure.

"So, slide it," she said impatiently.

"The thing with puzzle boxes is you have to move the parts in the right order to get them to open."

"Will we hurt it if we move various parts and pieces while we try to figure it out?"

"Not unless there's some sort of booby trap built into it. In which case, a wrong move will usually break a small vial of acid or solvent that destroys or dissolves the treasure in the middle of the thing."

"What are the odds we can get this thing to open on the first try?" she asked in quick alarm.

"Zero." He studied the box for a moment more and added, "This looks like a tricky one. The first order of business is to get an idea of how many moving parts it has and where they are."

She nodded, leaning close to his shoulder to study the box as he tugged and poked at each side. They found various panels, springs, hinges and connection points, and over time got a feel for the thing.

"Check out that piece right there," she murmured. "Does it look like the flower would move independent of the surrounding inlay?"

"Looks like it. You have a discerning eye."

"Forensic scientist, here. You may be a detective and

answer why everything happens, but I make my living spotting subtle details that will tell me how it happened."

"Logical," he murmured. "Ready to give opening the box a try?"

"One sec." She photographed the box with various panels moved enough to one side to create a tiny crack in the exterior wood panels. "Okay. Go for it."

His gaze snapped to hers. Now there were words he'd been waiting to hear come out of her mouth for a very long time.

"What?" she asked quickly as she stared back at him.

His mouth quirked up in a half smile. "Never mind. If you don't get it, I don't plan to be the one to explain it to you."

"What? You mean the innuendo of me telling you to go for it? Exactly what 'it' are you referring to, Mister Carpenter?"

"Ugh. If you flatly refuse to call me Reese, I'll take Detective Carpenter over Mister. Mister Carpenter is my father."

"You're still on duty," she murmured. "That makes you Detective Carpenter."

"Stubborn woman," he muttered. He commenced fiddling with the box. And fiddling. And fiddling some more.

Nothing worked.

"Wanna give it a try?" he asked, passing it to Yvette. Might as well share the misery and have equal-opportunity frustration around here.

She worked on it for a while before passing it back to him. "I may need a drink stiffer than tea before we get to the end of this mystery," she declared ruefully.

He smiled at her, and she smiled back in camaraderie. It was nice. Really nice.

"We could always just take a hammer to it," he suggested.

"Perish the thought! It's evidence. We can't destroy it because we got impatient!"

He threw up his hands in surrender. "It was just a suggestion."

"Worst case, we can take it back to the lab and x-ray it. It sounds like there's metal rattling around inside it, somewhere. If we can get a good look at that, we should be able to figure it out."

"Cheater," he teased. "Giving up so easily, are you?"

She shrugged. "I'm pragmatic. I know when to cut my losses."

"And run?" he asked quietly.

She looked up at him, her eyes big and dark and serious. He could fall into those eyes and lose himself for a few decades if he wasn't careful. "Sounds like you're hanging up your badge and shifting to off-duty questioning, Detective."

"Guess I am. Let's take a break from that beast, shall we?" He lifted his chin at the box. "I've got a bag of marshmallows in the cupboard. Can I interest you in roasting a few of them over the fire? It's burned down to just about perfect embers."

Her whole face lit with joy, and he about fell over his own feet in shock. She was pretty all the time. But she'd just turned into a raving beauty right there in the middle of his kitchen. Holy moly. How did everyone miss how drop-dead magnificent this woman was when she smiled like that?

An overpowering need to make her do that again swept over him.

They carried the marshmallows and two long metal roasting sticks over to the hearth. They sat knee to knee and poked the sweets onto the sticks. He commenced carefully rotating his marshmallow, keeping it just the right distance from the glowing coals to gradually puff and turn a perfect golden brown. He watched on in horror as Yvette shoved hers close enough to the coals to catch on fire almost immediately.

She yanked it out and blew on it to put it out.

"Do you need a new one?" he asked.

She looked up, startled. "No. This is exactly how I like mine." To that end, she pulled the blackened, gooey mess off her stick, blew on it to cool it, and popped it into her mouth.

"Of course, that's how you like yours," he muttered, carefully withdrawing his evenly browned, perfectly puffed marshmallow from the fireplace and blowing on it to cool it.

"You mean because I'm not an anal-retentive over-roaster like you are?" she teased.

"No, because you're an impulsive, impatient sugar-burner," he replied.

"You live your way—I'll live mine," she retorted.

He shook his head and popped his marshmallow into his mouth. Mmm. Yummy.

Yvette had already put another marshmallow into the fire and incinerated the poor thing. She glanced up at him, catching him blatantly staring at her perfect profile. His cheeks heated. Hopefully, she would think it was the warmth from the fire doing that.

"Tell you what, Reese. Why don't you try one my way for a change? See if you like it."

"Only if you'll try one of mine."

"Deal," she replied, her eyes glinting in challenge.

She blew out the charred remains of her marshmallow

and pulled it off the stick. "Open up," she ordered play-fully.

He opened his mouth for her, and it was damned sensu-ous having her slip that glob of crispy-crusted goo into his mouth. He closed his mouth and captured her fingertips between his lips. She froze, her gaze lifting to his before she pulled her hand free. Slowly. Sexily.

"Like it?" she asked.

He liked the sweet softness of her fingers very much. He nodded, his mouth too glued together by melted sugar to speak.

"The burned part gives it a sharp undertone that nicely contrasts with the sweet, don't you think?" she said.

"I guess. But I still prefer my steaks with a char and my marshmallows without." He poked a new marshmal-low on his stick. "Okay. My turn."

He carefully roasted the bit of sugar to puffed, golden perfection. "Try this."

He held it out and she leaned forward. She grasped his wrist with her light, slender hand, and took the marshmal-low delicately from his fingers. *Did she mean to run her lips over the ends of his fingers like that?* She was certainly taking her sweet time sucking his fingertips.

His groin lurched to attention as her lush, rosy lips fi-nally slid sensually off the ends of his fingers. She sat back, her head tilted to one side and her eyes closed as she sa-vored the treat. *"Good Golly, Miss Molly." Yvette Colton was a closet hedonist.*

He could just imagine her eyes closed in ecstasy ex-actly the way they were now, her head thrown back, her entire body arched and relishing the pleasure he would give to her—

Dude. Don't be an idiot. Jordana would kill him if he laid a hand on her, let alone went to bed with her. This was his partner's baby sister, for crying out loud. His partner's very grown-up, very sexy, and if he wasn't misreading her, very flirty sister. They weren't exactly snowed in, but a storm was raging outside, and they were cozy and alone in front of a crackling fire in the dead of night. It didn't get too much more romantic than this. And she seemed to feel it, too.

She startled him out of his lascivious thoughts with, "You have a bit of marshmallow on the corner of your mouth. Right here." Using the pad of her thumb, she rubbed the corner of his mouth lightly.

"Did that get it?" he asked, his voice noticeably huskier than usual.

"No. Hmm." She leaned forward slowly, her gaze locking on his. "Guess I'll have to get it this way."

She closed the distance between them very slowly, giving him plenty of time to pull away. But he didn't. He sat perfectly still, unable to believe that this beautiful, fey creature was leaning in toward him, closer and closer.

Gently, so lightly he barely felt it, her mouth touched the corner of his. Her lips were soft and plump, and then—

Jesus, Mary and Joseph. That's her tongue.

She licked the corner of his mouth. It was a quick little flick with just the tip of her tongue against his skin, but there was no mistaking it. All of a sudden, there wasn't nearly enough oxygen in his living room. Either that or he was no kidding hyperventilating.

Cripes. He hadn't done that around a girl since he'd been about thirteen and first started noticing them as anything other than annoying not-boys.

"There," she whispered. "That's better."

Moving as slowly as she had, giving her fully as much time to withdraw as she had given him, he lifted his right hand to the back of her head. Threaded his fingers beneath that heavy, warm twist of hair gathered at the base of her neck, and gently, gently, urged her forward.

He brushed his lips across hers lightly, more an invitation than an actual kiss. She lifted her chin a bit and he tucked his a bit, and their lips met again, this time fitting together a little more firmly, a little more definitely a kiss.

Her mouth was softer than the marshmallows and tasted every bit as sweet. The fire was warm on the right side of his face, the room cool on the left side of it. Light and dark. Hot and cold. Yin and yang. As opposite as Yvette and him. And yet, they fit each other.

Not one to overdo on a first kiss, he lifted his mouth away from hers a few inches and whispered. "There. Now, *that's* better."

Danged if she didn't reach up, this time her fingers twining into his hair, to tug him forward once more, murmuring a little breathlessly, "Where do you think you're going? Come here, cowboy."

Chapter 6

Profound relief came over Yvette as Reese swept her into the circle of his arms and drew her all the way into his lap. He might be big and strong, but he was infinitely gentle with her. His jean-clad thighs were muscular under hers, and the bulky sweatshirt cushioned the hard physique beneath it just enough to make her new seat imminently comfortable. The overall effect was one of being surrounded in safety and warmth.

"You're so delicate," he murmured. "It feels like I'm holding a hand-blown crystal bird when you're in my arms."

Thank God. He didn't call her small, or heaven forbid, childlike. "I assure you, I won't break."

"Good to know," he sighed as his lips closed on hers. He didn't go in for the slobbery tonsillectomy, thank goodness. Rather, he kissed with finesse, his mouth alternately brushing across hers and moving more deeply against hers.

He kissed really well. Or maybe she was just really out of practice. Oh, God. Did a person forget how to kiss properly? Was she being a total geek?

He lifted his mouth a fraction of an inch away from hers. "What's on your mind?"

"Why do you ask?"

"You tensed."

He'd felt that? Dang. The man was tuned in to her big time. Oh, right. Observant detective in the house. Note to self: for once, the detective's intense observational skills were delightful. Fantastic, even.

"I was wondering where you learned to kiss like that," she murmured.

"Behind the gym in tenth grade, I suppose."

"First girlfriend?"

"Not exactly. Best friend's older sister. She wanted to practice kissing and only dragged me out behind the school to perfect her skills."

Yvette snorted. "That's what she said."

He grinned against her mouth, and it was the most delicious sensation having his lips curve against hers, warmth and humor permeating the kiss. She ran her fingertips over the short hairs at the back of his neck. They were as neat and orderly as the rest of him.

But then he tilted his head slightly and deepened the kiss. The humor drained from him, and something darker, hotter, sexier emerged from him. Her breathing accelerated, and excitement at the sudden danger of him made her tingle.

She'd always had a thing for bad boys, which was why she was single now. As maturity and common sense had invaded her dating choices, she had no interest in the drama and heartbreak that came with immature bad boys. Which left her knowing to choose sensible, boring men. Emphasis on boring. Single seemed like the better option for her.

But Reese apparently was both sensible and had this hidden other side. Who knew?

His arms tightened fractionally around her, and he made a faint noise in the back of his throat that sounded a whole lot like frustration. As in male, sexual desire being tightly reined in. Regarding her? Bless the man. No male had looked at her with anything other than the most passing of interest ever since she'd gotten back to Braxville.

His big hands moved, one sliding down to her waist, and the other up to cup the back of her head. Still, he was slow and careful in his movements, as if he cherished this moment and wanted it to be perfect.

She grew a little impatient and took the lead, kissing her way across his jaw until she reached his ear. She nipped his earlobe lightly and then swirled her tongue into the shell of his ear. He groaned aloud, then, and his arms tightened significantly around her. She shifted her weight, throwing her thigh across his hips until she straddled his lap. Better. Now she was at the right height to kiss him without having to tilt her head back.

Oh.

And to notice the hard ridge behind his zipper that she was now straddling in the most suggestive possible way.

She probably ought to climb off the poor man before she made him any more uncomfortable. She lifted herself to her knees, but Reese swiftly pulled her back down with effortless strength that stole her breath away altogether. He did turn to one side, though, shifting her far enough off his lap to remove the wildly intimate contact of their nether regions. Fair. But all the while, he never broke the kiss that had become blatantly sexual, now.

He ran his tongue along her lower lip, and then caught

its plumpness lightly between his teeth. She gasped into his mouth and was shocked to realize she was arching her back, lifting her body up and into him eagerly. Thankfully, his forearm tightened across her shoulder blades and supported her because she was starting to feel more than a little boneless, here.

He slid his mouth down the column of her neck, and she threw her head back, giving him unfettered access to her throat. His mouth was fiery hot against her skin as he kissed the frantic pulse there. His lips slid lower, into the vee where the top of her shirt unbuttoned.

The hand at her waist came around front and fiddled at her neck for a moment and her shirt opened a little more. He took advantage of the exposed skin to kiss a little lower on her chest. He stopped at the upper reaches of her cleavage, though, and kissed his way back up to her throat and then across her collarbone as far as her shirt would allow. An urge to rip the garment off completely surged through her.

Her palms slid restlessly across his neck, under his chin, traced his jaw and cheeks. Flesh. She wanted flesh. To that end, she slipped her hands under his sweatshirt. Darn it. T-shirt. She tugged at the soft cotton impatiently.

Better. Warm, smooth, male skin.

Dang. The man had no body fat. At all. She felt only muscle and more muscle under her hands, hard and unyielding. Like the man himself. She might not always agree with him, but she could respect his certainty of who and what he was.

Reese slid off the hearth, taking her with him, and stretching out at full length on the thick, soft flokati rug in front of the fireplace. His body was a warm wall of man and muscle and she gloried in pressing into him. Their legs tangled together and his forearm was a living pillow beneath her ear as he leaned down to kiss her again.

She welcomed him with open arms, loving the way his sweatshirt rubbed lightly against her chest as he braced himself above her. He kissed her long and slow, taking his time, in no rush to advance his cause, for which she was incredibly grateful.

So many guys just fell on her. Kiss, tongue, grope, go for the bra hooks…as if it was a checklist to be hurried through en route to equally hurried sex. But Reese… Reese took his time, savoring every step along the way. She actually had no idea if sex was even his end goal here. She got the impression that possibly this was all he had in mind tonight.

Honestly, she loved how it took the pressure off her to put out, how she was able to just relax and enjoy the moment without having to mentally steel herself to say no and be blasted by accusations and recriminations about being a cock tease.

Eventually, Reese propped himself up on an elbow and smoothed her hair back from her face. He murmured, "I could look at you all day and all night and never get tired of doing it."

"I don't know. After a while your eyeballs might start bleeding."

"Why do you put yourself down like that?" he asked, tilting his head curiously.

"Saves other people the trouble of doing it, I guess."

He smiled a little. "Spoken like the baby of a family that engaged in a lot of teasing."

"Spoken like a man who knows my siblings."

"I know one of them quite well, and Jordana teases and makes jokes to lighten stressful situations." A look of concern flashed across his face. "This isn't a stressful situation for you, is it?" He sat up quickly.

She sat as well, but more slowly. "Not at all. In fact, I have been thinking about how nice it was not to feel pressured to end up in bed with you, tonight."

"For real?" he asked quietly.

"For real," she answered firmly. "You're a gentleman, and I really, really appreciate that."

He smiled a little sheepishly. "I've been called old-fashioned a time or two. Women looking for a hookup don't appreciate my desire to get to know them before I sleep with them." He shrugged. "First, I want—" He broke off.

"What?" she asked, dying to know what he wanted before having sex. Not that she was looking to—

Oh, who was she kidding? She was totally looking to have sex with him eventually.

"I want to get to know a woman. Have a personal connection. An actual relationship."

"Wow. That's enlightened of you."

He glanced up quickly as if checking to see if she was being sarcastic or not. She smiled and added, "I mean it."

She leaned forward, placing her hand on his cheek which was warm and smooth with just a hint of razor stubble starting to roughen it. She kissed him chastely, but found herself lingering over the kiss. Never in her life had she liked kissing a man the way she liked kissing this one.

He sighed and dropped a light kiss on the end of her nose. "It's getting late, and the roads have to be awful by now. I shouldn't have kept you this long. I'm sorry. It was selfish of me."

"Do you see me complaining?" she asked tartly.

He smiled and rose smoothly to his feet, then held a hand down to her. She laid her hand in his bigger, callused one, loving how his grip swallowed her whole hand. He tugged her to her feet. "Give me five minutes to warm up the truck and put the chains on my tires, okay?"

He went outside and she carried the mugs and marshmallows back to the kitchen. She studied the puzzle box sitting on his kitchen table. What secrets did it hold?

Reese came into the kitchen on a blast of cold air and commented, "I'll bring that box into your lab in the morning for you."

"Thanks."

"Bundle up. It's getting nippy out there."

Nippy hardly covered the way the cold hurt to breathe in and made her face feel stiff and numb. Frigid was more like it.

Reese followed her around to the passenger side of his truck and put his hands on her waist to steady her as she climbed in. She loved how his big hands spanned so much of her waist. Huh. Normally, she hated feeling small. But she liked it with him. Maybe because he seemed to like it so much.

He closed the door carefully behind her and then climbed in the driver's side. He backed out of his garage and turned out into the street, or rather the white sheet of snow roughly where she estimated a street to be.

Snow blew horizontally through the beams of his headlights, like crystalline diamond dust. She was silent, letting him concentrate on his driving. But after he made a left turn where he should have turned right, she piped up. "The Dexter house is in the other direction. That's where my car is parked."

"Do you have chains for your tires?"

"No."

"Exactly. I'm driving you to your house tonight. I'll pick you up in the morning and take you to your car, then. Assuming the storm has blown through by then and driving conditions have improved."

"That's way out of your way. It's too much trouble—"

He cut her off. "I didn't ask your permission. I told you what I'm doing."

"You're so high-handed!" she exclaimed. "And stubborn! And a know-it-all."

He shrugged, appearing unconcerned. "Do you have a safer idea?"

Safer? No. More convenient? Absolutely.

He must have taken her silence for consent to his plan because he said, "What time should I pick you up? Is eighty thirty too early? I have a meeting at nine."

"I—no. I mean yes. You can pick me up at eight thirty." She added with a huff, "That's fine." How did that man always seem to get the best of her? It was infuriating!

He pulled into the driveway of her Cape Cod cottage with its long porch and peaked roof covered in a thick blanket of white. He put the truck in Park but said, "Don't get out. I'll come around and help you."

"Reese. I can walk to my front door all by myself."

"And yet, I'm going to help you. My boots have cleats, and I can see the sheet of ice on your sidewalk. Last thing I need is for the forensic scientist working on my big murder case to break her leg."

There he went again, being right. Darn him.

He lifted her out of the truck, set her on her feet and wrapped his arm around her waist. In his big, fleece-lined rancher's coat, he felt like a bear giving her a hug. She was chagrined when a big gust of wind hit, and her feet did slide out from under her about halfway to her front door. Reese caught her and steadied her until she regained her balance, and they made it up the steps and to the door without further incident.

She unlocked the door and, hand on the knob, turned to thank Reese.

He beat her to the punch, though, and said, "Thanks for tonight. Get some rest and call me if you develop any dizziness, nausea, vomiting or disorientation."

She recognized a list as warning signs of a concussion. "Will do."

"I'll see you in the morning." He leaned down, gave her one last lingering kiss and then gently pushed her inside.

In the morning, indeed.

She was shocked to realize she was practically floating through her house as she hung up her coat and got ready for bed. Man. She had it bad for him. She even set her alarm a half hour early so she'd have extra time to get up and get ready.

Her bed was icy cold when she climbed under the covers, and she missed the warmth of his embrace as she settled down to sleep and dream of marshmallow kisses.

The storm was still howling around her house when her alarm jangled, waking her from a delicious dream of a certain hot detective and his amazing kissing skills. Well, fudge. She'd been hoping to wear something cute to work today, but instead, she was going to have to go full Michelin Man.

She pulled on thin wool long johns, jeans, a white turtleneck and a thick sky-blue ski sweater with a ring of snowmen around the yoke. She pulled her dark hair back in a long clip at the back of her head and took extra care with her makeup this morning. She stomped into a pair of thick-soled after-ski boots and laid out her puffy down-filled coat, light blue hat with its jaunty white pom-pom, mittens and a long scarf.

Exactly at eighty thirty, Reese's big silver truck turned

into her driveway. She could set a clock by that guy. Although, truth be told, it was reassuring to know he would always be exactly where he said he would be, when he said he'd be there. She'd dated enough flakes in her life to appreciate a punctual man.

She hurried into her cold weather gear as he walked up her sidewalk and opened the door for him just as he hit the front porch. "Hi there," she said brightly.

"Good morning. Are you always this chipper first thing?"

"Not usually before a cup of coffee," she answered, laughing. "I just happen to love a good blizzard. Always have."

"Were you the type to build a snowman and make a fleet of snow angels?" he asked as he opened the door for her.

"Absolutely. You?"

He climbed into the warm cab of the truck. "I was more the snow fort and piles of snowballs type."

"You have brothers, don't you?" she asked.

"Two younger ones. It was usually me in the fort with my brothers tag-teaming me from outside."

"In our house, snowball fights usually lined up girls against the boys."

"That doesn't sound fair," he protested.

She shrugged. "We girls usually lost, but we also usually got even by dumping snow down the collars of the boys' coats."

"Wow. Vicious."

"The motto of the Colton women is, Don't Get Mad. Get Even."

He grinned over at her. "Duly noted."

They drove a few minutes in silence, and it dawned on

her that he wasn't heading toward the Dexter house and her car this morning, either.

"Where are we going?" she asked.

"My nine o'clock interview cancelled. Thought you might like a cup of coffee, or maybe some breakfast, before we go pick up your car."

"Why Mr. Carpenter," she teased in a thick southern belle accent, "are you asking me out on a date?"

He glanced over at her, his eyes unaccountably hot. "What if I am?"

"Well, I do declare." She fanned herself with an imaginary fan.

He grinned. "I'll take that as a yes."

They pulled in to the local diner, which was blessedly open and surprisingly busy. Apparently, a number of businesses had either closed or were opening late today, and given the number of children in the joint, schools were obviously closed, too.

A couple got up to leave just as they stepped inside, and the waitress waved her and Reese over to the table as she cleared it. They slid into the booth, and Yvette was abruptly aware of lots of stares, some surreptitious, some open, in their direction.

She murmured, "Why are people looking at us? Do I have mascara running down my face or something?"

"No. You're perfect. They're all staring because I'm with the prettiest girl in town."

She smiled shyly at the warmth in his voice. "Flatterer. Actually, I think it's because they're jealous of me being with the most eligible bachelor in Braxville."

He snorted. "I think one of your brothers probably holds that title."

"All my brothers are officially off the market these days. Or hadn't you heard?"

"That's what Jordana said. I'm happy for them."

"Or maybe it's just the dozens of women you've dated before, pitying me for being your next conquest."

Reese gave a wholly satisfying snort at that notion. "I don't date local women."

Really? Now, that surprised her. "Why not?" she asked.

"What if I have to investigate one or arrest one, someday? How awkward would that be?"

"So, you don't plan to date me, then?" she asked in a small voice.

"You're different. You're on the force."

"Hmm. You strike me as the type who wouldn't date someone you work with."

"Yes, but I don't really work with you. Our paths cross in our individual jobs from time to time, but you're not in my chain of command, and I'm not in yours."

"How do you know I won't commit a felony, someday?"

He tilted his head to study her for long enough that she had to suppress an urge to squirm. "Do you think of yourself as capable of committing a serious crime?" he asked.

She shrugged. "I suppose in the right circumstances. Like if someone I loved was in mortal danger, I might be capable of violence. Or if a child or helpless animal was being hurt, I might go after the abuser."

"Those would be classed as justifiable crimes. I doubt you'd be prosecuted in either scenario."

"What about you?" she asked curiously.

"Same. I've been known to be protective of my friends and family." He paused, then added, "Unfortunately, engaging in a certain amount of violence is a potential part of my job. My least favorite part of it, in fact."

"Have you ever…you know…shot anyone?" She asked the last part in a hush.

"Thankfully, no. But I have to be prepared mentally to do it."

"Does the idea bother you?" she asked.

"Of course, it does. I hate the idea of taking a life. I would consider it a complete failure on my part if I couldn't talk a person out of the thing that would force me to shoot them. My job is to prevent violence, not meet violence with violence. That's the last resort."

"That's a progressive view, Detective."

He shrugged. "It's the ethical and moral view. Has nothing to do with being progressive."

"That's you. Mr. Ethics-and-Morals."

Darned if his eyes didn't get that sexy glint in them again. "I'm not always an uptight good guy, you know."

"Do tell." She leaned forward with interest to hear this one. "When, exactly, do you set aside your white hat and superhero cape?"

"That's for me to know and you to find out."

"Challenge accepted," she declared immediately. Their stares met, and sexual lightning crackled back and forth between them. It was a wonder they weren't blowing this place apart with it.

Sudden awareness of being in a very public locale with half the town looking on burst over her. She broke the stare and looked away hastily.

"How's the back of your head feeling this morning?" Reese asked neutrally enough.

"Sore where I hit it, but I took a couple of aspirin when I woke up and the headache's mostly gone."

"Good. Means you probably didn't get a concussion. I was worried about you last night. You looked on the verge of puking, there, for a while."

"I was on the verge. But I was determined not to barf in front of you," she confessed.

He smiled. "In my line of work, I've seen most of the human bodily functions any number of times."

"Have you ever delivered a baby?" she asked.

"Two. Messy, but totally cool."

He leaned back and took a sip from his water glass before changing the subject. "How's your family doing? Y'all have been through a rough time recently, what with the arsenic thing and then the murdered bodies in a building the Colton Construction Firm built."

"If only that was all we were dealing with," she sighed.

"Oh, yeah? What's up?" He sounded genuinely interested, and not just like a nosy neighbor. Maybe that was why she gave him a baldly honest answer. That, and he would just ask Jordana what she was hinting at if she didn't go ahead and tell him herself.

"My parents aren't exactly doing great. They've had some sort of major falling out, but I'm not sure what it's about. It seems serious, though. They treat each other like polite strangers these days. Mom's totally giving Dad the cold shoulder."

He frowned a little. "Your mom is capable of giving anyone the cold shoulder? No way. She's one of the warmest, kindest people I know."

She shrugged. "At least my siblings seem to be happy for the most part. The whole gang seems to have found true love." She added wistfully, "Except for me, of course."

"Maybe you've already found it and you just don't know it, yet."

Her gaze snapped up to Reese's, and his eyes were shockingly serious. Was he talking about himself? They barely knew each other. They'd made out once over marshmallows. Holy moly.

A friendly looking older woman wearing an apron approached the table. "Hey, Reese. Some weather we're having, isn't it? How are the roads?"

"Hey, Lola," he answered. "It's bad out there. Forecast calls for it to clear up around noon, though. I expect it'll take the snow plows a few hours to clear the major roads after that."

"Great. Maybe by quitting time I'll be able to get home without risking my neck. What can I get you kids to eat?"

"The special," Yvette and Reese said simultaneously.

"How do you want your eggs?" the waitress asked, pencil poised over a pad.

"Sunny-side up," Yvette answered.

"Over hard," Reese supplied.

"Bacon or sausage?" Lola asked.

"Bacon," Yvette answered promptly.

"Sausage," Reese chimed in.

It figured. The two of them never agreed on anything. Yvette mentally rolled her eyes.

"Toast or biscuit?"

"Wheat toast, buttered," Reese supplied.

"Can I substitute a bagel?" she asked.

"You bet."

Lola moved over to the pass-through window to the kitchen and shouted out their order.

Yvette smiled ruefully at Reese. "We're pretty much opposites in every way, aren't we?"

He shrugged. "We both wanted the special. That's agreement after a fashion. And, honestly, I like the fact that you're confident enough to do your own thing without feeling a need to imitate me."

"Keep that in mind the next time you're in the lab trying to tell me how to do my job," she retorted.

He grinned and poured her a cup of coffee from the steaming pot Lola set on their table. "Black?" he tried.

Yvette threw him a withering look. "Cream and sugar, of course. You can pretty much think about what you'd choose, do the opposite, and you'll get me right."

He rolled his eyes as he passed her the pitcher of cream and sugar dish. "I should've guessed you'd want your caffeine to taste like ice cream after the way you enjoyed those marshmallows last night."

She smirked knowingly. "The way I liked them best was on you."

Abruptly, his blue eyes were smoldering, the color of a flame burning super hot. "See? We agree again. I like marshmallows best on your lips, too. Or on the tip of your tongue. Or in the sweet, dark recesses of your mouth. Remind me next time to try out some marshmallow crème on other parts of your anatomy."

Suddenly it was her turn to be unaccountably out of breath. "Uhh, sure. That sounds—" she searched for a word. Sticky didn't convey the romantic vibe she was looking for. "—amazing."

"It's a date."

Wowsers. If she wasn't mistaken, she'd just agreed to have sex, or at least sexy foreplay with the hot detective.

Thankfully, their breakfast arrived before she burned to a cinder where she sat, charred to nothing by the heat in Reese's eyes. They ate quietly. Maybe he was as disconcerted by the direction of their conversation as she was.

She insisted on paying for the bill, both in thanks for last night's rescue and in gratitude for the rides he was giving her in his big, safe truck. The looks and side-eyes continued as they left the diner, and she was vividly aware of the light touch of Reese's hand on the small of her back as they reached the door. Was that just common courtesy, or was he sending a subtle signal to the single men in the room that she was taken? Either way, her heart pitter-pattered at the light, possessive touch.

"What's on your agenda today?" he asked as they pulled into the parking lot of the police department.

"Getting this rascal open." She patted last night's puzzle box resting on the seat between them.

"Shout out if you get stuck," Reese offered.

"Will do. What about you?" she asked as they walked carefully toward the building. "What are you going to do with yourself now that you don't have that interview this morning?"

"I'm going to go back and review the whole murder case one more time. See if anything jumps out at me in light of the recent information you provided about the murders happening at different times of year. That, and the fact that Markus Dexter has been paranoid and secretive for a long time."

"Shout out if *you* get stuck," she offered.

"Will do." He opened the building door and held it for her, saying as she slid past him, "Oh, and Yvette, would you mind dropping by my desk at some point to make a formal report about last night? I already filed a preliminary report, but I'll need a statement from you to make it official."

"Sure."

"I'll look forward to seeing you."

They traded quick smiles and parted ways in the lobby of the building. Reese headed for his desk in the squad room, and she headed downstairs to her lab. What a great way to start a day. She felt refreshed and energized after her meal—and conversation—with Reese. She counted it a victory that they seemed to have moved past their bickering to a more flirtatious brand of teasing. Marshmallows and making out would do that with a guy, apparently.

Chapter 7

A quick X-ray of what she was starting to call That Blasted Box down at the morgue revealed one fascinating piece of information. Nestled in the exact center of the puzzle box was a metal key.

The rest of the box was made of wood, however, and the X-ray was not helpful in showing her how to open it. Which sent her to the internet and a deep dive into how Chinese puzzle boxes were built. She figured out quickly enough that this one had been handmade, which was not good news. It meant that the builder could have constructed it to open unlike any traditional puzzle box.

But she did learn enough about how the boxes were built in general to begin moving panels and pressing hidden buttons. Reese's suggestion to just smash the thing resonated through her mind ever more frequently as the day aged.

She was hunched over the stupid thing concentrating intently, her neck and shoulders cramping, and only sheer, cussed stubbornness keeping her poking and prodding at the box when a hand landed on her shoulder without warning. She jumped violently, leaped out of her seat and spun around, hands coming up defensively in front of her before she was even conscious of moving.

"Easy, Yvie," Reese said, stepping back and holding his hands up in the air.

"Sorry," she muttered, chagrined at her overreaction.

"That's some startle reflex you've got, there."

She winced. Unfortunately, she knew exactly where it came from. She'd had a coworker at Quantico who'd gotten excessively handsy with her until she'd taken an intensive, weekend-long self-defense class. The next time he'd snuck up on her and wrapped his arms around her waist, he'd gotten a nasty surprise in the form of a donkey kick to the groin and bloody scratches across his face.

He'd tried to press charges, but the senior lab supervisor had seen Yvette's attack as self-defense and promised to tell authorities about the guy's ongoing harassment of Yvette if the guy made a formal complaint. The handsy coworker had backed off. Soon after that incident, he'd transferred to another lab.

While she'd been grateful for the support, the jerk had gotten off with a stern warning to leave the female employees alone, and she was left with a hair-trigger startle reflex over being touched at work.

She sighed. "It's not you. I've had problems in the past with a male coworker grabbing me."

Reese's eyes widened, and then narrowed. He asked tightly, "Who is it?"

He thought she meant here in Braxville. "I had the problem in Virginia. Not here."

Reese relaxed fractionally, but the thunderous set of his

brows didn't ease. "If anything like that ever happens to you here, you tell me about it. Okay?"

"It's all right. I can handle—"

"Stop being so cussedly independent, woman. If someone harasses you or does or says anything the least bit inappropriate to you here, promise you'll tell me."

"Umm—"

"Promise."

It was her turn to throw up her hands. "All right, already. I promise. But I've had a self-defense class. I can protect myself."

"I believe you. But I can kick someone's ass into last week. And if someone around here lays hands on you without your consent, it'll be needed."

Who knew Reese would go all caveman over protecting her right to consent? And who knew she would find it wildly attractive to have a man go all macho and protective on her behalf like this?

She gave herself a mental shake. "Change of subject— I found out what's inside the puzzle box."

"You opened it?" he exclaimed. "Show me how it works."

"No, I x-rayed it. There's a key inside. I haven't figured out the whole mechanism, yet. I think I've got it about half solved, though. Stupid thing is built in layers—puzzle boxes nesting inside puzzle boxes. Whoever built it was freaking diabolical. Maybe you can figure out the next layer?" she asked.

"I'd love to stick around and help you, but I've got that interview from this morning in about fifteen minutes. I thought I'd pop down to see if you'd eaten today."

Food? Oh, right. She glanced at the big clock on the wall over the door. It was going on three o'clock. She shrugged. "I'll grab something when I get hungry."

"No wonder you're no bigger than a hamster. You don't eat enough."

"A hamster?" she squawked. "I remind you of a rodent?"

He grinned. "A cute, cuddly rodent that you really want to pick up and hold and pet, except it'll bite the shit out of your hand if you try."

"I should punch you in the stomach again."

His grin widened. "You can try. But now that I know you're the impulsive type, I'll be on my guard."

"For the record, I don't generally run around attacking people."

"Good to know." He held out a paper sack. "I went to a deli for lunch, and I grabbed an extra sandwich. Just in case."

"If that's your afternoon snack, I'm not taking it."

"No, Yvie. I got it for you. Jordana said corned beef on rye is your favorite. I ordered it with extra mustard and light sauerkraut, exactly the opposite of how I would order it for myself."

"That's perfect!" she exclaimed. "Exactly how I like my corned beef sandwiches."

"Of course, it is," he replied wryly.

Whoa. He'd found out what her favorite sandwich was? In her experience, men didn't go to that kind of trouble unless they were seriously interested in a woman. "Umm, thanks." She took the brown paper bag and smiled up at him. "This was really sweet of you."

"I'd love to help you with that puzzle box, but I've got to run. Don't forget to come up and make a report about last night."

"I won't."

Except, after she ate the sandwich and went back to work on the box, time got away from her again. The next time she looked up it was nearly five o'clock. Rats. She locked the lab and hurried upstairs. Shift change was approaching, which meant not only were the day shift cops still at their desks, but the night shift guys were also milling around. She wound through the crowd to Reese's desk. He looked up from a file and his eyes lit with pleasure.

Warmth filled her belly as she smiled back at him.

"Here to make that report?" he murmured.

"Affirmative."

"Have a seat," he said formally.

She perched on the hard wooden chair beside his desk, and he pushed a yellow legal pad toward her along with a pen.

"I need you to write down what happened last night at the Dexter home in as much detail as you can remember."

"I can remember a lot of detail. I'm a forensic scientist after all."

"Then it'll be a long report."

"Okay," she said doubtfully, anticipating a bad case of writer's cramp. Biting her lower lip, she started to write. Out of the corner of her eye, she was vaguely aware of other cops checking out what she was doing at Reese's desk. Gradually, she became aware that Reese was starting to scowl. The longer she wrote, the grumpier his expression became. Finally, she looked up directly at him. "Am I doing something wrong?"

"Not at all. Continue."

"Then why do you look ready to rip the heads off bunnies with your bare hands?"

"Bunnies? I would never!"

"You know what I mean."

"Don't worry about it, Yvette. Finish your statement."

She put her head back down and wrote the last few lines, the part where Reese scared away the intruder and came upstairs to rescue her. As she laid down the pen, she heard a ripple of laughter behind her and turned to check it out. The laughter cut off abruptly, and a cluster of cops across the room looked away from her hastily, coughing conspicuously.

She looked back at Reese who did, indeed, look ready to commit homicide. "What am I missing?" she asked him under her breath.

"You're missing some of the young guys being jack-asses behind your back. Ignore them."

"Jackasses how?"

He sighed. "They're making faces at me because you're sitting at my desk."

She frowned. "I don't understand."

"They think you're attractive and are harassing me about having a thing for you."

"Oh. Well, then. I can take care of that," she said breez-ily.

She stood up and moved around the corner of the desk as Reese watched her warily. Before she could lose her nerve, she took his face in both of her hands, leaned down and planted a smoking-hot kiss on him, complete with pas-sion, heat and tongue.

Reese froze initially, but as his mouth opened against hers and she deepened the kiss, he abruptly kissed her back. His tongue sparred with hers and it was a duel to see who gave whom a tonsillectomy first. His hand came up and slid under her hair at the nape of her neck, urging her even deeper into the kiss. She melted into him, loving the way their mouths fit together, the deep, drugging suc-tion, the carnal intensity of their lips and tongues clash-ing and blending.

Blood surged through her veins, her heart pounded, and honest to goodness, her knees went weak. Hot dang, that man could kiss the stripes off a zebra. She could fall into him and blissfully drown—

They were in the middle of the squad room, for crying out loud!

She tore her mouth away from his and jerked upright, panting. His hand slipped from her neck as she pulled away. For his part, Reese stared up at her, his blue eyes glazed, looking rather hectic, himself.

"Right then," she managed to choke out. She made eye contact with him for the briefest moment and then her courage failed her. She turned and fled. It was all she could do not to break into a run as she scurried across the squad room.

But as she passed by the group of now slack-jawed beat cops, she did gather herself enough to say cheerfully, "Pleasure doing business with you, gentlemen. Oh, and he kisses like a god."

She made it out into the hall before she sagged against a wall to catch her breath. When was she going to learn to control her wild impulses? Lord knew, they got her into trouble more often than not. She could not believe she'd just kissed Reese Carpenter in the middle of the squad room. *And he'd kissed her back.*

Thankfully, she made it all the way back to the basement without running into anyone in the hall. Her face felt as if it was on fire, and her hair was falling out of its bun where Reese hand plunged his fingers into it. She must look like a complete mess. A well-kissed, complete mess.

Oh, God. She'd just completely blown it with Reese. No way would he forgive her for embarrassing him like that. What had she been thinking? She liked him. Really liked him. He was the first man in a long time that she'd been seriously interested in, as in potential long-term relationship material. They were so different from each other, but also shockingly compatible. And she'd had to go and humiliate the man, in front of his coworkers, no less. She was the biggest idiot *ever*.

If possible, her cheeks burned even more.

The worst of it was she knew better. If she'd learned nothing from having three mischievous older brothers, it was not to rise to the bait when they dared her to do anything. But today, she'd taken one look at those leering cops, and it was as if they'd dared her to do something outrageous to wipe those smirks off their faces.

She ducked into a ladies' room to redo her hair, but there was nothing to be done about the razor burn around her mouth, the faint swelling and rosy color of her lips, nor about the rather dazed look in her eyes. *Enjoy it for the last time, girlfriend. Because as sure as you're standing here, you chased that man far, far away from you.*

Reese Carpenter might have a secret wild streak of his own, but not while he was at work. Never while he was on the job.

Depressed and disappointed in herself, she peered out into the hallway. All clear. Mortified, she ran for her lab, sighing in relief to make it inside without being seen by anyone.

But no sooner had the door closed behind her than her personal cell phone rang. Grimacing, she pulled it out of her pocket to see who was calling.

Jordana.

She would love to ignore the call, but her sister knew where to find her and wasn't the sort to let go of a bone once she had it firmly between her teeth.

"Hey, sis."

"What in the heck did you just do?"

Summoning her best innocent voice, Yvette responded, "What are you talking about?"

"You kissed Reese Carpenter? In the freaking squad room?" Her sister's voice rose in pitch with every syllable. It was not often that Jordana Colton actually screeched.

"Oh. That. Yeah." God, she hoped the words sounded easy-breezy. Truth was, her stomach was in a total knot, now.

"What were you *thinking*?"

"I was thinking that the guys making fun of him and me deserved to be put in their places and shut up."

"And you thought kissing my partner was the way to do that? Do you know nothing about cops? That kiss is already the talk of the whole department!"

Yvette closed her eyes in chagrin. Jordana was right. Police departments were as rife with gossip as any other workplace. Maybe more so. "Okay, fine. You're right. I should have realized it wouldn't shut anyone up."

"I thought you two hated each other's guts. Is there something going on between you two that I should know about?" Jordana asked suspiciously.

"God, no." As soon as the words came out of her mouth, she knew them for the lie they were. Well, partially a lie. Yes, there was something going on. A truce, apparently. The mother of all truces, in fact. But no, she had no interest in her sister knowing about it.

Reese was like a brother to Jordana. Which, by default, somehow made her and Reese siblings in Jordana's mind. At least, that was how she'd described it to Yvette some months ago when Reese and Yvette had gone through a particularly bad patch of sniping at each other, and Jordana had intervened to referee. She'd told them that she loved them both and wanted them to get along like her other siblings.

That seemed a lifetime ago. And yet, now that she thought about it, she'd thrown him out of her lab in no uncertain terms a mere two days ago. All of a sudden, there definitely was something going on between her and the man who'd driven her crazy—not in a good way—for the past year.

What *was* she thinking? Two days ago, she would have laughed her head off at anyone who suggested that she kiss Reese Carpenter, ever, let alone in the squad room.

"Could you dial back on kissing my partner, Yvie? Your behavior reflects on me, too, you know."

"I'm sorry, J. I knew better. But I just got so mad when they all laughed at him and me."

Jordana laughed a little. "It's not as if you've ever had great control of your temper."

"Gee. Thanks. Love you, too, sis."

"Aww, c'mon, Yvie. I love you to death. But you and I both know you can fly off the handle when properly provoked."

She sighed. "Guilty as charged. I'll apologize to Reese the next time I see him."

"That's between you two. I'll do what damage control I can. I'll call it a joke. Make sure they all know there's nothing going on between you two. That you two can't stand each other."

"Umm, right. Sure. Thanks."

"You're still coming to Lou's retirement party, right?"

"I don't think so. Not after this—"

"Chicken."

Coltons were a lot of things, but chickens were not one of those things. In fact, it was a long-held family tradition that no Colton ever backed away from a dare. It had gotten her and all of her siblings in trouble from time to time over the years. And apparently, it was about to get her in trouble again, now.

"Fine. I'll go to your stupid party," Yvette declared.

Jordana hung up before she could call the words back.

Tonight, she had to correct her sister's mistaken impression of whatever was going on between her and Reese. Convince Jordana they were…

They were what?

Friends?

Friends with benefits?

Two people who hated each other's guts but were wildly attracted to each other?

Heck if she knew what they were.

One thing she did know. She did hate not being completely honest with her big sister. But honestly, it was none of Jordana's business what went on between her and Reese off duty…except that it was. Reese and Jordana were partners. They needed total trust, complete honesty, and to trust their lives to each other.

She had no right to interfere in their working relationship. She sighed and started to call Jordana back. Except a text came through to her phone that made her fingers freeze on the numbers. A text from Reese.

I'll be down in ten minutes to get you. Be ready to go.

Gulp.

Chapter 8

That man could be so bossy! So infuriating! Who did he think he was, ordering her around like that?

She interrupted her own tirade with a dose of cold reality. She owed him not only an apology, but a reckoning. If he wanted to come down here and chew her up one side and down the other, he had that right. She'd acted completely inappropriately and had embarrassed him. Time to face the music for her reckless behavior.

Glumly, she put away the puzzle box, powered down the lab equipment and locked the place up. Reese had barely opened the door before she turned off the lights, joined him in the hall and locked the door behind herself.

"Let's go," he said tersely.

At least the man had the good grace to get her out of the building before he ripped into her. That was classy of him.

Saying nothing to her, he strode out of the basement, leading her out the back way to a police-only parking lot behind the building. It was dark outside and his strides were so long and quick that she had to half jog to keep up with him.

He opened the passenger door of the truck for her and closed it behind her without comment. In fact, he drove out of the lot, turned down the street and made it all the way to the Dexter house, where her car was still parked, without breaking his stony silence. Was he that furious at her?

He pulled to a stop in the circular drive behind her little car and she blurted, "I'm sorry, Reese. I got mad that they were laughing at you—at us—and I didn't stop to think. I'm sorry I embarrassed you, and I shouldn't have done that in our mutual work environment. It was unprofessional and stupid. And given that I've been sexually harassed at work before, I should have known not to do the same to you—"

He leaned across the truck swiftly and kissed her hard as he swept his arms around her. He pulled her tight against his body and kissed her every bit as passionately as she'd kissed him earlier.

Shock stilled her in his arms. What did this mean? Was this some sort of revenge kiss? Or could it possibly mean he wasn't as mad at her as she'd thought? Was he punishing her? Saying goodbye? Showing her what she couldn't have in the future?

But then the kiss itself commanded so much of her attention that the little voices in her head faded into the background of his mouth moving against hers, his body moving against hers, his arms going around her and drawing her close.

His mouth was hot and wet and dark, and tasted of coffee. She threw herself into the kiss, gladly losing herself in him. In the moment.

Even now, he made her feel desired. Sexy. Beautiful. She reveled in the hardness of his chest, loved the strength of his arms. His breathing was fast and light, and she delighted in doing that to him as he kissed his way across her jaw and took the lobe of her ear lightly between his teeth. If this was a last kiss goodbye, she was going to miss this more than words could express.

"Next time you want to kiss me like that, do it in private, okay?" he murmured against her neck, just below her ear.

She froze. Had she heard him correctly? Next time? He was prepared to kiss her again, as in continue a relationship with her?

"Of course," she panted. She tilted her head back to give him better access to her throat, and he took immediate advantage of it to kiss the pulse fluttering wildly at the base of her throat.

His lips moved on the delicate skin there. "Because I don't want to have to stop kissing you again once we get started like that."

She leaned back far enough to look at his shadowed face as he lifted his head to stare down at her. His eyes were hard to see in the dim interior of his truck. "Does that mean you forgive me?" she asked in a small voice.

"Yup."

"Are you mad at me?"

"Nope."

"Are you sure?"

He continued to stare down at her in the electronic glow of the dashboard for a long moment. "Yes. I'm sure."

She smiled up at him tentatively. "I can't tell you how relieved I am. I was terrified I'd blown it with you."

He smiled crookedly. "Are you kidding? I'm a hero, department-wide."

"Why?" she blurted.

"You're generally considered to be the unattainable ice

queen. The gang was pleased to discover you're human after all."

"Don't BS me. They're teasing you like crazy over it."

"Absolutely." A smile started with an upward curve of the corners of his mouth and spread slowly across his face. "But they're all jealous as hell of me."

"Why?"

"That was some kiss you laid on me."

"Mmm. It was, wasn't it?"

His mouth descended toward hers again. "Yes, ma'am. It was."

The windows of his truck were completely steamed up when Reese finally pulled away from her with a sigh. "I'm not making love with you in the cab of my truck. At least not the first time. But if we don't stop soon, that's exactly where we're headed."

She looked around, measuring the distance between the seat and the dashboard. "If you push your seat all the way back and I straddle—"

"Stop." There was enough pained discomfort in his voice that she took pity on him and didn't finish describing what she had in mind for christening his truck.

"You going to Lou's retirement party?" he asked casually.

Crud. She'd totally forgotten about that. "I think I'll skip—"

He cut her off. "I could really use you to show up, even if just for a few minutes."

"Why's that?"

"Your, umm, attention to me over the past couple of days is causing a lot of talk. It's interfering with me doing my job."

"I'm sorry," she said quickly.

"It's okay. I just need you to show up at the bar, be casual around me for a few minutes while I'm casual around you, and then you can split. But Chief Hilton's asking questions about whether or not you and I can work together professionally or not. I'd hate to have the, umm, recent incidents impact our performance reports."

Gulp. The last thing she wanted to do was hurt Reese's career or chances at promotion. And goodness knew, she didn't need any reprimands in her permanent file about harassing a coworker. Not if she wanted to get hired by a big, prestigious forensics lab in a year or two.

"I get it. Not to mention I owe you one for saving my neck at the Dexter house."

"You don't owe me for that. I was just doing my job," he protested.

"Nonetheless. I'm the one who's caused you problems with the boss. It's up to me to fix it."

She climbed in her car and followed him downtown to Dusty Rusty's. The parking lot was close to full with the muscular pickup trucks a lot of the cops favored, and she winced as she parked her little car among them.

She spotted Reese parking and waited for him to go inside ahead of her. Giving him enough of a head start that nobody would suspect they'd arrived together—she hoped—she took a deep breath, climbed out of her car and trudged toward the bar.

Casual. She could do this. They still hated each other's guts and were just enjoying a temporary truce. Reese was an uptight jerk. He made her crazy.

Yeah. Crazy to kiss him senseless and get inside his pants.

Drat. The I-hate-Reese pep talk was a total flop.

Plan B: go inside and ignore Reese. It was what she would have done a few days ago.

Okay. She could do that. She stepped inside and was

bombarded by heat and noise and the overwhelming smell of beer. And man sweat. Ugh.

Did the fire marshal know this many cops were all crammed into Rusty's tonight? She was half tempted to call the fire department and report a building capacity violation. Until she spotted the fire chief bellied up to the bar. Sigh.

"Hey, Yvie!" Her sister's voice rose above the din.

She turned toward the sound but couldn't see Jordana in the press of big bodies. Lord, she hated being short, sometimes. She stood on her tiptoes, craning to see around the crowd and finally spotted her sister's auburn hair between the shoulders of a couple of big guys hunched over the bar.

"Beer?" Jordana's boyfriend, Clint, shouted at her when she finally reached the bar.

"Hate beer," she shouted back. "I'll have a seltzer water with a twist of lemon." Not booze but it looked like a drink. Saved a whole lot of explanations about how she had so little body mass that she was a complete lightweight when it came to drinking. And besides, she made a practice of never drinking with her colleagues.

Eventually a glass was passed to her filled with clear, fizzy liquid, ice and a lemon section. Jordana and Clint had their heads pressed together and appeared to be having an intense conversation, so she picked up her drink to leave.

"Don't go," Jordana shouted. "We have something to tell you."

She turned back to the couple, who looked so in love they practically glowed. A frisson of jealousy shivered through her belly. Must be nice to find that great a guy and have him fall head over heels for you. She noted the way Jordana leaned into Clint's side and how he angled his body protectively beside her. Yeah. That. Having a little of that would be nice, someday.

"What's up?" She leaned in close to avoid having to shout at the top of her lungs to be heard.

"I've decided to move to Chicago to be with Clint. His vacation is over and he has to go back to work. I'm going with him."

She stared, shocked. Of all her siblings, Jordana seemed the most connected to Braxville. She was a cop, here, and everything. "What about your job? You love being a cop."

"Tyler has offered me a job in his company." Tyler was their oldest brother and a partner in a high-end security firm.

"It's based in Wichita, not Chicago," Yvette responded, confused.

"He's opening an office in Chicago and wants me to head it up."

Yvette looked back and forth between Jordana and Clint, who were still doing that glowing thing, darn it. "Well, of course, I'll miss the heck out of you, but I'm happy for you guys."

Jordana reached up to push her hair back and Yvette spied a sparkle on her sister's left ring finger. She squealed and grabbed Jordana's hand. "Lemme see! He proposed? When did this happen?"

"This afternoon. After I accepted Tyler's offer and it was official that I'm moving to Chicago."

The diamond was big and beautiful, surrounded by a ring of smaller baguettes and more diamonds across the band. "Dang, sis. That thing is a lethal weapon. Punch someone with that and they're going *down*."

"Hopefully, the security business will be slower paced than police work."

Yvette grunted. Not bloody likely.

Clint grinned ruefully at her. "I keep trying to tell her

to ease off the pedal a little, but I doubt that's going to happen any time soon."

Yvette laughed. "Good luck with that. We Coltons tend to live life at ninety miles an hour with our hair on fire."

"I'd noticed that," Clint replied dryly.

Yvette leaned forward and hugged her sister. "I'm so happy for you two. Now, if you'll excuse me, I have to go find your partner and act casual around him so Chief Hilton will stop asking if Reese and I can work together like adults or not."

She turned away fast to avoid being quizzed by her sister and plunged into the crowd. The trick at a party like this, where she knew a lot of people but none of them were close friends, was to keep moving and always appear to be headed across the room toward someone.

She kept an eye out for the police chief, Roger Hilton, and for Reese. If she could catch the two of them together, or at least in visual contact with each other, she could stroll up to Reese, act casual for a minute or two and then get out of here.

Rusty's opened up in the back to a big seating area with dartboards along one side and a dance floor taking up the back half of the party space. TV screens mounted along the ceiling opposite the dartboards played several different sporting events at the moment. Thankfully, they were muted and weren't competing to be heard over the noise of the whole police department, most of the fire department, most of the off-duty EMTs from the county hospital, and a host of other people from around town who knew Lou Hovitz.

Dang. Popular guy. If she retired tomorrow and threw a party, maybe a couple of her siblings might show up— if they weren't busy doing laundry or something equally important. She supposed her mom would come. Lilly was loyal that way.

Yvette continued to move back and forth through the crowd in search of her twin targets, to no avail. Funny how lonely it was possible to feel in the middle of a big crowd. She'd left behind all her friends of the past several years in Virginia when she'd moved back to Braxville, and she felt that loss keenly now.

"Why the long face?" a male voice shouted in her ear.

She jumped and spun around to face Reese. "Where did you come from?"

"I've been playing darts. Your sister just kicked my ass, again."

"We have a dartboard in my dad's billiard room. Jordana's been throwing darts her whole life. She's the Colton family champion."

"Are you kidding me?"

"God's honest truth," she shouted back.

He swore under his breath and then said to her, "Thanks for coming tonight."

"Do you know where Roger Hilton is? He's the one guy who needs to see us getting along tonight."

"He's dancing with his wife. Been out there a while."

She turned her gaze to the mass of people currently boot scooting their way around the dance floor. It was so crowded she couldn't spot the Hiltons at all. She leaned in close to ask Reese, "Should we wait for him to come off the floor and then go over together to say hello to him or something?"

"I have a better idea. Dance with me."

Reese grabbed her drink and set it down on the nearest table along with his half-empty beer. He grabbed her around the waist and spun her out onto the dance floor before she even had a chance to say no.

The music was just changing into a country song made for two-stepping, and Reese confidently began shuffling around the floor with her. She hadn't two-stepped in years, but she relaxed and let him guide her around the floor to the quick-quick-slow-slow rhythm. As it came back to her, she let her feet move on autopilot.

Reese wore a crisply starched white shirt with the sleeves rolled up to reveal fine dark hairs on his forearms. His jeans were probably pressed and starched within an inch of their life, but she didn't dare glance down to find out.

His hand was firm on her waist as he guided her smoothly around the crowded floor, his thigh occasionally rubbing against hers. She had to tilt her head back to look up at him which threw her more than a little off-balance. More than once, she had to catch herself by tightening her hand on his shoulder.

After two or three of those balance checks, each of which pulled her closer to him, she realized she was more or less plastered against him, her chest rubbing against his, her belly rubbing against the zipper of his jeans. Her breath came faster, and it had nothing to do with the dancing. Nope, her dance partner made her think about doing all kinds of hot, naughty things to his delicious body.

The song ended and the next one was slow and sexy with sultry vocals that melted her from the inside out. At least she hoped it was just the song. Otherwise, it was Reese having that dramatic effect on her.

He stared down at her, his normally blue eyes black in the dim light of the bar. Or maybe his pupils were so dilated that his eyes appeared black. Either way, his gaze smoldered with intense heat. Oh, dear. Was he feeling the incendiary attraction between them, too?

His hand pressed against her back, drawing her even

closer against him until her thighs nestled on either side of one of his. They were in intimate contact from her knees to her shoulders, and everywhere she touched him, he was hard and burning hot.

Her right hand rested on his shoulder, and her left hand curled around his waist, where she noted there wasn't even a hint of an inner tube. Nope. This man was hard and lean, all muscle and restless energy.

And right now, that energy was aimed squarely at her. It vibrated through her, breaking the bonds between the molecules of her body until she felt like nothing more than a mass of tangled, separately tingling nerves. Taken all together, she was one giant hot mess.

Reese turned her in a slow, swaying circle, gradually spiraling her through the couples dotting the dance floor until the two of them were tucked in the back corner of the room, in the darkest, most heavily shadowed bit of the floor.

His head dipped down toward hers, and his mouth brushed against her temple. It was the lightest of kisses. It could even have been an accident. But then he murmured, "Is it just me, or is something definitely not casual happening between us?"

She pressed her eyes shut in chagrin. It was all she could do to stop herself from crawling all over his big, yummy body, right here, right now.

"We've got to dial this back," he muttered. "You know. For our careers."

"Right. Careers." Good grief. When did she get so breathless? All they were doing out here was swaying back and forth in slow motion. Nothing athletic that would steal all the air from her lungs like this.

She realized she was leaning in to him, craving the heat of his body, reveling in the feel of it pressed tightly against hers. They fit together perfectly. He was taller than her, but not so much so that her small stature made her feel like a half-grown child next to him.

His arms surrounded her, holding her snugly against him. Given the quick rise and fall of his chest against her breasts she surmised he was relishing the contact between them as much as she was.

Casual. Careers. Truce. The boss.

Nope. Nothing was distracting her from her pool of liquid heat forming in the pit of her belly, yearning toward the hard, sexual promise of Reese's body to fill that hungry void.

He turned to put his back to the room, effectively hiding her from everyone else in the joint. One of his hands left her back and reached between them, tilting her chin up. He leaned down and kissed her carnally, his tongue plunging into her mouth in a rhythmic imitation of sex. She surged up into the kiss on her tiptoes, her own tongue swirling around his. The smooth glide of lips on lips, the wrestling tangle of their tongues, the mingling of breath, stole what little breath she had left.

Gasping, she dropped back to flat-footed on the floor, burying her face against his shirt. He smelled of man and something tangy and citrus and delicious. Even the scent of him sent waves of need rolling through her.

"Let's get out of here," he murmured against her temple.

"Right. Yes." Her mind skipped like a needle jumping to another track on an old vinyl album. "But, umm, casual. Boss. We have to be seen by Roger."

"Screw casual."

"I won't wreck your career." *Ta-da*. She *was* capable of forming a complete sentence!

"Screw that, too. Let's go." He surprised her by pushing her backward toward the wall behind her. She stumbled, shocked as it gave way and a blast of cold slammed into her shoulder blades.

A door. Rear exit, apparently.

Reese spun her outside and the door closed behind them.

"My coat—"

"I'll text your sister to pick it up," he muttered against her neck.

She threw her head back, loving the feel of his mouth on her bare skin. "Oh, that'll go over great with her." She stopped speaking while a head-to-toe shiver made her momentarily incapable of speech, then continued breathlessly, "No way will you be able to convince her there's nothing going on between us if we flee the scene of the crime without even grabbing our coats."

"I don't care what she thinks," he murmured as he caught her earlobe between his teeth and bit down gently.

"You say that now. Have you ever seen my sister get a bone between her teeth and refuse to let go?"

He laughed a little, a sexy rumble in his chest that she felt through her whole body. "Yeah, actually. I have." He straightened, throwing his arm over her shoulder and tucking her tightly against his side. "C'mon. It's freezing out here."

He hurried her over to his truck and piled her inside. From behind the bench seat, he pulled out a thick wool blanket that he threw over her and tucked in around her.

Moving around to the driver's side, he climbed in, started the engine and pointed at a rotating dial. "Give the truck three minutes and then crank that all the way to the right. It'll start throwing heat out at you."

He opened his door again.

"Where are you going?" she blurted.

"Inside to get our coats."

"Mine's cream wool with a belt—"

He interrupted gently. "I know. I work with you. I've seen you come and go from the office every day for the past year. I'm familiar with your various coats."

"You know my coats?" she asked incredulously.

"My favorite is the light blue ski jacket," he commented casually as he climbed out. She stared, openmouthed as he shut the door and jogged off into the darkness. He paid attention to her *coats*? What did it mean? Was he merely observant, or did his attention to detail related to her mean... more?

No answers had come to her by the time Reese blew back into the truck cab on a gust of frigid air.

"Man. It's getting cold out there," Reese commented, pushing her coat across the now warm cab at her. "Feels like another storm may be blowing in."

"I should drive my car home," she said, reaching for the door handle.

"I'll drive you. Roads will already be getting icy."

"I have to get my car home, sometime," she replied dryly.

"It won't hurt anything spending the night here. I imagine a bunch of vehicles will end up being here overnight. Lots of cops inside are drinking and will know better than to drive afterward. Local rideshare guys are gonna get some good business out of Lou's party."

"You had a beer when I first saw you. Should you be driving?" she asked.

He ducked his chin a little. "I always buy one beer and dump half of it down a toilet. Then I carry it around the rest of the night."

"You don't drink?" she asked in surprise.

"Not often. And certainly not when I have to drive home. How about you? What was that in your glass?"

"Selzter water and a lemon," she confessed.

He laughed a little. "Who knew we were such a couple of stick-in-the-muds?"

"Speak for yourself, Detective," she replied tartly.

He grinned broadly at her. "I'll keep the secret if you will."

"Deal," she replied, smiling back.

Honestly, she was relieved not to chance the bad roads in her lightweight car without four-wheel drive or chains for her tires. Her father and brothers had been trying to talk her into trading her fuel-efficient little car in for something bigger and heavier, suited to the bad weather that was known to blow in at this time of year. But to date, she'd resisted. She'd forgotten how bad these sudden blizzards could be out here on the Great Plains.

Ruefully, she said, "I'm trying to repair my reputation in the department. Leaving my car here in a blatant advertisement that I've gone home with someone else isn't going to help matters one bit. As much as I appreciate your offer to drive me home, I need to get my car out of here."

He sighed. "Fine. I'll follow you to your place. If the roads are too bad for you or you get in trouble, I'll be there to help. And, be careful. There are black ice patches on the roads."

Black ice was the bane of Kansas roads at this time of year. The sun warmed snow and ice during the day into wet puddles. Then, at night, when temperatures fell below freezing, the puddles froze into sheets of clear ice that allowed the black pavement to be seen below. Hence, the name. The stuff was glass smooth and treacherous to drive on. Braking on a sheet of it was impossible. A car might as well be on an ice-skating rink.

"Will do." Reluctantly, she shrugged into her coat, climbed out of the truck and tromped through drifts of snow already a foot deep to her car. Reese helped her brush the snow off her windshield and windows while the interior of the car warmed up.

When she was ready to go, she flashed Reese a thumbs-up and he trudged back to his truck and climbed in. With him following a safe distance behind, she did, indeed, drive home exceptionally cautiously and arrived without incident in her driveway. She trotted out of her garage to Reese's truck, and he rolled down the window as she approached.

"Would you like to come inside? It's not late. Have you eaten? I can cook for us," she offered.

"Do you know how to cook?"

She snorted. "You don't have to sound so surprised. I've made it into my midtwenties, which means I've been eating for years all by my little self."

He rolled his eyes and turned off the ignition. "Yes, but is it edible?"

"Come in and find out. I dare you."

"You really have to stop daring me to do things. One day, you'll get in over your head."

"Never," she replied stoutly, opening the door from the garage into the house and kicking out of her boots in the mudroom.

"Big words, little girl," he teased as he followed her into her cozy kitchen.

"Who are you calling little?" she demanded as she turned on the lights and started pulling out food.

Grinning, he backed her up against the wall beside her refrigerator and kissed her long and leisurely. Goodness. She could not get enough of kissing that man. Belatedly, she realized her hands were full of lettuce, carrots, tomatoes and celery. He stepped back, and she plunked the food onto the counter, then pulled out a cutting board and knife.

"Can I help?" he offered.

"Sit." She pointed the big knife at the kitchen table.

Grinning, he threw up his hands and sat. "Truce. It's still in effect, right?"

"As long as you don't make fun of my cooking, it is."

"Yes, ma'am." He grinned cheekily at her.

Those bedroom eyes of his were at it again, sparkling sexily and making her think about things she'd like to do with him on the kitchen table that had nothing to do with food. Dang, that man was lethal.

She forced her attention to the task at hand. Supper. She had a couple of nice steaks in her fridge, and she put a cast-iron skillet on the stove to heat up. When it was sizzling hot, she dropped in butter and seared the steaks quickly on both sides to seal in the juices. Then, she put the whole pan in the oven to finish off the sirloins. While they cooked, she boiled eggs, chopped romaine lettuce, ham, carrots, celery, onions and bacon, and put together a decent Cobb salad if she did say so, herself.

She put Reese to work snapping green beans and steamed those with garlic and butter after he was done. Just as she set the salad on the table the oven timer went off. She peeked at the beans, which were bright green, aromatic and tender. *Yes.* She whisked the steaks out of the oven to rest, plated them and the beans, and set the meal on the table with a flourish.

It was pure luck on her part that everything came together at once, but she was totally willing to take credit for it with Reese.

She sat down beside him and smiled. *"Bon appétit."*

"I have to admit, I'm impressed."

"You haven't tasted it yet."

He cut into his steak, and juice mingled with the butter. It was medium rare, succulent and tender. Again, sheer luck. But what Reese Carpenter didn't know about her hit-or-miss cooking skills wouldn't hurt him.

He groaned with pleasure. "Oh. That's a fine piece of meat."

His gaze snapped up to hers, startled. "Sorry. I didn't mean that the way it sounded."

She stabbed a piece of her steak daintily with her fork and waved it at him airily. "Never fear. I take no offense at the double entendre. I'm nobody's piece of meat."

"No kidding," he replied heartily.

"Meaning what?" she demanded. "Don't you think I'm attractive enough to be seen as meat?"

He put down his utensils and threw up his hands. "You are totally meat-worthy. But I in no way think of you like that—"

She burst into laughter. "I'm just messing with you."

He scowled momentarily but then dissolved into a grin. "So that's how it's gonna be, huh? Duly noted. Just remember, payback's a bitch."

"Bring it, buddy."

Clearly, he planned to delay his retaliatory teasing for he fell to his meal with enthusiasm and little talk ensued.

Near the end of supper, she finally worked up the courage to ask the question that had been bugging her ever since Reese forgave her in his truck. "How bad was the razzing after I left the squad room today?"

He looked up from his last bite of steak and grinned. "Actually, it went dead silent. Everyone was so shocked they didn't know what to say. First time I've ever seen that bunch speechless."

She winced. "I'm so sorry."

He leaned back with a sigh of pleasure. "That was a helluva good steak. Thank you."

"I don't have anything snazzy to offer you for dessert.

I do have ice cream and some fresh strawberries I can slice over it."

"I'm stuffed. Nothing for me, thanks," he replied.

She leaned back, as well. "How did Jordana find out about our, umm, squad-room kiss so fast? She called me about thirty seconds after I got back to the lab."

"I expect somebody texted her." A frown crossed his brow. "Was she mad?"

"At me? Oh, yeah. She said it reflects on her and that she considers us both to be her siblings…which makes it weird, apparently."

"Hmm. Gonna have to have a chat with her about you, I guess."

He didn't sound thrilled at the prospect.

The elation she'd been feeling at his forgiveness evaporated. "I'm sorry—"

"Stop apologizing already," he interrupted. "You've done nothing wrong."

"Well, I did lay a big wet one on you in the middle of our mutual workplace."

"Which I willingly—correction, *eagerly*—participated in. That kiss took two people, in case you hadn't noticed."

She answered sarcastically, "I had noticed, thank you."

He snorted with laughter. "I do love a woman with a dry sense of humor."

"That's me. The Sahara Desert."

She started to get up to do the dishes, but Reese reached out, grabbed her wrist and tugged her back down into her chair. "Oh no, you don't. You cooked. I'll do the dishes."

"If that's how you roll, I'll cook dinner for you every night."

This time it was her gaze that snapped to his, startled and chagrined.

Darn her mouth! When was she going to learn to think about what she said before the words just popped out?

"It's my pleasure to clean up," he responded blandly enough. But she caught the look of—something—in his eyes as he turned away. She couldn't tell if that was speculation or cold, hard terror in his eyes at her crack about doing this every night. Behind his back, she squeezed her eyes shut in chagrin. She was a total mess around him.

Sleeves rolled up and sponge in hand, which was possibly the sexiest look she'd ever seen on him, he said over his shoulder, "I forgot to ask if you've gotten into that puzzle box yet."

"No, but I'm close. I think there's only one layer of the puzzle left. Sucker has four layers to solve."

Reese murmured, "Which begs the question, what does that key open that's so important?"

"Dexter—assuming it was Dexter and not his wife—went to a whole lot of trouble to hide the key, that's for sure."

Reese replied, "Using the X-ray image of the key that you emailed me, I did a little preliminary research on it. My guess is that it's some sort of a safe-deposit box or locker key."

"Interesting."

"I showed the image of the key to the guys at all the local banks in Braxville, and they said it's not one of theirs."

"A bank in Wichita, maybe?" she suggested. "Or possibly Kansas City?"

He nodded and picked up a dish towel to start drying. "I had time to check with a few Wichita banks, today. I'll email the image to the rest of the Wichita banks tomorrow."

"If you don't get a hit, let me know. The FBI maintains

an exhaustive key database that I have access to as a forensics investigator."

He looked over his shoulder at her and nodded. "Thanks. Will do." He put the last plate onto the dry towel he'd spread out beside the sink. She had a perfectly functional dishwasher, but she'd enjoyed sitting here watching the hot, macho man washing dishes. There was something unbelievably attractive about a man doing a domestic chore with ease and comfort.

She stood up and went over to the sink to wrap her arms around his hard, lean waist from behind. "Thanks for doing the dishes. And thanks again for forgiving me about the whole kiss thing."

He turned in her arms and wrapped his arms around her shoulders. Resting his chin on top of her head, he said quietly, "I'm not the giant ass you seem to think I am."

"I don't think you're a giant ass. Maybe just a little one. Sometimes."

His chest rumbled with silent laughter. "I love how you call me out. Keep me honest."

"I thought you were the one who always calls me out. You pick on how I do my job and how I run my lab all the time."

"I don't pick on you," he disagreed. "And I don't tell you what to do. I make helpful suggestions."

She laughed aloud at that. "Right. Forcefully."

"I'm sorry if I've been a jerk. I just really wanted to see you succeed."

Startled, she leaned back in his arms to look up at him. "Come again?"

"There was a lot of skepticism in the department about hiring a woman, and so young a woman, for your position. I was on the hiring review committee, though, and you were by far the most qualified candidate for the job. I've been in your corner since before you were hired."

"For real?"

He flashed that crooked smile of his again that was so endearing and irresistible.

She said softly, "And here I thought you were busting my chops and trying to chase me out of the department."

"Nope. Exactly the opposite."

She reached up and laid her palm lightly on his cheek. "Thank you, Reese."

"You don't have to thank me. You earned the job, and you've been knocking it out of the park ever since you got here. All the credit goes to you."

"Well, shoot. Now I'm embarrassed," she confessed.

"Don't be. Own the space you've earned."

"When did you become such a feminist?" she queried.

"Since my partner on the force showed me that women are every bit as good at police work as men, and since her sister showed me women make first-rate forensic scientists, too."

"Surely, your mother had something to do with this enlightened attitude."

He chuckled. "She would blister my butt if I was anything less than respectful to any woman. And I don't mess with my mama."

"I hear you. I wouldn't ever cross mine, either."

"Your mom is a sweetheart. She took care of my dad in the hospital after his heart attack. She gave him just the right combination of kindness and tough love he needed to get back on his feet and change his eating and exercise habits."

Yvette smiled fondly. Her mother had often been a distant figure in her life, with a big family to care for, her husband's career to support and demanding career of her own. But she never for a moment doubted that Lilly loved her as fiercely as she loved all her children. Her mother had always called her *My special gift* and *My littlest angel*.

Reese commented casually, "Did anybody tell you your dad's coming to the police department tomorrow to turn himself in?"

"No." She'd temporarily forgotten about the arsenic case in the kerfuffle over the puzzle box, her mad crush on Reese and the whole kissing-in-the-squad-room fiasco. "Is it going to be bad for him?"

He shrugged. "There could be press. When is it ever good when reporters and cameras are around?"

Yikes. Not encouraging.

She led Reese into her sitting room, which she'd decorated like an English country cottage. The furniture was casual and cozy, a blend of old and new. The sofa and curtains were a buttery-yellow floral print, but their femininity was balanced by the masculine weight of the massive stone fireplace.

"Pretty room," Reese commented.

"It doesn't give you hives to be surrounded by all this girly stuff?" she asked doubtfully.

"I happen to like girls quite a lot. In my experience, they tend to come with girly stuff."

She smirked. "Sort of like men come with smelly socks, empty beer cans and butt-crack scratching?"

"You really don't like men much, do you?"

Her gaze fell away from his. "I like you."

"Why don't you like men in general?"

She sighed. "You'd have to be a single, reasonably attractive woman of dating age to understand."

"Try me."

"In high school and college, too many guys I knew were hopelessly immature and focused mainly on getting laid as often as possible. The word *no* wasn't always in their vocabulary. Some of them got angry and aggressive." She shrugged. "A girl learns to be cautious."

"Cautious how?"

She shrugged. "You don't take drinks or food from strange men in case they're drugged. You don't go to parties alone—always go with a couple of girlfriends—and for goodness' sake don't leave alone. Take a girlfriend to the bathroom with you. Don't engage with guys who smell like booze—I could go on, but you get the point."

"Didn't you meet *any* education-focused guys interested in pursuing serious careers and whose parents taught them how to treat a woman right?" he asked.

"I probably did, but I was so turned off by the other kind that I couldn't see the good ones hiding among the bad ones."

"We're out here. You just have to look for us."

"No offense, but you were the biggest jerk of all when I got to the department. Although, in your defense, you never came on to me."

"I'm sorry if I came off like a jerk. I just wanted you to make it, here. I should have trusted you to be able to handle being the first woman in your position."

"Is there still resistance to me in the department?"

"Not after today."

She rolled her eyes and sighed. "I'd prefer to be judged on my professional merits and not how I kiss."

He reached out and tucked a stray strand of her hair behind her ear. His fingertips traced the rim of her ear lightly. "Never fear. Everyone thinks you're scary smart and darned good at your job."

Thank goodness. "That's a relief, at least."

He smiled warmly at her.

"Why was it I hated you, again?" she asked.

"Because love and hate are only a hair's breadth apart?" he offered.

Love? Whoa. That was a big word. But he had a point. The sizzling friction between them this whole past year had morphed into something much more sexual and intimate in the blink of an eye. That wouldn't have happened if a lot of that simmering tension hadn't already been driven by attraction, unconscious or otherwise.

She cast about for a more neutral topic of conversation and ended up blurting, "What are you going to do for a partner once Jordana leaves the department?"

Reese froze, staring at her. "I beg your pardon?"

"Surely, she told you first. She's moving to Chicago to open up an office for my future brother-in-law's security firm."

"I…she…sonofabitch." He whirled away, shoving a hand through his dark hair, standing it up on end.

"Ohmigosh. She hasn't told you, yet. God. I'm so sorry." She stepped forward and touched Reese's arm tentatively.

He whirled, all but knocking her over with the violence of the movement, and ended up having to wrap his arms around her tightly to keep from knocking her right off her feet.

"Sorry," he muttered.

"No, I'm sorry. I just assumed. I'm so stupid—"

He kissed her ferociously, and she absorbed his anger, and what felt like something akin to grief, into herself in silence. But then his anger shifted. Intensified. Turned into something dark and sexy and dangerous.

He surged against her, kissing her with his whole body, and she flung herself at him in return. She couldn't get enough of this man. He backed her up against the front door and planted his thigh between hers, effectively pinning her in place. Not that she minded one bit. Her nether regions rubbed against the rough denim and her breath caught at the delicious sensation.

His hands plunged into her hair and his tongue plunged into her mouth, and she returned the favor, inhaling him even deeper into their kiss.

He must have realized he was crushing her for he turned suddenly, dragging her with him until his back was against the door and it was her turn to press into him, kissing him with all the pent-up intensity that had been building between them for months.

His mouth slashed across hers and she met him halfway. Their kiss was wet and hot, a sparring match between two aggressively attracted people who were rapidly spinning out of control. And it was glorious. The ridge behind his zipper was big and hard, and she pressed her belly hungrily against it. The peaks of her breasts rubbed against his chest, and her entire body felt light and energized, tingling and eager for more.

Gradually, Reese's mouth eased away from hers, and his hands stilled their roaming path across her back. She leaned back to look at him questioningly.

"I'm sorry," he sighed. "I shouldn't have fallen on you to take out my frustration."

She smiled a little. "Depends on what kind of frustration you're talking about."

He smiled reluctantly. "I just—losing another partner— it was a surprise—didn't see it coming."

"Another partner?" she echoed. "You've lost one before?"

She was still sprawled all over him, so she felt his entire body tense. His eyes shut down as if he'd just flipped an off switch in his brain. Whoa. She stepped back quickly, snagging his hand and pulling him away from the door and over to the sofa.

"Sit down. Talk to me, Reese. What giant nerve did I just hit?"

He shook his head and started to stand up, but she pushed on his shoulders, pressing him back down to the cushions. Not that she could brute force him into doing anything, of course, but he went along with her pressure.

"Talk."

He closed his eyes tightly for a moment, and when he opened them again, they were bleak. "I lost my first partner a few years back. She died. Shot in an arrest gone bad. I saw the gun. Too late. Tried to draw my own weapon. Wasn't fast enough. She went down." He stared over her shoulder at nothing, obviously seeing the whole thing again in his mind's eye. "So much blood. Bullet hit her aorta. She died in under two minutes. No time for an ambulance to get there. No backup. Just me holding her as her life slipped away…"

"Oh, Reese. I'm so sorry. I had no idea. I'm such an idiot."

"You had no way of knowing."

She said in a more upbeat tone, "Well, Jordana isn't dying. She's just moving away to be with her fiancé. Clint proposed today, by the way."

"Good for them. I hope they're happy."

She said dryly, "They're freaking delirious. It's disgusting."

Hah. That got a tiny smile out of him, at least.

She said, "She'll be back to visit all the time. Her whole family is here in Braxville. You're family to her, too."

"She's the irritating sister I never had," Reese said ruefully.

Thank goodness it was Jordana who'd been relegated to that role and not her. She channeled her mother for a moment and asked him, "Can I get you a cup of tea? Or a stiff shot of whiskey?"

He snorted. "You are a Colton, aren't you? When in doubt, offer food or drink."

"That's us. Always stuffing our faces."

"Then how do you stay so tiny?" he asked with a hint of humor in his voice.

Yep. He was doing better. The first shock of finding out his partner was leaving the force had passed, and he was going to be okay. She waved a casual hand at him. "I only dine on the souls of my enemies and drink the blood of small children. Keeps me trim."

That made him laugh reluctantly. "You don't fool me. You're not the evil ice queen folks in the department make you out to be."

"Don't tell them that!" she exclaimed in alarm. "I've worked hard to cultivate that image."

"Why's that?" Reese asked.

"Have you counted how many single, horny men there are in the Braxville PD? This is a small town, and eligible women are few and far between. The last thing I needed was for the whole police force to try to date me."

"Jeez. I'm sorry—" he started, moving to rise.

She grabbed his arm quickly. "You're fine. We have a truce, remember?"

"Right. Truce. You're sure you don't want to stop this—whatever this is—before it goes any further?"

"Positive," she answered immediately. More hesitantly, she asked, "How about you? Do you want to call things off?"

"Absolutely not."

They traded looks that were by turns warm and abashed. He cleared his throat. "Well okay, then. I'm glad that's settled. And now, I really do need to get out of here."

"But if we just decided to extend the truce—"

"If I stay any longer, we're going to pass way beyond a truce to a full-blown peace treaty," he interrupted.

"What's wrong with that?" she demanded.

He stood up, moving swiftly for the door. "I'm not a one-night-stand kind of guy. If we do this, we're going to do it right."

She frowned. "We're not doing anything right now."

"Patience, Yvie."

"Have you met me? I don't have a patient bone in my body!"

He laughed low and husky. "Ahh, this is going to be a fun ride."

She scowled darkly at him. "You'd better buckle up, buster."

"Roger that." Grinning, he reached for the doorknob.

"What am I going to do with you?" she asked rhetorically.

"You're going to come over here so I can kiss you goodnight and thank you for that delicious dinner, and then you're going to show me out. Otherwise, the neighbors are going to wonder whose truck is in your driveway in the morning."

"I barely know my neighbors' names. Stay."

"Don't tempt me. I make it a policy never to sleep with a woman on our first date."

"I thought sorting files in my lab was our first date."

He laughed a little, sounding pained. He drew her into a hard hug and dropped a kiss on top of her head. "Ahh, you are a firecracker. You're going to keep me on my toes, aren't you?"

"Baby, I'm no firecracker. I'm a tactical nuclear bombshell."

"Truer words were never spoken," he replied, grinning.

She did, indeed, walk him to her front door. A soft glow came from outside, peachy light from the streetlamps illuminating the blanket of fresh snow that had fallen in the past few hours.

Reese drew her into his arms, kissing her slowly and thoroughly. She kissed him back, throwing herself into the kiss with abandon. She loved everything about how he felt against her, his body hard and fit, his mouth warm and resilient, his tongue wet and sexy and impudent.

She sucked at his tongue, pulling it deeper into her mouth, and he groaned in reaction. Just when she thought she might have broken down his resolve to leave and convinced him to follow her back to her bedroom, he straightened all at once and took a hasty step back.

"Lord, woman. You're more temptation than I can stand up to."

And yet, he'd just backed away from her.

"Stay," she said softly.

"Not tonight. But soon. When we're more sure of each other."

What more was there to be sure of? She was totally sure she wanted to sleep with him.

"Dream about me, tonight," he said quietly, dropping a quick kiss on the tip of her nose. He opened the door and stepped out onto the porch.

"Maybe I won't dream about you," she tossed out.

"I'll bet you a dollar you do," he tossed back.

"You're such a know-it-all," she groused, smiling.

"It's not being a know-it-all if I actually do know what I'm talking about."

Laughing, she walked to the edge of the porch where the snow got deep and his footprints sank deep into the fluffy blanket of white on her sidewalk. "You keep telling yourself that, big guy."

"God, I love smart-mouthed women."

"Smart being the operative word."

He turned and strode back to her swiftly, kissing her hard and fast one more time. "Dream of me," he ordered her.

Darned if she didn't dream about him that night, too. Lovely dreams about dancing in the dark, smoking-hot kisses and laughter. Lots of laughter.

It was hard to be mad at him for being right, or for owing him a dollar, though, when she woke up the next morning with a smile on her lips.

Chapter 9

Reese looked around the lobby of the police building, which had been set up for this morning's press conference. A raised dais held a podium and several light stands. In front of it, a dozen reporters already milled around, and more were coming into the building every minute. Broadcast vans lined the entire perimeter of the parking lot, their satellite-uplink dishes already pointed skyward.

He recognized several of the journalists from national news shows and winced. This was going to be a circus—a big three-ringed mess of one. He'd tried to warn Yvette obliquely last night, but he doubted she'd caught the hint as to how bad this was going to be.

Chief of Police Roger Hilton strolled up to him. "Everything ready to go? Colton knows what to do?"

Fitz Colton was turning himself in this morning to face charges in the arsenic-poisoning cases. The plan was to allow him to make a statement to the press first. Then, the police chief would speak. And then Reese would drop the bomb. A bomb he would've been fine lobbing a few days ago. But now that he'd gotten to know Yvette better, he was hating himself for having volunteered to be the bad cop in this scenario.

Fitz and his lawyer were in on the plan and had agreed to participate in it as part of his plea deal, but none of Fitz's kids had any idea what was coming, today. It was important that the family's reactions be authentic and believable if this little charade was going to work.

The lobby continued to fill as the nine o'clock start time for the press conference approached. Two of Yvette's brothers, Brooks and Tyler Colton, walked in together and stood near the back, taking in the crowd with less than pleased expressions. Brooks's fiancée, a schoolteacher, wasn't here this morning. But Tyler's fiancée, Ashley Hart, walked in with Bridgette Colton—Yvette's other sister besides Jordana—and the two women made their way over to the Colton brothers. Neil Colton walked in with his girlfriend, Braxville mayor, Elise Willis, but they separated immediately as she headed for the press corps to say hello to some of the more famous journalists here this morning.

Jordana was at her desk right now, unaware of the circus forming out here. He would text her in a few minutes to come out if she didn't wander out on her own to check out the rising din of close to fifty journalists milling around chatting with one another and making last-minute adjustments to makeup, lighting and camera angles with their crews.

Yvette was the only other child of Fitz Colton not here yet. And she should walk in any minute expecting to go to work. He hated ambushing her like this, but the plan required her to walk in unprepared for this fiasco.

Honestly, he was surprised she wasn't here yet. Her

workday technically started at nine in the morning, but she often could be found in the lab before seven o'clock. Perhaps his prediction had been true and she'd slept in late, dreaming of him. He smiled a little in anticipation of teasing her about it later.

A hand touched his elbow and he turned, startled. *Jordana.*

"What the hell is this?" she demanded under her breath.

"I guess word got out that your father was going to turn himself in, today."

"Jeez Louise. What a mess. Can we get all these people out of here? It's five degrees outside. They won't stick around for long if we can move them outdoors. I'll call my dad and tell him to delay coming in—"

"He's due in any second. You need to let this play out."

"The news cycle is as much about entertainment as facts. They'll nuke him!"

"It's too late to stop this thing," he responded. "If you send away national media outlets at this late moment, they'll make a story out of that and accuse the Braxville Police Department of a cover-up on behalf of your rich, powerful father. For your old man's sake, you have to let this press circus happen. His arrest has to appear fair and unbiased."

"I *know* that. But this sucks."

He couldn't resist giving his partner a tiny warning of what was coming. "Brace yourself. The worst thing you could do is intervene on his behalf with the press. Today— as long as the cameras are rolling—you have to be a police officer first and Fitz Colton's daughter second."

"God, I hate this," she said fervently.

At least she didn't argue with him about not intervening in the coming proceeding. It had been a calculated risk not to brief her on the plan, but Roger Hilton and the district attorney had agreed with Reese's assessment that Jordana wouldn't agree to play along with it.

He said quietly, "Call Clint. Ask him to come over and give you some moral support. And in the meantime, a bunch of your siblings have gathered in that back corner. Why don't you go hang out with them? I'll handle the questions from the press directed at us police that Roger can't answer. It would probably be best if a non-Colton detective fielded questions about the Fitz Colton investigation."

"Yeah. You're right. Thanks for taking the bullet."

He winced. A bullet indeed. He had no doubt she would want to empty a whole clip of ammunition into him by the time this press conference was over.

Whew. One Colton sister handled. Now, if only Yvette would get here so he could coax her to go down to her lab and avoid this whole show. Because a show was exactly what they had planned for today.

Yvette turned in to the police department's parking lot and stopped her car. The entire lot was crammed with vehicles, and the whole front of the thing was lined with television broadcast vans with network names sprawled over their sides. Many of them were major national news outlets.

Oh, God. This had to be about her father.

Panic erupted under her breastbone. Not good. So very not good.

She drove around to the auxiliary parking lot behind the building and found a spot in the very back of the lot, tucked in a corner next to a huge snowbank that butted practically right up against the side of her car. Good thing she was tiny and could squeeze out of the few inches she could get her door open.

She slipped and slid across the icy parking lot, skating her way into the police building. She was sorely tempted to bolt down the back stairs and hide in her lab, far from the cameras and noise. But her whole family would no doubt show up to support her father, and her absence would be glaring, not to mention disloyal.

Reluctantly, she headed toward the front of the building. Fitz had always been an intimidating figure in her life. She didn't know him very well—he worked long hours through her childhood building his beloved company, and he had a naturally gruff personality. He hadn't been a bad father. He just hadn't been a good one.

As she emerged into the main lobby, she gaped at the mob crammed into the large space. Good grief. She recognized every face in the entire front row of reporters crowding the podium. All the national news shows were here. Ugh.

Why couldn't a tsunami have hit or a volcano have erupted somewhere else in the world today to sweep the Colton Construction arsenic story out of the news cycle? Not that she wished a disaster on anyone else, of course, but she hated this with every cell in her being.

She spied Reese's familiar back in front of her and moved toward him. He turned as she approached, his worried eyes lighting with a brief, intimate smile for her.

"There you are," he murmured. "I was wondering if you were going to get here before the big show begins."

"This is awful. Isn't there anything we can do to get these people to go away?"

He shrugged. "It's a free press. They can cover whatever they deem newsworthy."

"And the fall of a rich, powerful man makes for a great headline," she said bitterly.

"I'm sorry about all of this, Yvette. I would shield you from every bit of it if I could. In fact, why don't you just go on down to your lab? I'll text you when this is over—"

"I'm a Colton. We stick together."

He sighed. "Yeah, I figured you'd say that. It was worth a try, though. Your brothers and sisters are gathered in the back." He pointed toward the left back corner of the room. "That way." He added, grinning slyly, "Since you can't see them over the crowd."

"You're hilarious, Jolly Green Carpenter," she shot back, grinning.

She stepped away from him and her petite frame was swallowed by the mob. He was still trying to verify that she'd made it back to the cluster of Coltons when a ruckus erupted by the front door behind the crowd. Lights went on, cameramen turned their equipment to face the back of the room and journalists talked into their microphones.

He spied Lilly Colton's red hair first, as she was climbing out of a black Town Car. He did feel bad for her. She was a kind person, and this scandal had to have been hard on her. Her natural compassion couldn't have been at ease with the idea of her husband and his partner sickening and killing some of their employees.

Fitz climbed out of the car behind her. The vehicle pulled away from the curb. They must have hired someone to bring them down here. The blackout windows would have kept rotten vegetables from being lobbed at them as they drove through Braxville, at any rate.

Predictably, the press rushed Lilly and Fitz as they headed for the building, stopping them from even reaching the front doors of the police department. Reese sighed and spoke into the microphone clipped to the collar of his suit coat. "Can we get a few uniforms outside to usher Mr. and Mrs. Colton into the building?"

Quickly, several cops cleared the way, and the couple stepped inside. Lilly peeled off to join her children—thank God. At least she would be surrounded by loved ones when the feces hit the fan. Of course, unlike her children, she knew what was coming.

The district attorney hadn't wanted to tell her what was going down today, but Fitz had rebelled at the idea of keeping her in the dark. He'd complained that his marriage was already in the toilet and keeping this secret from her might push Lilly over the edge. The DA had caved, but only if Fitz made sure Lilly swore not to warn her children about it in any way. This plan relied heavily on genuine reactions out of the family.

Fitz made it to the dais and stepped up to the podium. He pulled a folded piece of paper out of the pocket of his suit coat and spread it out before him. The room went expectantly silent as he cleared his voice.

"Thank you for coming today, ladies and gentlemen, although I hardly think this moment warrants such attention. At any rate, as you all know, Colton Construction, in which I'm co-owner, stands accused of using arsenic-laced wood products, obtained from China some years ago, in one of its construction projects. In the ensuing years, several employees have become sick, and a few have passed away from complications likely related to exposure to this toxic wood.

"I am here today to turn myself in to the police to face charges relating to these sad events. Furthermore, as the majority partner in the firm with a fifty-one percent stake in the company, I would like to announce that I have decided to sell Colton Construction. In accordance with a plea deal I have struck with the Braxville District Attorney's office…"

Reese tuned out as the statement droned on. He'd been in the room when Fitz's statement was drafted and agreed upon, and he knew that a detailed explanation followed of how the proceeds from the sale of the business would be disbursed through a neutral, third-party attorney agreed upon by Fitz and the DA.

While Fitz read on, Reese craned to see over the crowd, to find Yvette's face in the melee, to check in on her and make sure she was doing all right. Of course, this wasn't the part where things would get ugly.

There she was. She looked pale, her features drawn in stress. Did she feel bad for her part in proving the wood from the Colton project was the source of the arsenic that had poisoned the Colton workers? He sincerely hoped she didn't feel guilty for helping put her father in this uncomfortable situation. He'd done that to himself when he'd gone along with Markus's plan to cut financial corners and use the cheap Chinese wood that was known to be treated with toxic chemicals.

The arsenic acted as a pesticide to protect the wood from insect damage, but was outlawed for use in the United States for precisely the reason that it caused cancer in the people who handled it and worked with it.

He tuned back in to see where Fitz was in his statement.

"...and all remaining proceeds of the sale will be put into a trust fund administered by a neutral third party. Its funds will be available to pay for medical bills and expenses for the affected employees and their families, including the survivors of deceased employees.

"I will also personally be establishing a scholarship fund for the children of the affected employees to defray the costs of their higher education. I regret the decisions that led to this tragedy and accept responsibility for my part in it. I promise to do everything in my power to make it right for the affected Colton Construction employees and their families."

Fitz had balked at promising anything, but the DA had

stood firm and insisted that the verbiage be in the statement. He wanted Fitz on the record with his word of honor.

Assuming that's worth anything. Reese wasn't so sure of that, anymore. At least Yvette didn't seem to have inherited her father's…flexible…sense of right and wrong. Besides, it wasn't like Fitz could ever make it right for the employees who'd died.

As soon as Fitz stopped speaking and looked up from the paper before him, the journalists shouted all at once, yelling questions about how much money would go to the employees, whether or not he was going to serve jail time, and whether or not the plea deal included any further admission of guilt.

To Reese, standing just to one side of the podium, the din was deafening. And it wasn't even directed at him. Dang. No wonder people talked about the press going into feeding frenzies.

The police chief stepped up to the podium and held up his hands for silence. It took a while for the reporters to settle down. He made a brief statement that the Braxville Police Department was committed to seeing the law enforced and investigating the charges fully and impartially. Then he said, "I'll pass any questions you have to the officer in charge of the investigation, Detective Reese Carpenter."

That was his cue. Reese stepped forward. Here went nothing.

He spoke into the microphone. "The arsenic investigation is an active case, and therefore, I'm not going to be able to answer any specific questions about evidence or the details of the case. I can tell you we have passed the case to the district attorney for review and that Mr. Colton has cooperated fully with the investigation so far. Before I take any questions, I would also like to speak for a moment about another major investigation the Braxville Police Department is involved in. As many of you are already aware, several months ago, the remains of two individuals, a man identified as Fenton Crane, and a woman, Olivia Harrison, were discovered hidden in the walls of another Colton Construction project. Today, not only will we be arresting Mr. Colton for the arsenic poisoning, but we will also be arresting him in connection with those murders—"

He was drowned out by a shout of surprise and a spate of questions that erupted from the crowd in front of him.

More important, many of the cameras swung around to capture the reaction of the Colton family to that shocking announcement. It was exactly why he hadn't told Yvette or Jordana what was coming today, and why only Lilly had any warning at all in advance of the announcement of Fitz's arrest for murder.

Predictably, the family looked equal parts shocked, alarmed and furious. Their expressions of dismay were everything he and the district attorney could have hoped for. Lord, he hoped those reactions were enough to convince Markus Dexter that Fitz Colton had really been arrested for the Harrison and Crane murders.

Otherwise, he'd just put that poor family through hell for nothing.

Eventually, the lights and cameras swung back to him.

He squinted into the blinding lights, trying desperately to see the Colton family's reactions, trying at least to find Yvette's petite silhouette in the cluster of siblings, to give her what silent moral support he could. But he couldn't pick her out at all. All he saw were black silhouettes before him. He couldn't make out any faces past the front row of reporters.

Someone called out, "Do you have proof that Fitz Colton killed that couple? What is it?"

Reese answered, "The Harrison-Crane case is also an

active investigation, and I'm not at liberty to comment on any specific evidence we've collected regarding the case. Also, I'd like to remind everyone that, while we know the identities of the two victims, we know very little about their past lives or what circumstances brought them to their tragic ends. We cannot speculate on whether or not they were a couple or even if they knew each other. The Braxville Police would like to ask anyone in the public with information regarding the final days of Ms. Olivia Harrison or Mr. Fenton Crane to contact the Braxville Police Department." He recited the phone number for the tip line and gave out the general email address of the department.

He spent the next fifteen minutes repeating himself over and over that he couldn't share any details of the evidence on either investigation while reporters tried every way they could to trip him up and get him to reveal some new morsel of evidence.

Finally, the question he'd been waiting for was asked. A reporter called, "Where's Fitz Colton's partner, Markus Dexter? Is he going to be charged in the arsenic investigation and murder case, too?"

Reese leaned in to the mike. "Fitz Colton is the majority partner in Colton Construction, and with regard to the arsenic case, the responsible party for any actions taken by the company as a whole. As for the murder investigation, we're uncovering new evidence on a daily basis. Dexter is not the person we're looking into right now with regard to the Harrison-Crane murders."

"And that evidence implicates Fitz Colton?" the reporter followed up. "Hence his arrest?"

He smiled and shrugged. "I'm sorry. I can't comment on that. I can only repeat that Mr. Colton will be questioned after this press conference with regard to the Harrison-Crane case." He made darned sure to give the answer in a tone indicating that the evidence did, indeed, point to Fitz as the killer.

Time to wrap up. "Thanks for coming today, everyone. If you have any further questions, you can contact the public affairs officer for the City of Braxville." He turned off the microphone and stepped off the stage, craning to search over the crowd for Yvette.

He didn't need to see her face to know exactly how she would have responded to the surprise arrest of her father for the Harrison-Crane murders. She would be livid. She knew better than anyone that the evidence so far *didn't* point at her father, but pointed squarely at his business partner.

Fitz had agreed to play along with this charade in an attempt to coax Markus Dexter out of hiding. If Dexter believed he'd been cleared, the hope was that he might return to Braxville, or at least show his face to law enforcement wherever he was. A nationwide BOLO—be on the lookout—for Dexter had already been issued.

As it turned out, Fitz had been eager to help smoke out his old partner. He was pissed as hell at Dex for getting him and his beloved company into the arsenic mess by talking him into purchasing the tainted wood, and he wanted to see Dex hang if he'd actually committed the two murders and used a Colton building to hide the bodies.

Predictably, Reese was mobbed after the press conference by reporters trying to get a scoop and to trick or bully him into revealing something he hadn't during the press conference. He finally resorted to answering every question with a blunt "No comment," as he pushed through the crowd toward the back of the lobby.

He *had* to find Yvette.

Chapter 10

Yvette's face was on fire. She couldn't breathe. Her chest had an iron band around it.

Holy cow. This was a panic attack. She had to get out of here, away from all these people. And at all costs, she had to avoid Reese. What in the heck was he doing, accusing her father of murder? She knew all the evidence in the murder cases—she'd personally logged in most of it in the stupid investigation. Even though she'd passed the most important testing off to other labs to avoid any appearance of conflict of interest and to avoid accusations of her tainting the evidence, she did know the results of all that testing.

And one thing she knew for sure: n o way was her father the killer.

It was a wild miscarriage of justice.

Her brothers and sisters murmured angrily among themselves, and she became aware that they weren't talking with her. Of course not. To them, she was the Judas. The forensic scientist who'd apparently—and secretly—set up their father for a crime he hadn't committed. She felt their emotional withdrawal as acutely as she felt their physical withdrawal from her.

It was subtle, but all of her siblings had moved away from her, circled around Lilly, turned their backs to her just enough to shut her out of their mutual circle of concern for their dad and of support for their mom.

Miserable, she turned and wriggled into the crowd, using her small stature to slip between reporters in the crush of bodies. She had no idea where she was headed. Just…away.

"You're Fitz Colton's daughter, aren't you?" a reporter asked, shoving a microphone under her nose. "Do you have a comment on your father's arrest?"

"Uhh, no," she stammered.

Another journalist closed in on her. "Hey, aren't you the forensics chick for the Braxville Police?" To the first reporter, the second one said, "She's Fitz Colton's kid, you say?"

Both journalists turned on her. "You investigated your own father? Proved he's a murderer? How does he feel about that?"

"No comment."

"Hey, guys! Colton's own daughter is the one who put him in jail for the double murders! This is her!"

And it was on. The press corps mobbed her, hemming her in so tightly she couldn't move and could barely breathe. Lights glared in her eyes, microphones were shoved in her face and a cacophony of voices shouted in her ears until she couldn't make out anything anyone said. Which was probably just as well.

She put her head down and did her puny best to push

through the crowd, but to no avail. She might as well have been standing in a cage made of arms and elbows and microphone wires.

The panic from before magnified until she was breathing so fast and shallow she started to see black spots and feel lightheaded. The questions and accusations bombarded her mercilessly, and she felt as if she was drowning. An urge to shout for help nearly overcame her.

How could Reese have done this to her? Heck, to her family and her father? It was wrong on so many levels. Fitz didn't kill those two people. Of that, she was completely convinced. There was no evidence whatsoever to tie him to the murders. He wasn't the one who'd fled town when the bodies were uncovered. Nope, that had been his partner, Markus Dexter.

As for her, she totally wasn't so dumb as to process the evidence in a case against her own father like these reporters were accusing her of doing. She knew better than that. She'd mailed all the important evidence having to do with the Harrison-Crane murders to other labs to process. She only catalogued evidence as it came in and then figured out what tests to run and where to send it. It was Forensics 101. Never create even the appearance of a conflict of interest.

However, she also knew that, having been identified as a Colton, her only choice was to say nothing—nothing—to the press. Her professional reputation, her entire career really, rode on her keeping her mouth shut right now.

She looked around frantically for help in escaping the aggressive attention of the journalists, and saw Reese step down off the dais at the front of the room. He plunged into the crowd, and it looked for all the world like he was headed straight at her.

He might be able to help her get out of here, but he was the *last* person she wanted to see. She made a right turn and hooked her arm around the smallest journalist she could find, urgently pushing the woman aside. Must get away from Reese. But fleeing him in this mob was like swimming in peanut butter for all the progress she made.

Without warning, a hand gripped her elbow and she turned sharply to give Reese Carpenter a piece of her mind over his ambush of her father, hack, her whole family. Except it wasn't Reese.

The man before her was older than Reese, a bit taller, with brown eyes and dark blonde hair. In great physical shape for a man in his fifties, this man held himself crisply upright.

"Oh! Uncle Shep," she blurted. "When did you get here? And why are you here?"

Quickly he led her toward the back of the building, away from the crowd of reporters. "I got here in time to catch the end of the press conference. And as for why I'm here, it's to lend moral support to my brother and my favorite niece. Are you okay, Yvie?"

"No, actually. I'm not."

The former navy officer and Fitz's younger brother wrapped her up in a big, warm hug that was exactly what she needed right now. His cashmere coat was soft against her cheek and warm from the heat of his body.

"It's all wrong," she mumbled against his chest. "He didn't do it."

"I know, kiddo. My brother may be a giant jerk at times, but he's no killer. Of course, you're in a position to help prove that. Is there anything I can do for you? Bring you food? Take you out for a coffee? Slip you out the back and get you away from this zoo?"

She looked up at her uncle gratefully. Over the years, he'd had a way of always being there for her when she needed him. Even though his navy career had taken him all over the world, he'd stayed in contact with her, calling her from ships to tell her stories of the exotic ports he'd seen. Now and then she randomly got a package in the mail from him with some pretty trinket from far away. He'd been good to all his nieces and nephews, but the bond between the two of them had always been special.

When the triplets took up all the oxygen in the house, and quiet Yvie had been mostly ignored, he'd come home on leave and taken her to Kansas City on a special adventure, just the two of them. They'd gone to a baseball game, visited a museum and he'd even taken her to high tea in a fancy restaurant. He'd been the one who'd seen her when everyone else did not.

He'd made it home when she broke her leg falling off a horse when she was thirteen. He'd coaxed her back into the saddle by riding behind her and holding her in his arms until she wasn't afraid anymore. He'd taught her how to drive the car whose keys her father had carelessly tossed across the breakfast table and then left for work when she turned sixteen.

Uncle Shep had even been there for her senior prom. He'd walked her down the stairs from her room and sent her off with a kiss on the cheek and a whisper about how beautiful she was and how proud he was of her. Fitz had worked late that night.

She smiled up at her uncle in gratitude. "Thanks for always being here for me when I need you most. You're the best."

He responded as he always did, "Nope, that's you. You're the best."

They traded fond smiles.

"Where are you off to now, Yvie?"

"Down the rear stairwell."

"Not the parking lot to get away from the jackals?" he asked as he eyed the wall of bodies in the front lobby.

"I'm swamped with work in the lab. And a bunch of it pertains to the murder cases."

"Fair enough. Go prove Fitz's innocence. The whole family's getting together for supper tonight, though. You'll be there, right?"

Gee. This was the first she'd heard of it. Talk about feeling left out.

"Yeah. Sure," she answered dejectedly.

Just what she needed. To be interrogated by the entire Colton clan about what evidence the police had on Fitz. Especially since she couldn't talk about it any more than Reese had been able to. Maybe Jordana would back her up if the whole gang came at her hard.

Shep gave her one last hug. "You head on down to your lab and I'll run interference up here so nobody follows you."

"I love you so much, Uncle Shep."

His eyes brimmed with warmth. "I love you, too, Yvette. I'm so proud of you. Now, scoot. I see a few reporters straggling this way."

"Bye." She turned and made a beeline for her lab.

She made it inside and leaned her back against the door while she caught her breath. Safe.

Well, not entirely safe.

As sure as she was standing here, Reese was going to try to barge in here and talk to her about her father's arrest. She had nothing to say to him, however.

Not only was it a gross miscarriage of justice, but he'd gone behind her back. As the department's forensic scientist, that offended her, and as the woman he was allegedly dating, it infuriated and hurt her in about equal measures.

As a deep sense of betrayal set in, so did certainty that she never wanted to see him again.

To that end, she locked the lab door from the inside and scrunched a towel along the bottom of the door so no light would shine out into the hallway. There. Now maybe everyone, especially Reese, would think she'd gone home for the day. Just maybe she could work in peace.

She turned around to face the tall shelves stuffed with evidence from the original Dexter house search, the boxes of files from the man's office, and that cursed puzzle box taunting her on her desk. Somewhere in that mountain of evidence, there had to be something to prove Dexter had killed Olivia Harrison and Fenton Crane.

Sheesh. Now she was doing exactly what she'd accused Reese of—deciding who the killer was and then looking for evidence to prove it.

She was a scientist. Dispassionate. Factual.

Let the evidence speak for itself.

Deep breath.

She strode over to her desk, determined to open the puzzle box today or just resort to smashing the thing.

It took about an hour, but at long last, a flat wood panel slid to the side, and a small black-velvet-lined compartment in the middle of the box was revealed. Nestled inside it was a metal key. After photographing it and donning latex gloves, she picked it up and turned it over, looking for any identifying marks. Nothing. It was just a key.

But to what?

Obviously, it was important, or at least secret, for one of the Dexters to have gone to all this trouble to hide it. She couldn't rule out the wife having hidden this key, but it was much more in keeping with Markus Dexter's character to carefully hide a secret key.

First things first. She dusted the key for fingerprints

and lifted a partial of what looked like a thumbprint. It was a nice, clean print, though, and had enough arches, loops and whorls that she ought to be able to make a positive match with it.

She pulled out the sample prints of both Markus and Mary Dexter. It took her under a minute to verify that the partial print was Markus's. Yep. That was his key… to something.

She made a wax impression of it and then bagged and tagged the key as evidence. Meticulously, she wrote out the steps she'd used to open the puzzle box. That done, she reassembled, bagged and tagged the box. It was too big to fit in the safe she used for valuable evidence, but she did put the key in the safe.

Time to dig into the evidence collected from the Dexter house search. The first bag she opened contained a men's wooden hairbrush with black bristles. Gray hairs threaded through them. Given that Mary Dexter was blonde, it was a good bet the gray hairs were Markus's.

He hadn't given a DNA reference sample before he skipped town, so she was pleased at the prospect of getting one now. If any old DNA evidence was found on the bodies, they could compare it to Dexter's. Both corpses were currently being examined by a forensic archaeologist who specialized in old crime scenes.

She extracted several hairs from the brush that still had follicles attached to them and bagged them carefully. Although she was trained and qualified to process DNA, her lab in Braxville didn't have the proper DNA-sequencing equipment, let alone certification by the FBI. She boxed up the sample for shipping and quickly walked it down the hall to the mail chute. She hurried back to her lab and locked herself in once more.

It was cowardly to hide from Reese like this, but she

was so mad at him right now she didn't trust herself not to punch him in the nose when she saw him. How dare he accuse her father of a crime there was *no* evidence to tie him to?

How could she have trusted him? She thought he was a good cop, an honorable man. Apparently, he was neither. Jerk. And to think, she'd been halfway to falling a little in love with the man. Last night, she'd even dreamed of them married and happy together. Gah!

She threw herself into her work with a vengeance, plowing through most of the remaining evidence from the Dexter house. The two seized laptops were both password protected, so she packed them up and mailed them off to a computer forensics lab in Chicago. Not that she expected Markus Dexter to have been dumb enough to leave behind a smoking gun on his computer. He didn't even put names in his address book. He surely wouldn't incriminate himself any other obvious way.

The five o'clock shift change started overhead with stomping boots, scraping chairs and faint voices talking and laughing. Reluctantly, she packed up for the day and headed out.

She cringed at having to face her family tonight. They would no doubt demand to know everything about the investigation of Fitz, and all she could say was that she had no idea what evidence the Braxville Police had. She prayed the clan believed her. She would hate to have them think she'd betrayed them and Fitz by trying to prove he was a killer behind his back.

She peeked out into the corridor. Clear. She literally ran for the back staircase, scurried up it and raced across the parking lot. She nearly spun out on a patch of ice in her haste to get out of the lot, but finally, she turned onto the street and breathed a sigh of relief. Lord, she hated sneaking around like this.

Debating whether or not to go home and change before heading over to her folks' place, she ultimately opted to procrastinate a little longer and change into more casual clothes. Once home, it became even harder to force herself to leave the security of her little house to go face the music. She dawdled over changing into jeans, letting down and brushing out her hair and redoing her makeup.

Eventually, the moment arrived when she could think of nothing else to do to get ready to go to her parents' house. With a sigh, she scooped up her keys and trudged out to her car.

As she approached her parents' massive estate, she caught herself slowing down more and more, well below the speed limit.

Ugh. When had she turned into such a chicken?

Since Reese Carpenter had put her in an impossible situation. That was when.

She decided that, if things got too nasty, she would claim to have an early meeting in the morning and flee the family gathering. It wasn't great as escape plans went, but it was a plan.

The entire circular drive and the concrete pad between the main house and the carriage house were crammed with cars. Oh, joy. The whole clan was here in force tonight. Her gut and her jaw both tightened.

If she was lucky, she would be able to slip into the kitchen and blend in with the crowd without anyone realizing she'd only just arrived. Goodness knew, she'd done it enough times over the years.

When she opened the back door, the smell of her mom's world-famous chili and a wall of noise assaulted her. It sounded like everyone was talking at once while crowd-

ing the huge kitchen and hanging around the massive is-
land in the center of it.

"Hey! Look who the cat dragged in!" her brother Neil
exclaimed.

Darn it. Busted. An assortment of her siblings and their
significant others stopped what they were doing to turn
and stare at her. "Hey, everyone," she mumbled. "Carry
on with what you were doing."

After a brief chorus of hellos, the whole gang went back
to talking and laughing, and her moment in the spotlight
blessedly passed. She was ridiculously relieved, but she
was also perplexed. She'd fully expected to be jumped
and interrogated within an inch of her life the second she
showed her face. What was up with them not having anything to ask her about Fitz's arrest?

Also, everyone seemed surprisingly cheerful for a
bunch who'd just found out their father had been arrested
for murder.

Weird.

Her mother came over from the stove and gave her a
hug. "How are you holding up, darling?" her mother asked
sympathetically.

"Umm, fine. I'm just buried at work."

"I can imagine. It's not often Braxville has two big
criminal investigations going at one time."

"How are you doing, Mom?"

Violet smudges under her mom's eyes gave away the
strain that Lilly was operating under. Yvette also recognized in her mom's face a certain transparent quality to the porcelain skin she'd inherited from her mother.
Her skin did the same thing when she was exhausted and
stressed out.

"I'm fine, sweetheart."

"Are you sure? No offense, but you look tired."

"It's been a little rough. But all bad things pass eventually."

"How can you say that? Dad was just arrested for murder!"

"Fitz texted to say he'll be here any minute. He'll explain what's going on."

"Fitz is coming?"

"Yes, dear. He's out on bail."

The whole idea of her father having to be out on bail for anything set Yvette's teeth on edge.

"Talk to him when he gets here, honey. He has already spoken with the other children, but nobody could find you this afternoon and you weren't answering your phone."

"I had a lot of work to do," she mumbled.

"I'll let him explain."

Yvette frowned. That was an unusual undertone of steel in her gentle mother's voice. Great. What had her dad done now? Fitz and Lilly had been on precarious marriage footing more than once over the years, usually because Fitz was being an ass. Most of the time it had to do with him ignoring Lilly and/or the kids and choosing his company over his family.

The second-to-last person on earth she wanted to talk to right now was her father. Tonight's gathering was obviously going to be a casual affair as evidenced by the big pot of chili on the stove, a huge pan of baked potatoes on the counter and a buffet of stuffed-baked-potato fixings in bowls beside that. Because it was a work night, family members would undoubtedly come and go based on their work schedules.

But apparently, everyone would be expected to stick around at least until Fitz arrived. He was the patriarch of the whole clan, after all.

Yvette had just finished eating a stuffed spud and was

rinsing her plate in the sink when the kitchen door opened on a gust of freezing-cold air. Two men burst inside and she turned around to greet her fath—

Reese. What on God's green earth was he doing here? He wasn't family! And he certainly wasn't welcome here the very same day he'd arrested the head of the family for a crime he didn't commit!

"Hey, shortcake," Fitz said casually, giving her and the wet plate a perfunctory hug before stepping around her to grab a plate of his own and load it up. He added, "Eat up, Reese. There's plenty of food."

Yvette moved over to Reese's side and muttered angrily, "You have some gall, showing your face around here."

Surprisingly, it was her father who responded. "Take your foot off the accelerator, there, 'Vette. Reese gave me a ride home from the police station. Least we can do is feed the boy by way of thanks."

Thanks? *Thanks?* Her father didn't owe Reese Carpenter thanks for anything!

Reese murmured to her father and she caught part of what he said. "…looks like she wants to kill me…should go…"

"Gimme a second to talk her down off the bridge and get a bite to eat. Then I'll take you up on that ride to the airport you offered."

What ride to the airport? And how was it her father managed to sound so condescending to her all the darned time? Sometimes, she got really tired of being treated like she was twelve years old around here. She turned away from both men with a huff and stomped out of the kitchen. Her father might have just told her in not so many words to cool her jets, but it didn't mean she had to stay in the same room with a Judas.

"Wait up, 'Vette."

God, she hated it when he called her that. She was neither a retired soldier nor a car. She stopped in the hallway without turning around to face her father.

He stepped into her field of vision and she looked up at him reluctantly. He was a big man, and she was the only one of her siblings who'd inherited nearly none of his features. They all teased her about being made of the leftovers after the rest of them were created.

"Before you go off half-cocked, there's something you need to know," he declared.

"What's that?"

"As part of my plea deal, I agreed to participate in a sham arrest. The cops are hoping to draw out Dex. If he thinks I'm being charged with the murders, maybe he'll come out of hiding."

"You…they…what?"

"That whole business of me being arrested for the murders was an act. The press conference was a setup. I'm as eager as the next guy to see that bastard partner of mine's sorry ass behind bars, so I agreed to help. Your mom knew in advance, but the cops wanted to be sure the rest of the family reacted in genuine surprise this morning."

"Did Jordana know? She's a cop."

"Nope. Nobody but me, your mom, the district attorney and Reese. Oh, and my lawyer, of course."

"Of course," she echoed dryly.

But Reese had known. And he hadn't said a thing about it to her. He'd let her go into that press conference and get blindsided, and then get jumped by a pack of rabid reporters. Her family had turned on her, her police colleagues had turned on her and he'd abandoned her to face all of their silent blame alone.

As if his casual pronouncement explained everything and made it A-OK, Fitz turned away from her and headed toward the stairs. "I'll be down in a sec, Reese. I'm already packed."

Packed to go where? Why now, in the middle off all these messes involving his precious company? What business could possibly be more important than being here in Braxville to support his family? All of her siblings were involved in the events of the past six months at Colton Construction in one way or another.

She looked over at Reese and asked tightly, "Where's he going?"

"The airport."

She huffed. "And flying to *where*?"

"I didn't ask."

"Are you lying to me?" she snapped.

"No!"

"Why should I believe you?"

"I've never lied to you, Yvie."

"Hah! You sure as heck didn't tell me about this morning's circus."

"That's not lying. That's omitting telling you something. And I did suggest there might be press present when he turned himself in."

"Same difference." She drew breath to lay into him more, but Fitz came downstairs just then carrying two big suitcases. As in *big*. The kind of bags a person could live out of for weeks or months.

Lilly rounded the corner form the kitchen and asked Fitz coldly, "Do you have everything you wanted from the house?"

"I left instructions with my assistant on where to ship the boxes in my closet."

"Fine." Lilly turned and left, her expression as icy as Yvette had ever seen it.

What on earth?

She stared back and forth between Fitz and Reese. "What am I missing? What's going on?"

Fitz answered lightly, "Oh. That. Your mother and I are getting a divorce."

"A...*what*?"

"Your mom will explain. I have to go. Don't want to miss my flight. Reese? You ready to roll?"

Reese took a step toward her. "Is there a time soon when you and I can talk?"

She looked up at him frigidly. "I have nothing to say to you."

He winced fractionally but replied evenly enough, "Fair. But I have things to say to you."

"Like what?" she snapped.

"Not here. Not now. Be with your family tonight. Tomorrow is soon enough for what I have to say."

Hah. As if.

Reese sighed and grabbed one of Fitz's big suitcases. He didn't make eye contact with her again. Fleeing the scene of the crime, was he? Along with her coward of a father? She was so speechless with shock she just stood there as the two men strode down the hall and out the back door.

The door closed, leaving behind only the distant din of her family talking and laughing as if nothing had happened. As if her family had not just imploded before her eyes.

Her feet felt like blocks of wood as she stumbled into the kitchen. Her mother and Jordana were standing side by side at the sink, rinsing dishes and loading them in the dishwasher.

"Mom?" Yvette asked in a small voice. "Dad just told me. Are you okay?"

Lilly turned around and dried her hands on a dish towel,

leaning a tired hip on the counter. "I'll be fine, darling. Really."

"But—" she rushed forward and wrapped her arms around her mother's waist, hugging her tightly. Still slender and athletic, her mother felt strong. Stronger than she'd expected. In fact, it ended up being her mother hugging and comforting her and not the other way around.

When the shock abated enough for Yvette to think again, she leaned back to stare up at Lilly. "What happened? Was it the arsenic thing and the murder thing?"

"Oh, honey. It's been building for a lot longer than that. Years. Decades, really. Maybe since even before the triplets came along. Your father always loved work more than family. He has never been…emotionally available. I stayed in the marriage for you kids. And to be honest, because it was more convenient to stay than to go. But in the past six months, the situation has changed."

"So, it *was* the investigations and the bodies?" Yvette pressed.

"Not exactly." Lilly continued, her voice tightening, "I did agree to stand by your father through the arsenic investigation. His attorney felt strongly that a show of family unity would be important in gaining enough public sympathy for Fitz to avoid going to jail. But now that the whole fiasco is concluded, I'm free to move on. And that's exactly what I plan to do."

Yvette studied Lilly intently. Her mother looked almost transparent she was stretched so thin. She stepped forward once more to embrace her mother. "Oh, Mom. I'm so sorry."

Lilly accepted the hug but turned away soon enough, her eyes suspiciously moist, and left the kitchen.

"Way to go, Yvette," Jordana muttered, hurrying after Lilly.

She stood alone in the kitchen feeling like a heel for making her mom cry. She'd been trying to comfort Lilly. But as usual, she'd zigged when she should have zagged with her family. She purely sucked at being a Colton.

"Hey, kiddo. Why the long face?"

Uncle Shep. On cue. There to look out for her when no one else saw her.

"Oh, Uncle Shep. Mom just told me about the divorce. You do know that just because your brother is divorcing my mom, you'll still always be family, right?"

He smiled crookedly at her. "You always did have a giant heart. Don't worry about me. I'll be fine. I'm just worried about your mother. She's been through so much…"

She reached out and gave Shep's hands a squeeze. "You'll be there for her, won't you?"

"If she'll let me."

"She loves you to death. Of course, she'll let you," Yvette assured him.

A strange look flashed through her uncle's dark brown eyes. She couldn't tell if it was hope or something else altogether, more akin to chagrin. "Go be with your mom and your brothers and sisters. I'm going to head back to the carriage house and not intrude tonight."

"But—"

He turned her by the shoulders and gave her a little push toward the living room. "Go."

Chapter 11

Saturday morning dawned gray and damp, the clouds low and pregnant with snow. The forecast was for more snow, and possibly lots of it, starting in late morning. Perfect. She could get to the lab, hunker down, and as the weather deteriorated, nobody would be dropping by to bother her. Nobody, as in Reese.

She finished going through the evidence collected from the Dexter house without finding a single thing of interest, let alone anything that pointed at Markus Dexter as a murderer. But it wasn't as if the guy was going to keep around the blunt object he'd killed two people with after all these years.

She continued working on cracking the codes he'd used for his address books and managed to decipher about half of them. It was clear the man had a thriving nightlife. An almost continuous string of initials dotted his evenings, many with late-night meeting times beside them. How could his wife have had no idea he was going out so much to meet other women?

She ate the lunch she'd packed for herself and finished up her final report on the arsenic investigation in the afternoon. Her final findings were moot now that the plea deal with her father was complete, and she could've just written up a few paragraphs and called it good. But she finished the job to the best of her ability anyway. She'd always believed any job worth doing was worth doing well.

Ugh. She was starting to act like Reese. His persnickety procedures were rubbing off on her. She corrected herself: she'd been careful and professional long before he'd come along and tried to tell her how to do her job, thank you very much.

At long last, the two big work tables in her lab were cleared off. All the Dexter evidence was sorted, labeled, cataloged and shelved. The samples from the arsenic investigation were analyzed and packed up, and she was even done with the massive collection of files from Dexter's office. Well satisfied that order had finally been restored in her lab and in her life, she closed up shop, turned off the computers and lights and headed home.

She was surprised to realize it was nearly eight at night and that close to a foot of snow had fallen since this morning. Man. Kansas was really getting clobbered this winter. More snow was falling lazily now, thick enough to be pretty but not a blizzard.

The parking lot was blanketed in a thick layer of white, and her little car looked like an overfrosted cupcake with mounds of snow on the hood and roof. She wasn't even going to be able to start it and defrost the windows until she cleared the snow away from her tailpipe.

She trudged around the back of her car and bent down to start pulling snow away from her car's exhaust with her mittened hands.

The shadow came at her fast, a flash of black out of the corner of her eye, barreling at her in snow-muffled silence. She started to turn. Started to fling up her hands. Started to shout. But the attacker was on her too fast, tackling her hard and driving her to the ground.

It turned out that the snow wasn't thick enough to cushion her from slamming hard into the pavement beneath. Her shoulder hit hard and her head snapped to the side, slamming into the concrete with enough force to make her jaw ache from the impact.

She saw stars, dazed.

The weight on top of her was massive, and she tried to draw a breath, but nothing happened. Her diaphragm was paralyzed, the breath knocked out of her. Panic shot through her as she sucked ineffectively at the cold air. The stars turned into bright lights before her eyes and then narrowed down to a gray tunnel.

"Bitch," a male voice snarled.

She vaguely saw something dark and long—an arm maybe—lift up over her and then swing down fast toward her face. She managed to turn her face away from the blow, but the impact caught her over her ear on the left side of the head.

The explosion of pain inside her skull was absolutely excruciating. So that was what it felt like to have her head split open like a melon.

Blackness rushed toward her. Blessed oblivion, and she embraced it. Anything to escape the spearing agony roaring through her head.

And then there was only darkness and silence.

* * *

Reese straightened up, leaning on the snow shovel for a second to catch his breath. The streetlights cast soft pink circles of light, and the heavy blanket of white lit the night with a soft glow that was beautiful and quiet. He loved the silence of a good snowfall.

He'd already finished shoveling his driveway and that of his neighbor across the road, an elderly widow. He'd just made a quick run across his driveway again with the shovel to push aside the inch of snow that had fallen while he was working on Mrs. Weintraub's drive. He went on call at midnight and needed to be able to get his truck out of his garage by then.

The vigorous exercise had helped work off some of his frustration at Yvie for being unreasonable last night. He reminded himself that she had good reason to be mad at him for not telling her about the sham press conference. He really wished he could have been the one to tell her it had all been an act. Fitz hadn't been exactly gentle or sensitive about breaking that news to her. But it was what it was. All he could do now was get her to listen to his sincere apology and do everything in his power to make it up to her until she forgave him.

It didn't help matters that her old man had sprung the news of his divorce from Lilly on her like that, either. He really wished he could've been there to comfort Yvette last night, but she wanted nothing to do with him at the moment.

It looked like the snow was letting up a little. He hoped Yvie was okay, that she'd remembered to go shopping and lay in groceries before this storm hit. The forecast was for as much as a couple of feet of snow, all told. The town was going to be completely snowed in soon—assuming it wasn't already.

He was tempted to run by her place to check on her, but she'd been so mad at him last night he figured he'd better give her a day or two to cool off before he tried to reason with her. A passionate woman, she was.

That, and he suspected some of her ire last night was directed at her father and not actually at him. He probably ought to let her sort that out on her own. One thing he knew, though. Unlike her old man, he was not about to abandon her.

He'd never liked Fitz Colton much—the guy had strutted around acting all self-important and as if he was the sole benefactor of the entire town for as long as Reese could remember. Granted, Colton Construction had provided a lot of jobs over the years. But that didn't make Fitz some kind of hero to Braxville.

This latest move of Fitz's, though—divorcing his wife and leaving his family to face the fallout of his screwups— that was massively selfish. A serious jerk move.

How was Yvette even his daughter? She was nothing at all like him—

His phone vibrated inside his coat. Crud. The department wasn't so overwhelmed that it was already having to call him in, was it? It was barely nine o'clock.

He pulled out his phone and stared at the caller ID in a combination of shock and profound relief. Yvette was calling. Thank goodness.

"Hey, Yvie. I'm so glad you called—"

"It's not Yvette. This is Lilly Colton. Is this Detective Carpenter?"

Alarm slammed into him. Why was Yvette's mother using Yvie's phone? Something bad had happened, as sure as he was standing here. Oh, God. Not Yvie.

"Yes. This is Detective Carpenter. What's wrong?" he

asked sharply. "Why are you calling me on Yvette's phone? Where are you? *Where is she?*"

"I'm at the hospital. Yvette was brought in a little while ago. You might want to come down here."

He was already sprinting for his garage, slipping and sliding on the fine sheen of snow left over from shoveling the drive. "What happened? Is she okay? How bad is it?"

"We don't know much. She's unconscious. She appears to have suffered blows to her head."

Blows, plural? What the hell? His detective radar fired off hard. Had she been *attacked*? An image of Olivia Harrison's desiccated body flashed into his head, the entire back of her skull bashed in. And that was when the panic hit him. He asked with faint hope, "Did she fall?"

Lilly's voice lowered, and it sounded as if she was cupping her hand around the phone. "The ER doc thinks someone hit her. That's why I'm asking you to come down here. I think maybe the police should get involved."

He leaped into his truck and it roared to life. "I'll be there in fifteen minutes. I'm already pulling out of my driveway."

"Then hang up and drive carefully. I'll meet you in the ER waiting room and take you back."

The strain in Lilly's voice was palpable. It was bad, indeed, if an experienced nurse like her was that freaked out.

It was all he could do not to floor the gas pedal as he made his way across town to the hospital. Only the deep snow and impaired visibility held him even close to the speed limit.

Yvie attacked? By whom? Where? How? How bad was it? Unlike in television, he knew that most people regained consciousness relatively quickly after being knocked out. But she'd been out long enough to be found and brought to the hospital. And she was still unconscious. That was not good. Not good at all.

Hang on, Yvie. Don't you die on me. And then he started praying.

He parked outside the hospital and ran, slipping and sliding, to the emergency room. When he burst through the doors, he immediately spotted Lilly waiting by the double doors leading to the examining rooms. Without a word, she turned and swiped her identification card to unlock the doors.

He followed her swiftly down a hallway to a small room full of quietly beeping monitors. In a bed in the middle of all kinds of equipment lay Yvie, small and pale, covered in tubes and electrodes.

His heart literally skipped a beat. If there was any way he could trade places with her right now, he'd do it in an instant.

"What's her condition?" he asked low.

"Guarded. She's going down for an MRI in a few minutes to check for swelling or—" Lilly took a deep breath, "—or brain damage."

"What happened? What do you know?"

"Someone found her unconscious in the police parking lot, lying on the ground behind her car. It appeared she'd been digging out her tailpipe. There were, umm, tracks in the snow. I gather it looked there might have been a scuffle. An ambulance was called. She was dangerously chilled when she got here, and the officer who found her said there was snow accumulating on her coat. So, she might have been there for a while before someone found her."

His pulse was racing faster and faster as Lilly spoke and he had to talk around a lump in his throat when he asked, "Is she warmed up, now?"

"Yes. They put an electric blanket on her in the ambulance, and we've got one on her now." Lilly glanced at one of the monitors. "Her body temperature is almost back up to normal."

His impulse was to reach out and take Yvette's hand, which lay limply outside the covers with a clip over her index finger, but right now Yvette needed him to be a cop, first.

He squeezed his eyes shut for a second and then asked briskly, "You said she had been hit in the head?"

"Yes. There's a small bump on the right side of her head, here. It's consistent with a fall." Lilly pointed out the bump visible under Yvette's still damp hair.

He nodded.

"And then there's this much larger bump on the left side of her head, over her ear. It's elongated and consistent with her having been struck by—" Lilly's voice cracked, and she paused for a moment before continuing in an admirably professional tone, "—consistent with a blunt object like a club or a pipe."

He swore under his breath. "Right. Do you mind if I take a few photographs of the wounds?"

"Not at all. It's why I called you down here, Reese. Somebody attacked my baby."

He paused in the act of taking out his phone to wrap his arms around Lilly in a brief, hard hug. "I'll find out who did this to her." She shuddered in his arms for a moment, then took a deep breath and stepped back, smiling bravely at him.

"Thank you," she murmured. "It has been a rough week."

"Yeah. You've been through it, haven't you? I'm sorry about everything that's happened, Mrs. Colton."

"Please. Call me Lilly."

"Lilly. Call me Reese."

They traded brief smiles, and then he turned to the business of documenting Yvette's injuries. He mentally girded himself and asked, "Are there any other injuries?"

"Minor scrapes on the right side of her face, but that's it. Nothing else."

He let out the breath he'd been holding. Thank God. She hadn't been sexually assaulted. "Was anything taken? Her purse? Her car?"

"I don't know. She didn't have her purse on her when they wheeled her in. I don't know if it was left behind in the parking lot. I found her cell phone in the pocket of her jeans."

He reached for his phone to make a call, but another nurse came into the room just then. "We're ready to take her down for the MRI. Do you want to come with her, Lilly?"

"Of course." Lilly looked up at him apologetically. "You won't be able to come with us. Do you mind waiting in the lobby?"

"How long will the MRI take?"

"About an hour, all told."

"I think I'll run over to the police station, but I'll try to be back by the time she gets out. Call me if there's any change in her status. *Any* change. And if she wakes up, I want to know immediately."

Lilly nodded, already unhooking monitors and helping the other nurse prepare Yvette to move. He stood back watching helplessly. He hated not being able to do anything to help, but he was completely out of his element here.

Lilly and the other nurse wheeled Yvie's bed out of the room and headed off down the hall quickly. He had a lot to do in the next hour, so he hurried out, determined to be back by the time Yvette's MRI was finished.

He headed for the police station and didn't have to ask

where Yvette was found, because several cops were in the parking lot, using bright flashlights to examine the ground behind Yvette's car. The area was already taped off, and he noted with approval that the police were staying outside the taped area to conduct their search.

"Howdy, guys," he said tersely. "What have we got?"

Joe Brennan came over to join him. "Hey. Did you hear what happened to Yvette Colton?"

"Yeah. I just came from the hospital."

"How's she doing, man?"

"Still unconscious. They're doing an MRI now to check for swelling or bleeding in her brain."

The other cop swore. Police in general took it hard when one of their own went down.

"What happened? Who found her?" Reese asked.

"I did," Brennan answered. "I came out to my SUV because I forgot the sandwich my wife packed, and I saw a big pile in the snow behind Yvette Colton's car. It looked weird, so I went over to check it out. And it turned out to be her. She was covered in about an inch of snow and out cold. I called for an ambulance and then carried her inside."

"What was her condition then?" Reese asked tersely.

"She was a freaking popsicle and bleeding from a gash in the side of her head. Her pulse was thready. I yelled for some guys and they brought blankets and we lay down on either side of her. Made a human sandwich to try to warm her up."

"It looked like that gash was more than just a fall, so I went ahead and taped off the area behind her car as a potential crime scene, and then I dragged Eric's ass out here to help me take some pictures of the tracks and the blood and look for any evidence."

"Find anything?" Reese asked.

"No sign of a weapon. But I've got a good blood-splatter

pattern on the rear fender of her car. Looks to me like some asshole hit her with a short object."

"Did you find her purse?"

"No. Does she usually carry one?"

Reese nodded. "It's pink. With little leather butterflies on the flappie thing and butterflies going up the shoulder strap." He held his hands about eight inches apart. "It's about that big."

"Haven't found it. Her car's still locked but we looked in the windows. Didn't see it there, either. Maybe she left it in the lab?"

"I'll run in and check. Thanks for being on top of all of this. And thanks for taking care of her, Joe."

"She's one of us," the cop intoned grimly.

Reese catalogued pleasure that the guy counted Yvette as a full-fledged member of the department, but his over-riding emotion was panic. Yvette had been attacked and left to freeze out here. Had Joe not happened to stumble upon her, who knew how long she'd have lain out here. Would she have frozen to death before someone found her?

A cold, hard kernel of fury formed in his gut. He was going to find her attacker and by God make whoever it was pay for doing this to her.

He jogged down the stairs to the basement and spied the open door to the forensics lab as soon as he reached the long hallway. He swore under his breath and unsnapped the holster holding his pistol under his left armpit. Approaching the lab carefully, he stood to one side of the door and shoved it wide open.

No movement.

He spun inside low, reaching for the light switch and throwing the lights on.

Ho. Lee. Cow.

The entire crime lab was in shambles, ransacked from

top to bottom. He scanned it quickly for any sign of movement. Nothing.

Moving as fast as he could among the wreckage, he made a circuit around the room, clearing it. Nobody was hiding in here. Without touching anything, he backed out of the room and pulled out his cell phone.

"Hey, Joe, it's Reese. Looks like Yvette's lab has been broken into. I need you to come down here and tape it off as a second crime scene."

He examined the door carefully, paying close attention to the lock and card scanner outside the door. There were no signs of tampering or violence against the locks. Then how did the intruder get in—

Of course. Yvette's ID card. It would have been in her purse. Her missing purse. The assailant mugged her in the parking lot, knocked her out, stole her ID and came in here looking for something. But what?

They would have to do a complete inventory of the lab and figure out what, if anything was missing. But later. Now that he knew Joe Brennan had things well in hand here, he needed to get back to the hospital.

Joe arrived with a fat roll of yellow crime-scene tape and glanced in the lab. The guy whistled. "Wow. That's a right royal mess. I assume Ms. Colton didn't leave it that way?"

Reese laughed reluctantly. "She's as big a neat freak as I am."

"Damn. That bad, huh?"

"Tape it off. Don't let anyone in. The whole lab's gonna have to be inventoried to see if anything's missing."

"This what her attacker was up to, you think? Robbing her lab?"

"Looks that way."

"She keep anything in here like medications or controlled substances?" Brennan asked.

"Nope. Anything like that would be checked into the evidence locker." Which was upstairs and untouched.

"Want me to get started cataloguing the damage in there?" Brennan asked.

"If you don't mind. I'm going to head back to the hospital and wait for Yvie to wake up and give me a statement."

"Give her my best," Joe called after him as he spun away and hurried toward the stairs.

He only prayed she woke up to receive the well-wishes of her colleagues. Afraid like he couldn't ever remember being afraid, he headed back toward the hospital and Yvette.

Chapter 12

Yvette might have faded out in blackness, but she faded back into featureless, blindingly bright white light. Loud, pounding noises echoed all around her until her head literally felt like it was splitting in two. So excruciating was the pain that she willed herself to fade back out into blessed oblivion.

The next time she regained consciousness, it was quiet with only a faint, steady beeping noise to interrupt the deep silence. Her eyes fluttered open, and she was lying semiupright in a dim room. It looked like a hotel at first glance, but then the IV tower beside her with a tube leading to the back of her wrist registered.

Hospital.

Ahh.

She was cold. Was there another blanket? She told her

hands to reach down to her thighs to check, but they only lifted weakly and fell back to her sides.

Something big and dark moved swiftly out of the shadows, startling her badly. She flinched away and her head exploded into the worst headache she'd ever had the bad fortune to experience. She heard a faint moan, presumably from her own throat. But she hovered in this strange place of detachment, her body present but seemingly far away from her. All except that pulsating, daggerlike pain stabbing the backs of her eyeballs. It was all too real and present. She squeezed her eyes shut and prayed for unconsciousness again. But this time, her body didn't cooperate. She was becoming more alert, more aware of the pain in her skull by the second.

"Easy, Yvie. It's just me. I won't hurt you."

Reese. Hurt her? Of course, he wouldn't hurt her. What was he talking about?

He approached her bed, his hands held out away from his sides in what she presumed was some sort of show of no intent to harm her.

She blinked in an effort to clear her vision—her right eye was a little fuzzy—to no avail. Two of him stood in front of her. She noted idly that if there had to be two of any man, he was a good one to duplicate.

"Hey, Yvie," the twin Reeses murmured gently. "How are you feeling?"

She felt like crap on a cracker, to be honest. Weird. Her thoughts weren't reaching her mouth. There was some sort of disconnect in her brain. Or maybe this was all some strange dream. What was he doing here? How did he get here? Confusion coursed through her fuzzy thoughts.

"Do you need me to call the nurse?"

Why would she need a nurse? What was wrong with her? How did she get here? Still, the questions didn't make it out of her head into verbal speech. What was wrong with her? Why couldn't she talk? Fear blossomed in her belly as she nodded, but the pain of moving her head was so excruciating that she stopped doing it right away.

Thankfully, Reese seemed to figure out that she needed some blanks filled in and obliged. "You're in the hospital, Yvette. You're going to be fine. You've had an MRI, and there's no bleeding in your brain. They're monitoring you here overnight as a precaution to make sure no more swelling develops in your brain."

Whew. This not being able to talk thing would be scary as heck, otherwise. As it was, it was annoying as heck. Was there some swelling already? Was that why she couldn't talk?

Reese continued, "As far as we can tell, somebody jumped you in the parking lot of the police department and hit you in the head. Joe Brennan found you lying behind your car covered in snow. Your mom is here. She was on shift when you came in and has been popping in to check on you all night."

All night? What time was it? How long had she been here? Had Reese been sitting here with her the whole time? That was actually really sweet of him.

"Do you feel up to answering a few questions for me? We're trying to piece together what happened to you. Figure out who did it."

Oh. Never mind. He was here on police business. He wasn't here as a man who cared about her. This was Detective Carpenter. Disappointment coursed through her, and she felt moisture fill her eyes. Was she actually crying over Reese? Cripes. She was a mess.

He reached out gently with the pad of his thumb and wiped away a tear that escaped to track down her cheek.

"You're safe, Yvie. Nobody's going to hurt you again. I promise."

He seemed to think she was afraid, but honestly, she wasn't.

"Do you remember what happened to you?" he asked with gentle insistence.

She had to give him credit. He had a decent bedside manner while interrogating a girl. But that was all this was. He needed information from her. He leaned down over her, his blue eyes sparkling like bright sapphires, his lashes dark and long. Lord, his eyes were beautiful.

"Do you remember leaving the lab?"

She closed her eyes, thinking back. Did she remember anything about whatever had happened to land her here? An image of clean work tables came to mind. Right. She'd finally gotten through the mountain of evidence from the Dexter investigation. She recalled feeling satisfied at the cleanliness of the tabletops. She would have shut down the computers and turned off the lab equipment, then turned out the light, locked the door behind her and headed out. Although she knew what her usual routine was, she had no memory of actually doing it last night.

"Were you carrying a purse when you left the lab?" Reese asked.

She opened her eyes to look up at him. A purse? She had no idea. *Think.* She hadn't packed her lunch yesterday morning. Which meant she'd have grabbed snacks out of the machine down the hall to nibble through the day. It also meant she probably would have grabbed her cute little purse with the butterflies. Not that she had any actual memory of doing so, darn it.

As for carrying it when she left the lab, of course, she would have taken it home with her. It would've had her wallet and keys in it along with her cell phone and various other bits and pieces.

But she didn't specifically remember anything about last night after that image of the work tables. Did they find her purse in the parking lot, or had it been stolen in a mugging? Was that what this was? A mugging?

Frustration at having been the victim of a crime coursed through her. She had all the training she needed to defend herself. But she'd been mad at Reese—more interested in sneaking out of the precinct and avoiding him than in being aware of her surroundings. This was her own stupid fault.

The one thing she hated most in the whole world was feeling small and helpless. Yet here she was, lying in some dumb hospital bed because she hadn't been paying attention and someone had taken advantage of her being a complete idiot.

She was so mad at herself that the tears in her eyes welled up even more out of sheer frustration.

"Hey. Don't cry. I'm here. I won't leave your side. I'll protect you."

What? Oh. He still thought she was afraid. He didn't realize she was angry at herself. She opened her mouth to try to force words out, to explain his mistake to him, but a spill of light from the hallway made her turn her head toward the door.

Mistake. Screaming pain ripped through her skull, and she groaned wordlessly.

Her mother moved over to the bed and picked up her hand. "Hi, sweetheart. Is your head hurting a lot?"

She nodded fractionally, but even that much movement sent the bad men with knives to work on the backs of her eyeballs again. She pressed her eyes shut against the pain.

"It has been long enough that you can have another ampule of morphine. Would you like to take it now?"

For the relief of a powerful painkiller, she was willing to nod one more time. Her mother fiddled with the IV tower out of Yvette's line of sight for a moment.

"There, darling. Give that a minute or two to hit your bloodstream, and you should feel better. It may make you sleepy, though."

Yvette got the impression that the comment about her getting sleepy was aimed more at Reese than at her. And indeed, Reese commented, "I promise I won't bother her if she falls asleep."

"Good," Lily answered tartly. "My baby needs her rest."

Amusement coursed through Yvette. Gentle Lilly turned into a mama grizzly bear when one of her kids was upset or hurt.

Reese murmured, "She's not talking at all. Is that normal?"

Lilly glanced down at her, and Yvette knew her well enough to see the worry hidden at the back of her mother's gaze. "She did take a blow on the part of her skull just where the speech center lies. If there's even the slightest swelling in that part of her brain, it could impede brain function in that area. It would explain why she may not be able to talk just yet."

Her mom must have realized Yvette was hearing that with alarm, for Lilly looked down at her and added, "Don't worry, sweetie. It's a totally temporary thing. The MRI showed no brain damage or bleeding in your brain. As soon as the anti-inflammatories in your IV kick in, you'll be talking up a storm."

"Good. We need to know what she can tell us about who did this to her as soon as possible," Reese added.

"Cool your jets, Detective. The first priority is her health. And right now, she needs to rest."

He threw up his hands in surrender, and Yvette smiled

faintly as the cool relief of the morphine flowed into her bloodstream and her eyelids drifted shut.

Reese waited until Yvette had been asleep long enough to be sure she wasn't going to wake up again soon and then stepped out of her room. He headed down the hall to an empty seating area and pulled out his phone.

"Hey, Jordana, it's Reese."

"What's up? What time is it?"

"Umm, it's about five thirty in the morning. Sorry to call so early, but I figured your mom hasn't had a free moment to call you what with pulling a shift here at the hospital and trying to stay on top of Yvette's condition."

"What condition?" Jordana sounded a whole lot more awake all of a sudden.

He filled her in quickly and finished with, "Look. I know it's none of my business, but Yvette is feeling a little…ostracized…by all of you, right now. My impression is that she thinks you're blaming her for not catching whoever murdered the bodies in the wall and for her dad having to get arrested to try to smoke out Markus Dexter. Hell, it's possible she's blaming herself for your folks' divorce."

"That's crazy."

"Just sayin'. She could use a little Colton love."

"Got it. Thanks. I'll call in the troops."

Alarmed, he added quickly, "But not right now, eh? She just got a morphine drip and passed out. Later today will be soon enough."

"But she's gonna be okay, right?"

"According to your mom, her loss of speech is temporary until the anti-inflammatories kick in. Other than that, she appears only to have a smashing headache."

"Any leads on the mugger?"

He lowered his voice instinctively, not wanting Yvette to hear him, even though she was a full hallway away from here. "Whoever mugged her appears to have swiped her Braxville PD identification card and broken into the forensics lab. The perp totally trashed the joint."

"Anything stolen?" Jordana asked quickly.

"Nobody can tell yet. It's a war zone. We're gonna have to go through and straighten out everything and then inventory every single piece of evidence in the whole lab."

"Ugh. What a nightmare that'll be."

He grimaced. "That's an understatement."

"Okay. Well, I guess I know what I'm doing after I round up the siblings and drag them all over to the hospital to shower Yvie in TLC. I'll head over to her lab after that and have a look around. See if I can figure out if anything was taken."

"I'm sticking around the hospital in case Yvie wakes up and can talk. I'm going to need a statement from her about what happened."

Jordana's silence was just a breath too long. She knew full well he didn't need to stick around the hospital for her sister to wake up. A nurse could call him just as easily if Yvie regained the ability to speak.

"Okay, then. Call me if her condition changes?" Jordana asked lightly.

"Will do." He debated for a moment and then added, "By the way, Yvie let it slip to me that you're moving to Chicago. She felt terrible about mentioning it when she realized I didn't know yet."

"Ohmigosh," Jordana said softly. "I'm so sorry. It should have come from me. It's just that I've loved working with you so much and I hate to leave the department behind."

"Tell you what. You have my blessing to go to Chicago

and make lots of beautiful babies with Clint if I have your blessing to date Yvie."

"Hah! I knew there was something going on between you two!"

"Do we have a deal?" he pressed.

"Just so long as you know I'll have your head on a platter if you break my baby sister's heart."

"I'd expect no less of you," he replied dryly.

"Deal."

He disconnected the call and pocketed his phone, shaking his head. Jordana was not kidding. She would tear him up if he ever messed up with her baby sister. He hated to think what the Colton brothers would do to him if he broke Yvie's heart.

But it was worth the risk. She captivated him in a way no other woman ever had. He was thirty-one years old for crying out loud. He'd dated enough women to know how special she was, and furthermore, to know how perfect she was for him. He would like to think he was right for her, too. His steadiness and organization seemed like a good foil for her impulsiveness and creative chaos. If nothing else, she made him laugh and was endlessly interesting to be around.

Before the siblings got wind of it, he definitely owed her an apology for not telling her about the fake arrest plan for her father. Surely, she would forgive him for that. She was a smart woman and would understand that they needed all of the Colton kids' reactions to the announcement to be genuine and unrehearsed. Television cameras caught everything, after all.

He approached her door and was startled to hear voices coming from inside Yvie's room. He stopped outside, unsure of whether or not to barge in. If it was a doctor doing an examination or something, maybe he should wait out here—

"…swear she's going to be all right?" a male voice said from inside.

"I swear. I'll take care of our little girl."

That was Lilly Colton. Had Fitz flown back from wherever he'd jetted off to when he'd heard Yvette was hurt? But how was that possible? Reese's impression was that Fitz had headed outside the United States.

"She's all I have, Lilly. I can't lose her," the man said.

Lilly answered low, "We're not going to lose her. And you have me, too."

"Thank God."

Okay, then. Obviously, Lilly Colton had known for a while that Fitz was leaving and had already moved on to a new relationship. He hoped this guy treated her like gold. The way he heard it from Jordana, Fitz valued his business above all else in the world, including his family, and definitely more than his wife.

Reese heard rustling sounds as if Lilly and the man had moved together and were embracing. Definitely not a doctor, then. Who was this mystery man? And why was Lily calling Yvette their baby girl? Reese cleared his throat loudly and gave it a few seconds before he rounded the corner.

Surprise coursed through him, and just in the nick of time, he stopped his eyebrows from sailing up. Shepherd Colton? He and Lilly Colton were a thing? Since when? He sensed family skeletons lurking in the Colton closet. Ah, well. Every family had its own secrets and scandals.

"Any change?" he asked Lilly, lifting his chin toward the bed where Yvette slumbered in morphine-induced unconsciousness.

"No. If you want to go home and get some sleep, I can have the floor nurse call you when she wakes up."

"That's okay. I'll stick around. It's urgent that I speak with her the moment she's alert enough to answer a few questions. Even if all she does is nod or shake her head yes or no."

Lilly shrugged. "It's your neck and back in a bad chair."

Except no sooner had Yvette's uncle and mother left the room than an orderly wheeled in a pretty decent recliner chair for him, saying that Lilly had asked to have it brought in. He kicked off his shoes, covered himself with the blanket the orderly had left in the chair, leaned it back and closed his eyes.

But his brain didn't shut down right away. He replayed the conversation he'd overheard between Shep Colton and Lilly. The man had called Yvette all he had, and Lilly had referred to Yvie as *our little girl.*

Was it possible? Was the uncle actually Yvette's father? It would certainly cast a new light on the recent divorce announcement between Fitz and Lilly. Not that Reese cared one way or another who'd slept with whom in the Colton family. Given his own opinion that Fitz was more of a scumbag than not, he couldn't blame Lilly for stepping out on her business-obsessed spouse.

Did Yvette know?

She'd never once hinted at anything like that, nor had Jordana.

Nah. His money was on nobody knowing that. Assuming he was even interpreting what he'd heard correctly. Thankfully, it shouldn't impact the active investigation into the twin murders in the wall of the Colton-built warehouse. The case didn't require him to tell anyone that juicy little detail about Yvette's family.

Yep. That was one secret he would happily take to the

grave. No way did he want to kick the foundation of her family out from under Yvette's feet. What she didn't know about her parentage wouldn't hurt her. He only prayed he was interpreting what he'd heard all wrong.

But in his gut he knew he wasn't wrong.

He tossed and turned for a long time in search of sleep.

The next time Yvette woke up, stripes of diffused light came through the vertical blinds covering the window and the clock on the wall across from her bed said it was nearly ten o'clock. Based on the sun, that would be ten in the morning.

Reese was stretched out in the recliner in the corner, asleep. A blanket was draped over him, and his shoes sat on the floor beside the chair. Relaxed in sleep, his face looked younger. Less intimidating. She would have liked to get to know this Reese, the one who set aside his cop persona to relax and just be a guy. A good-looking guy with enough kindness in his heart to sit in the hospital with her.

She knew the second he woke up, though, his eyes would harden, he would don his badge and he would start in with the questions about what had happened last night.

What *did* happen? She thought back, and still was able to retrieve nothing beyond that one image of her work tables being cleared off.

She did remember details from before that, though, including taking her cute pink butterfly purse to work. It was a sure bet she'd taken it out of the lab with her. She never left her purse at work. Which seemed to indicate that she had, indeed, been robbed.

She had to give it to the mugger. It took guts to target someone coming out of the police department.

Too warm, she kicked off one of the blankets and found the remote control for her bed and the television. The pictures on the controls were self-explanatory, and she pushed the button to sit the bed more upright. The whir of the motor woke Reese, and he sat up quickly, rubbing his face.

"Good morning, Yvette. How are you feeling? Can you talk yet?"

She opened her mouth to try. "Hi," she croaked.

"She speaks!" He kicked the footrest down and padded over to the side of her bed in his socks. "I never thought I'd be glad to have a silent Colton woman commence talking at me, but dang, I'm glad you're able."

"That is the most sexist thing I've ever heard," she snapped.

He grinned. "Like I said. Welcome back, Yvette."

She scowled. "Is there a glass of water around here? My throat is parched."

"Lemme get a nurse. I don't know if you're allowed to have anything like that. I wouldn't want to do anything to harm you when we're just getting you back."

He stepped out into the hall and was back in a second. He put on his shoes, folded the blanket he'd been using and shrugged into his suit jacket. She sighed. Detective Carpenter had shown up for duty.

She said, "I took my pink purse to work yesterday. It has little butterflies all over it and going up the shoulder strap. If it wasn't on me when you found me, then it was stolen in the mugging."

He nodded briskly and pulled out his cell phone. He stepped out into the hall, presumably to call the station, while a nurse helped her go to the bathroom and return to her bed, hauling her IV tower with her.

The headache was a constant, dull ache, emanating from a line of sharp pain above her left ear. She reached up and encountered a bandage on the side of her head. "Do I have stitches?" she asked the nurse.

"They weren't necessary. But you do have butterfly bandages holding your head wound shut. If you mess with those, the doctor might put a couple of sutures in."

"Got it. No messing with the bandages."

Reese stepped back into the room still on the phone. "Is there anything else you can remember, Yvette? Anything you can tell us about your attacker?"

"I'm sorry. I don't remember anything about it. The last thing I remember is looking at the tables in my lab and being happy they're finally clean."

Reese snorted. Whether that was directed at her or something the person on the other end of the phone said, she couldn't tell.

He finished the call and came back into the room. He asked the nurse, "Any idea when Miss Colton can be released?"

"The neurologist wants to see her later today, and assuming she's doing well then, I should think he'd send her home." The woman turned to Yvette. "Do you have a roommate? Live with someone?" The nurse cast a suggestive glance in Reese's direction.

"No, ma'am," she answered.

"Well, you can't stay alone for a while. You've had a serious concussion. You'll need someone to keep an eye on you, watch out for dangerous symptoms to develop. While you rest today, you might want to think about who you'd like to arrange to stay with you."

"That's covered," Reese said briskly. "I'll be staying with her. Or rather, she'll be staying with me at my place."

Chapter 13

Yvette whipped her head around to stare at Reese, which was an exceedingly bad choice. Blinding pain ripped through her head and she had no choice but to collapse back on the soft pillow and close her eyes, breathing in short, shallow gasps until the worst of the pain passed. By the time she opened her eyes, the nurse was gone.

"I'm not staying at your house," she declared.

"Who will you be staying with, then? As I recall, all of your siblings are in relatively new romantic relationships, and you don't strike me as the type to play third wheel comfortably. Your parents are in the middle of a divorce and are stressed out to the max. By your own admission, you haven't made friends in town since you've moved back. Except for me, of course. And besides, I want to do it. I can take care of you, and I can see to it you're safe."

"But—"

"But nothing. Don't tell me you can take care of your-self."

Her mouth closed. That had, indeed, been what she'd been about to say.

"You heard the lady. You can't be alone for a while. Discussion closed. You'll stay with me. I have plenty of room, and I figure you'll get in less trouble at my house than you would in your own home."

She frowned at him, but she had to admit he was prob-ably right.

They were saved from any more debates by the arrival of her sister Bridgette, who looked as gorgeous as always. She was a golden person, golden skin, golden hair, golden, shining personality.

"Hey, Yvette. How are you feeling?"

"Like warmed-over mush," she confessed.

"I brought you a few little things—some mascara and gloss. A little blush. Oh, and a hairbrush and a toothbrush. A girl's gotta have a little confidence to face the whole Colton clan, eh?"

"The whole clan?" she echoed in dismay.

Bridgette leaned down and murmured, "Jordana has called out the troops and ordered all of us to stop by and visit you today. Which we're glad to do, of course. You should have called last night to let us know you were here. We'd have come by then."

"I was unconscious most of last night, I'm told."

Bridgette's blue eyes, so like their mother's, widened. "Just how badly were you hurt, Yvie?"

"It's nothing. I'll be fine." The last thing she needed was to have the whole family clucking over her like a bunch of worried chickens with their feathers all fluffed out. "Please, for the love of God, call off the reinforcements."

"Too late," Ashley Hart called from the doorway. She

was Neil's fiancée and fully as gorgeous as Bridgette. A socialite and philanthropist, she'd have been stunning even without the best beauty care money could buy.

Yvette groaned under her breath.

"Tyler's parking the car. He'll be in shortly," Ashley commented, breezing into the room. "And I think I saw Brooks and Neil pulling into the parking lot."

This time, Yvette didn't bother to muffle her groan.

"How's the new house coming?" Ashley asked Bridgette.

"Luke thinks it'll be done before Easter, but I'm betting it'll be at least Memorial Day before we're into it."

Tyler, the oldest and most serious of the siblings, came into the room and dropped a fond kiss on Yvette's cheek before moving to stand beside Ashley and looping his arm around her slender waist. Neil, the criminal attorney came in right behind him.

Yvette grumbled at her lawyer sibling, "Don't you have to be at court or something, Neil?"

"Nope. No big cases pending at the moment."

"Drat," she grumbled.

Everyone laughed as Brooks, one of the triplets, rounded the corner and demanded, "What did I miss?"

Yvette rolled her eyes as he came over and yanked on her big toe through the blankets.

She looked over at Neil in chagrin. "No wonder you were so hot and bothered to get out of the hospital before. I get it now."

Tyler piped up with, "Hey. At least you weren't shot, Yvie." He was fully recovered from the gunshot wound he'd suffered a few months back, thankfully.

"Nah. I was just mugged. Garden-variety crime. Nothing fancy like you," she retorted.

The conversation ebbed and flowed around her with her

siblings laughing and talking about their jobs and homes and general gossip. It turned out Ty and Ashley were planning to take a vacation soon, and a spirited debate over where they should go ensued with Venice and Maui emerging as the two front-runner choices.

When the conversation lagged, Yvette commented, "Gee, it's too bad Jordana's not here to enjoy this gathering of the troops that she arranged."

"Yeah. Where is she, anyway?" Neil demanded.

As if conjured by the question, Jordana turned the corner into the room no more than a minute later. "I see everyone's here," she commented. "That's great. I have an announcement to make. I've told Mom, and Yvie already knows, but I'm moving to Chicago to be with Clint, and I'm going to open up an office there for Ty's security firm."

Exclamations and congratulations were forthcoming, and Yvette was delighted not to be the center of attention as the others focused on Jordana. It was great of her family to show up like this, but frankly, the whole Colton clan at once could be a little exhausting.

Perhaps two minutes passed with nobody else coming into her now crowded room, but then one more body filled the doorway. Reese. The gang greeted him, and he joined in to the conversation easily.

Yvette noted that he and Jordana seemed to have come to an understanding, for the two of them were relaxed and joking with each other. Thank goodness. She would have hated to put a rift between them with her thoughtless revelation of Jordana's plan to leave the force and move away.

One by one, the siblings started to drift out, citing jobs and other obligations. Jordana was the last one left. She came over to Yvette's bed and leaned down, looking concerned. "Do you have any idea at all who could've jumped you in the parking lot, sis?"

"None."

"No enemies? Disgruntled exes?"

"You have to have exes for them to be disgruntled," she retorted.

Jordana smiled but the expression didn't reach her eyes. "I'm worried about your safety, Yvie. If last night's attack is related to a case you're working on, the attacker may not have gotten what he wanted."

"Meaning what?" she asked her older sister sharply.

Jordana sighed. "He might have meant you more serious harm than this."

"Are you tiptoeing around saying the attacker might have meant to kill me?" Yvette demanded.

"Well, yes," Jordana allowed reluctantly.

"I'd already thought of that," Yvette confessed.

Reese jumped into the conversation. "Don't worry, Jordana. I'm taking her back to my place and not letting her out of my sight. I'll see to it she's safe going forward."

Jordana nodded in relief. "Call me if you need help or you need me to spell you. Yvette can be a bit of a pill, especially when she's not feeling good."

"Hey!" Yvette exclaimed. "I'm an angelic patient."

Reese and Jordana both laughed at that.

A wave of fatigue washed over her and Yvette closed her eyes.

Reese murmured to Jordana, "Yvette's looking a bit droopy. Maybe we should let her rest a bit?"

Her sister took the hint, planted a quick kiss on her cheek and left.

"Thanks for kicking her out," she murmured to him.

"I knew it meant a lot to you to have your family rally around you, but you need your rest."

For the first time since she'd come back to Braxville, she felt like she was really home. She reached up to touch the bandages on the side of her head. "It's a heck of a way to finally reconnect with my family."

He smiled gently. "Maybe you can go a while without hitting your head again? It would help my blood pressure immensely."

Worried about her, was he? Okay, that made her insides feel even warmer and squishier. "I forgot what it's like to be part of a big family. Or at least, I forgot for a while what the best part of being a Colton is."

Reese did a strange thing. He frowned for a moment. His lips parted as if he was going to say something in response to that, but then he closed his mouth and turned away. What on earth?

Without looking back at her he mumbled over his shoulder, "I'm going to arrange for a police officer to stand outside your room. Once he gets here, I have some stuff to do. But, I'll come back in a little while to check on you. Get some rest, eh?"

"Umm, yeah. Sure." What was up with him? He kept blowing hot then cold with her, and it was confusing as heck.

The door closed behind him and silence fell around her. Alone at last. Her eyes drifted shut.

She dreamed of running after Reese as he strode away from her, calling for him to come back, and him never once turning around to even look at her.

She woke with a lurch, feeling lost and alone, abandoned by everyone she loved. Startled by how powerful her reaction to some stupid dream was, she reached up with both hands to dash tears off her cheeks. Sheesh. Since when had she become so sappy and sensitive?

From the doorway, a male voice boomed, "Yvette? Are you awake?"

Well, duh. She would be now if she hadn't already been. "Hi, Dr. Jones."

"I came to have a look at you and see how you're feeling."

"I'm feeling ready to get out of here."

The doctor smiled as he shone a blindingly bright little torture device of a light in her left eye. "All my patients say that."

She responded dryly. "You mean not everybody loves being poked and prodded awake every hour on the hour around the clock?"

His grin widened. "Well, I can see your ornery wasn't hurt in your mishap."

Not hardly. She was still ticked off at herself that she hadn't had more situational awareness when she went out to her car last night. She'd been so relieved not to run into Reese that she'd forgotten everything she knew about self-defense.

Another male voice spoke from the doorway. "What's the verdict, Doc? Can she go home today?"

She peered around the physician to see Reese leaning against the door frame looking long and lean and sexier than any one man had a right to.

"She can go home if and only if she's got someone with her around the clock for the next twenty-four hours. She's going to need to be woken up every couple of hours for at least one more day—"

Yvette groaned. "You're killing me with all this interrupted sleep. Is it really necessary?"

The doctor looked down at her sternly. "You have a serious concussion. Immediately after a serious head trama, there's a risk of you falling unconscious and slipping into a coma. You have to be woken up periodically to make sure that hasn't happened."

"Oh, please. I'm fine."

Reese spoke over her. "I'll see to it she's woken every two hours like clockwork. Any other care instructions?"

"I'll send her home with painkillers and antibiotics, and I need her to stay on anti-inflammatories for at least a week to prevent any swelling in or around the brain."

"Got it," Reese said briskly.

"Complete bed rest for the next day. She can only get up to go to the restroom. After that, limited activity for another three to four days. It goes without saying that she mustn't do anything that will shake her head or move it abruptly. No sports, no vigorous activity, no exercise."

"Party pooper," she mumbled.

Reese grinned at her and she gifted him with her blackest scowl.

The doctor left the room and Reese commented, "You're so cute when you're mad."

"Did you just call me *cute*? Now, I'm going to have to kill you. As soon as I can engage in vigorous activity, you're a dead man."

His grin widened. "I can think of a few vigorous activities I'd like to engage in with—" He broke off. "Sorry. That was out of line."

Her cheeks heated up until they felt on fire. He was thinking about sleeping with her, was he? "There's still the matter of you lying to me to deal with, mister."

"Me? I've never lied to you."

"What do you call not telling me about my father's fake arrest?"

"That's an omission, not a lie. I would never lie to you. We couldn't tell any of the Colton kids about it because the cameras were there to record your reactions. They had to be real."

She huffed. "I still don't like it."

"I didn't like doing it if that makes you feel better," he said soberly.

Actually, it did. But she wasn't about to admit that to him until he groveled a little more.

"I swear, Yvette. I will never lie to you—"

The doctor stepped back into the room and Reese broke off.

The neurologist boomed, "I've had a nurse send all your prescriptions over to the drugstore. They should be ready for pickup by the time you've finished the release paperwork and you're ready to get out of here."

For a man who worked around people with head pain a lot, the guy sure was loud.

"Thank you, Doctor," she said politely. She opened her mouth to forgive Reese for not telling her about the fake arrest of her father, but a nurse came in and shooed Reese out of the room.

The woman had a clipboard and shoved it under Yvette's nose. It took a half hour to wade through a mountain of documents with print too small for any reasonably sighted human being to read, but at long last, the woman held out a large plastic bag. "Here are your clothes and personal effects. Do you want me to help you get dressed?"

"No. That's okay. I can dress myself." Just how helpless did they all think she was?

She was dressed and seated on the edge of the bed, reluctantly admitting to herself that she had the beginnings of a monster headache coming on, when Reese came around the corner into her room.

"Let's spring you from this joint," he said jauntily.

"Thank goodness." She jumped off the edge of the tall bed and knives stabbed her brain from about fifty directions at once. Whoa. She paused until the pain subsided enough for her to actually see—

A hand gripped her elbow and Reese loomed beside her. Man, that guy was fast. That, and he could read her well. He must've seen the pain on her face and jumped over to support her.

"You okay?" he asked quietly enough not to send the knives back through her skull.

"Yeah. Sure," she mumbled.

"Liar."

"Just get me out of here. I hate hospitals."

He paced himself beside her as a nurse pushed her to the elevator in a wheelchair. When it opened on the ground floor, he jogged ahead and was waiting at the exit in his truck by the time she arrived. He helped her into the cab, shut the door gently and climbed in beside her. "I promise to drive like Grandma's soup and a couple dozen crates of fresh eggs are in the back of my truck."

"Thanks," she sighed.

He navigated out of the parking lot.

"I really do appreciate everything you've done for me. If you could just take me to my car, I'll go home and stay out of your hair for the next couple of decades."

Reese's frown was immediate and intense. "Did you not listen to the doctor? You can't be alone. The only reason he let you out of there was because I agreed to look out for you."

"Which I appreciate you doing. Deeply. But I'll be fine—"

"I swear to God, Yvette. If you tell me you can take care of yourself and don't need help one more time, I'm going to shout at the top of my lungs."

"Please, no," she blurted. Her head was already pounding.

"You're coming to my house. And that's that."

"You are so stubborn."

"Pot, meet kettle," he replied dryly.

She huffed and crossed her arms, sitting back in irritation as he drove past her house—literally past it—on his way across town to his place. Oh, he was just taunting her now.

However, by the time he pulled carefully into his garage and turned off the engine, she actually felt wilted and in need of painkillers and a nap, in that order. He opened her door and she moved to get out, but he stepped forward and shocked her by scooping her up into his arms.

"Reese! What are you doing?" She flung her arms around his neck to regain her equilibrium.

"I should think it's patently obvious what I'm doing," he said, using his hip to shut the truck door, and heading for the kitchen. He leaned down a little for her to turn the doorknob and entered the house with her. Another hip check to close the kitchen door and he strode through his house to—*ohmigosh*—his bedroom, where he deposited her on his bed and left to get her meds.

His room was neat and masculine. His bed looked handmade out of logs sanded smooth. She would bet he'd built it. There was something intensely intimate about lying in it, knowing he'd made it with his own two hands.

He came back, setting down several prescription bottles with her name on them and a tall glass of water. He'd picked up her medications for her? When? He must have raced out while she was filling out the discharge paperwork and gotten them.

He reached out again to pick her up so she could pull the blankets out from underneath herself. He set her back down on the soft mattress gently. Her arms still rested around his neck, and their faces were about a foot apart. Her heart fluttered at the sexy proximity of this man.

"I'm glad you're going to be all right," he murmured.

"When I got that call from Lilly that you were hurt—" Reese's voice cracked.

"I'm tougher than I look."

"You don't have to be tough for me, Yvie. I'll take care of you and keep you safe."

"You can't always be there for me."

"I can try."

Their gazes melted together, hers in gratitude and his in concern. His eyes were so blue and beautiful she could lose herself in them forever.

"Kiss me, Reese."

His lips curved up. "Thought you'd never ask."

"You were waiting for me to ask?"

His hand slipped out from behind her knees and he ran his fingers across her forehead ever so gently. "You don't seem to have had much luck with men. I didn't want to scare you off."

"And here I was, worrying that I'd scared you off."

He frowned slightly. "Why would I be scared of you?"

"I think it's safe to say I've proven I'm a bit of an accident risk."

His frown dissolved into a wry smile. "Truth. But I'm generally pretty good at anticipating trouble and heading it off."

She smiled up at him. "You obviously haven't hung out around me for long."

His mouth lowered slowly toward hers. "No, but I'm looking forward to doing so."

His lips touched hers lightly, preventing her from responding. Which was just as well. She was totally speechless. Did he just admit to wanting a long-term relationship with her?

His lips pressed against hers a little bit more firmly, and she threaded her fingers into his hair to tug him closer.

He resisted, and she finally mumbled against his lips, "I won't break."

"Still. Not gonna risk hurting you," he mumbled back, stubbornly refusing to increase the pressure of the kiss.

He did take his time, however, brushing her lips with his mouth, kissing his way lightly across her cheekbone to gently nibble her right earlobe. When she was panting a little and starting to feel more than a little hot and bothered, he lowered her shoulders to the stacked pillows and straightened. Took a step back from her.

"Lord, you're tempting," he murmured.

"Then don't stop."

"Doc said no vigorous activity for a week. If I don't stop now, there are definitely going to be vigorous things going on in my bed."

"Well…hell."

He laughed down at her. "Can I get you something to eat? Maybe a drink?"

"How about a stiff shot of vodka?"

"Can't mix your pain meds with alcohol."

"You're such a buzzkill."

"That's me. The old stick-in-the-mud."

She looked up at him quickly. "You're not a stick-in-the-mud. Far from it."

"That's not what you've spent the past year telling me."

"I didn't know you for the past year."

"And you think you know me now?" he asked, sitting down on the edge of the bed.

"I'd like to think so."

"Then how can you blame me for not telling you about your father's staged arrest? Not only was I doing my job, but I'm trying to catch Markus Dexter and solve a murder. You know Gwen Harrison. It's agony for her not to know who killed her mother and if that killer is still alive.

I would never do something like stage your dad's arrest just to harass your family. The Coltons have been through plenty in the past year."

She sighed. "I believe you. I was just so shocked and angry at the unfairness of the accusation I didn't stop at the time to think about why you'd have done it."

He reached out to tuck a strand of hair behind her ear. "Thank you for giving me the benefit of the doubt when you did stop to think about it."

"Don't thank me. I was trying to avoid running into you when I raced out into the parking lot last night and didn't pay attention to my surroundings."

"I'm sorry."

"You don't owe me any apology for that. I'm the one who didn't trust you. I'm sorry."

"If I accept your apology, will you agree to accept mine?"

"I guess so."

"Grudge holder, are you? Good to know," he teased.

She answered seriously, "Actually, I'm the least grudge-y of all my siblings and me."

He smiled warmly at her. "I'm glad the air is cleared between us. Now, I'm getting out of here so you can take a nap. You look exhausted."

She actually was, but she said stoutly, "I'm fine."

"Yvie." His voice was reproachful. "We've been over this before. You don't always have to be fine for me. You can show weakness or fear or sadness—or anything, really—and I won't think any less of you. I'm not your brothers. More importantly, I'm not your father."

And on that note, he turned and left the room, leaving her to stew in her own thoughts. He wasn't her father? That was an astute observation. How did he know that Fitz only seemed to value strength in his children? Although, she supposed to meet Fitz was to recognize that about him.

She did wish her father had paid more attention to her whcn she was a kid. Maybe told her, or at least shown her now and then, that he loved her. She wished he'd been at least a little proud of her. Heck, Uncle Shep had told her more often that he loved her and was proud of her than Fitz ever had. Sigh.

She dumped a pain pill out of the bottle on the bed stand and swallowed it with several gulps of water from the glass. As the sweet relief washed over her, she closed her eyes and let the deep silence of Reese's cabin in the woods envelop her.

Chapter 14

Reese cracked open his bedroom door to check on Yvette, but she was out cold. Good. She needed the rest. From watching her in the hospital, he knew she would likely sleep for several hours after taking one of her pain pills. He set an alarm for her next wake-up check and backed out of the doorway.

He went to his kitchen at the far end of the house and called the precinct. "Hey, Jordana. How goes the clean-up of your sister's lab?"

"Slow. The intruder really trashed the place." She added, "Oh, and speaking of which, we checked the logs, and it turns out Yvette's ID badge was used to gain access to the forensics lab."

"So the mugger knocked her out, stole her ID out of her purse and got into the lab?"

"Looks that way."

"Anything missing?" he asked.

"Yeah. That big puzzle box Yvie's been sweating over."

His partner might as well have punched him in the gut. That box again? What was so danged important about it? Or rather that key hidden inside it. "And the key?"

"It is logged into Yvie's database as being locked in her wall safe. Which, I'm pleased to report, the robber did not break into. So, the key should still be safe in there."

That was great news. "Any luck figuring out what that key unlocks?" he asked his partner.

"Nope. I've got emails out to every bank within a three-hundred-mile radius of Wichita. If it's a safe-deposit box, someone will respond."

"Hopefully sooner rather than later."

"Nobody except Yvette or Chief Hilton knows the combination to the safe. He's at his hunting cabin this weekend, and Yvette has been unconscious, so nobody has opened the safe to verify that the key's inside."

"If her paperwork says it's there, it's there," he replied confidently.

"How's Yvie?" Jordana asked.

"Tired. In pain. Trying to be tough."

"That sounds like her. Thanks for taking care of her. I'd have volunteered to take her to my place, but it's in chaos right now."

"Why's that?"

"Packing for the move," Jordana admitted.

He frowned. "I didn't realize you were going so soon."

"If you'd found the love of your life, would you mess around for long getting to her side?"

He envisioned Yvie, pale and beautiful against his pillow when he'd left his bedroom. "Nope. I'd get her as close to me as possible and keep her right there."

"There you have it."

"Holler if you need help packing," he offered.

"You're doing plenty looking out for Yvette. That's an enormous weight off my shoulders."

He disliked the idea of Yvie being perceived as a weight of any kind to her family. She was a lovely person and independent as all get-out. She hated being a burden to anyone. But it wasn't his job to fix the Colton clan's family dynamics.

Thoughtfully, he pulled out vegetables and a pot roast and got to work making a big pot of beef stew.

Surely, Markus Dexter was the intruder who'd bowled over Yvette in the attic of the Dexter home. There'd been no sign of forced entry to the house, which indicated someone with a key had been the intruder. Of course, Yvie might have left the door unlocked when she'd entered. He would have to ask her when she woke up.

If Dexter had been the intruder who'd gone looking for the puzzle box in his own attic, it stood to reason he was also the mugger in the parking lot and thief of the box from Yvie's lab.

And, if that logic was correct, the attack in the parking lot also indicated that Dexter was not averse to violence against others. Now that he thought about it, the mugger had hit Yvette in the head…which was the same way both Olivia Harrison and Fenton Crane had died. Blunt trauma to their skulls. Was her recent attack further proof that Dexter was the killer of Harrison and Crane?

He woke Yvette at the two-hour mark after she'd gone down for her nap, disturbing her just long enough for her to mumble at him to go away.

Smiling a little, he backed out of the room to let her sleep. About supper time and almost time for another two-hour check on Yvette, headlights coming up his driveway flashed through his front windows.

Who'd driven all the way out here after dark? He wasn't

expecting anyone. He shrugged into his holster and un-snapped the flap over his service weapon as the car parked in his driveway.

Standing to one side of his front window, he was startled when Lilly Colton got out of her car and headed up his sidewalk. He opened the door for her and she thrust a big deep casserole dish at him.

"What's this?" he asked. "And please come in."

"It's my world-famous banana pudding. Yvette's favorite."

"It's kind of you to think of her."

"She is my baby," Lilly said a bit tartly, sounding just like her daughter when Yvette was irritated. He grinned at the resemblance between mother and daughter.

"I'm glad someone remembers that," he retorted.

"You don't like us Coltons very much, do you?"

"I like most of you just fine. But to be brutally honest, I'm not a huge fan of your husband."

"Neither am I. That's why I'm divorcing him."

Interesting. She was divorcing him and not the other way around? "I'm sorry about that—"

She waved a brisk hand. "No condolences necessary. I should have done it years ago. I waited until all the kids were grown and settling down into their own lives. But now I wonder if I should've done it long ago and saved them having to put up with an absent father—" She broke off. "I'm sorry. You didn't ask to hear about my marital problems."

"I don't mind. You were my dad's nurse a few years back when he had a heart attack, and my family credits you with whipping him into shape and convincing him to finally take better care of his health."

She laughed a little. "Oh, dear. I hope I wasn't too hard on him."

"Not at all. You gave him exactly the kick in the pants he needed."

"Mom? I thought I heard your voice."

He whipped around to see Yvie standing in the doorway, her hair tousled, squinting at the bright light in his kitchen. "What are you doing out of bed?" he demanded.

"I'm not dead for crying out loud, and my legs aren't injured. I can walk."

Lilly threw him a commiserating look and said gently, "Sweetheart, you have a serious concussion. I'm sure Dr. Jones told you to stay in bed for several days and rest."

"I can't sleep twenty-four hours a day, Mom."

"No, but you can rest twenty-four hours a day."

"Thank you," he chimed in. "You heard your mother. Back to bed with you, Yvie. I'll bring you a bowl of *my* mother's world-famous beef stew, and if you eat all of that, you can have a bowl of *your* mom's world-famous banana pudding."

"Banana pudding?" she exclaimed, and then immediately winced. Her voice much lower, she continued, "Thank you, Mommy."

Lilly moved over to kiss her on the cheek and give her a gentle hug. "You're welcome, darling. If you need anything, you call me, okay? And, Reese, if you need a break from her, I'm happy to come over and sit with her while you escape for a bit."

"I'm not *that* awful a patient," Yvette complained.

"Then what are you doing out of bed?" he asked wryly.

"Fine. I give up. I can't fight both of you. I'll go back to bed, if just to get some peace and quiet." She called back over her shoulder as she disappeared down the hall, "And a bowl of my mom's pudding."

He took the opportunity to turn to Lilly and ask quietly, "How are you doing? I know it's none of my business, but you've really been through the ringer these past few months."

"It's kind of you to ask, and I'm surprisingly good. I have more support than I ever knew I had, and I'm at peace with my decision to leave Fitz."

Was Shepherd Colton part of that surprise support network? He was sorely tempted to ask Lilly why she and Shep hadn't told Yvette that he was her actual father, but it was emphatically none of his business.

Lilly left quickly after that and Yvette called out that she was starving, so he put the matter of her parentage from his mind.

Yvette had a secret. She loved sleeping in Reese's bed. Not only was it huge and comfortable, but it smelled like him. She could snuggle down under the thick comforter and feel completely surrounded by him even when he wasn't there.

He'd wanted to send a patrol car out to watch the house when he had to go in to work, but she'd argued nobody except her family knew she was out here, and she was perfectly safe by herself for a few hours. Reese hadn't liked it, but he'd eventually given in.

He made quick trips in to work after her first twenty-four hours of constant wake-ups ended, but he refused to talk about anything that was going on at the department with her. Which she took as a bad sign. He was avoiding stressing her out.

Gradually, her headache eased, and by day four it had mostly disappeared. She felt pretty good and was starting to get bored and housebound. When Reese went to the office on day five, she declared herself sick of being sick and got out of bed and dressed as soon as he left the house.

She picked the place up, raided the kitchen and discovered that he had all the ingredients for homemade spaghetti from scratch. She set to work pulling together a big pot of sauce and setting it over very low heat to simmer all day. Then, she built herself a fire in the fireplace. It was impossible not to remember the kisses they'd shared in front of it before. And yes. She wanted more.

To that end, she hunted around in his pantry and found some candles. She set the table for two and made a centerpiece of pinecones and some bright holly berries she brought inside. She stood back to observe her work. Considering that she was working within the limits of a bachelor pad to create a romantic atmosphere, she declared her efforts not bad.

She heard his truck pull into the garage, and she checked her makeup and hair in the bathroom mirror quickly. Thankfully, her mother had brought over a bag with some of her clothes and toiletries the day after she brought over the pudding.

She swept out into the living room just in time to see Reese step into the kitchen and stop cold. "What have you done? You're supposed to be resting!"

"This was restful. I'm bored to death, and cooking a nice dinner was relaxing. Think of it as therapy for me."

He hung up his coat and came over to kiss her leisurely. He confessed, "I like coming home to you like this every day. I look forward to seeing you the whole time I'm at work. Is that weird?"

"Not weird. No weirdness at all." In fact, it made her insides jump with pleasure and little warm fuzzies skitter across her skin.

He held her chair for her at the table. "You sit. I'll serve us."

She smiled when he set a plate heaped with a giant pile

of spaghetti and sauce in front of her. "Fattening me up so no other guys will look at me?" she murmured.

He slipped into his seat, grinning. "What if I am?"

"Then I'd say we're getting serious with each other." Whoops. All of a sudden, the light humor of the moment evaporated, leaving the two of them staring awkwardly at their plates.

"Forget I said that," she mumbled. "I'm an idiot and my mouth frequently gets ahead of my brain."

He smiled a little. "In my experience, your brain moves at light speed most of the time."

They dug into the meal and didn't talk much for a few minutes. But then Reese said, "If you're bored, maybe I could bring home something from your lab for you to work on a little? Nothing strenuous. If you promise not to overdo—"

"That would be amazing!" she exclaimed. "My laptop, maybe? That way I could get emails and keep up with correspondence on various pieces of evidence I've sent out for analysis."

"I'll bring it home with me tomorrow." He added carefully, "Seeing how you're feeling better, maybe now would be a good time to tell you that whoever mugged you in the parking lot also stole your ID badge and broke into your lab."

She gasped. "Was anything stolen?"

"The puzzle box was taken. And, umm, your lab was, well, trashed."

"What? How bad?"

"Jordana and a couple of the other guys have spent this week putting it back together as best they can. The department's insurance is paying for replacing the lab equipment that was damaged."

"What equipment? How damaged?"

"It's a few machines. You're safe. That's what matters."

She sat back, staring at him. The wreckage must have been bad, given the way he was avoiding her questions. "Was any other evidence taken?"

"Unknown. Jordana has been going through your database of logged evidence and trying to match it to stuff in the lab. But she's no forensics expert. I've been helping out where I can, but some of what you do is beyond my training."

"Gee. I'm glad you finally admit that maybe I know more about my job than you do."

He rolled his eyes.

"When can I go to the lab to check it out? Will you drive me in tomorrow?"

"The doctor said to rest."

"The doctor said three days after a day of bedrest. It has been five days since the incident. I'm fine."

Reese raised a sardonic eyebrow at her. "If I could erase the word *fine* from your vocabulary forever, I would do it in a minute."

She rolled her eyes back at him. "All right, then. I'm fully recovered, have no headache and am sick of being marooned out here in the middle of nowhere. I want to get back to my work. My important work that will help nail a murderer."

"You don't like it out here? I thought you'd find my cabin restful and quiet."

Darn it. He sounded hurt.

She sighed, her indignation broken. "I love it out here. I love the quiet and the trees, and your place is incredibly comfortable and pleasant. But I have a job to do, people depending on me. I need to get back to it. How would you feel if you were in the middle of a murder investigation and had to stop working on it for a week?"

"Which is pretty much what has happened this week," he said with a sigh. "I ought to be putting in sixteen-hour days on the Harrison-Crane case, and instead, I'm going into work a few hours a day in and around making sure you don't overdo it. Which I wouldn't have any other way, mind you."

She stared at him in dismay. "I don't want to keep you from your job. What you do is important."

He looked up quickly, meeting her gaze with surprising intensity. "You're more important. Hands down."

She stared back, stunned. More important to him than his precious career? Wow.

"And you're not mad about me taking you away from your work?"

He frowned. "Of course not. Family always comes before work no matter how important the work might be. It's not even an issue for me."

Oh. Huh. Maybe it was an issue for her because her dad had always put his work above his wife and kids. "You're sure about that?" she asked in a small voice.

He leaned forward and took her hand in his. "When I saw you in that hospital bed unconscious, my world… ended. And it didn't begin again until you woke up and spoke to me."

"I… You… We…" It wasn't often she was at a complete loss for words, but she was now. She reached out and laid her hand over his on the table. He flipped his hand over beneath hers and twined their fingers together.

"Yeah. That," he muttered in response to her stammering.

"We haven't even…we hardly know each other…it's too soon…" she tried.

"I know." He finally lifted his gaze to hers. "But there you have it. I fell for you like a ton of bricks."

Panic at how fast he'd fallen for her and she for him roared through her. "I have all kinds of quirks and flaws you don't know about. I'm a basically terrible person."

"Perhaps I should be the judge of that?" he suggested wryly.

"Easy for you to say. You're perfect," she snapped.

He laughed at that. "Oh, my dear Yvette. I'll never be half good enough for you. I'm just a hick cop from a small town in Kansas. You…you're royalty around here."

"God, I hate being a Colton, sometimes."

His gaze shuttered and slid away from hers. The same thing had happened once at the hospital. What had they been talking about then? Something to do with her father—

Reese stood up abruptly, carrying their empty plates over to the sink.

"I made a pie," she said tentatively.

"You bake?"

"I do. It's apple pie. It was the only kind I know how to make that you had the ingredients for. I didn't know if you'd like that or not."

"Apple pie is my favorite," he said in a muffled voice.

"Of course, it is."

"I guess that means you hate apple pie?" he asked.

"Nope. Love it. Warm with ice cream melting all over it."

"Glory be. We agree on something for once."

She looked over at him sharply. "How can you declare that you've fallen for me and then be snarky over how we don't agree on anything?"

"Haven't you ever heard that opposites attract?" He turned around, sleeves rolled up, wielding a towel as he dried the big pot she'd cooked the pasta in.

"I've also heard that opposites combust when combined, ultimately consuming and destroying each other."

He shrugged. "That may be true in a science experiment, but I think people whose weaknesses and strengths compensate for each other can be the strongest couples of all if they can learn to accept each other's differences."

"It didn't work out for my parents," she said sadly.

Reese replied tartly, "When the difference between two people is that one's an asshole and one isn't, that's not a great foundation for a relationship."

"You really don't like my dad, do you?"

"Nope. Not one bit. He let his partner talk him into doing something that would get people killed, and he knew it. He had a great family and chose to ignore it, and now he has bailed out on all of you and left you guys holding the bag for his crimes. The rest of you Coltons have to walk around this town bearing his name and his blame, while he's taken off."

"Do you know where he went?" she asked.

"I have an idea."

"Well? Where?"

"I'm not at liberty to say. One of his conditions for signing the plea deal was he didn't want anyone in his family to know where he's going to settle down next."

She sat back, shocked to her core. She realized her jaw was sagging open but didn't have the wherewithal to shut it.

Reese turned to look at her. He must have seen how that bombshell had hit her for he moved over to her side swiftly and pulled her out of her chair and into a big, tight hug.

Dishes forgotten, he bent down, scooped her off her feet and carried her into the living room, which was lit only by the light of a sluggish fire burning hot and slow. He sat down on the overstuffed sofa in front of the fireplace with her still in his lap.

"I'm sorry you had to find that out from me," Reese

murmured against her temple. "I'm a jerk for just springing it on you."

"I recall springing Jordana's move to Chicago on you,
so I'd say that makes us even. Do my siblings know? Oh,
God. Does my mom know?"

Reese winced and she put her palms on each side of
his face and forced him to look at her. "Does my mom
know?" she repeated.

He sighed. "I believe it was your mother who asked
for it. She wanted a clean and complete break from your
father."

She stared up at Reese in dismay. "What did he do to
her? She's not a vindictive person. She doesn't cut anybody out of her life like that."

He closed his eyes tightly for a moment. When he
opened them, their blue depths swam with pain. "You'd
have to ask her."

"You know more than you're saying," she accused.

To his credit, he replied candidly, "I do have an idea
why she did it. But that information is not mine to share.
You'll have to ask her."

"I will! Right now!"

"Maybe right now you should rest and relax a little after
overdoing way too much today."

"I made a pot of spaghetti," she said scornfully.

"And the rest of a nice meal, and you baked, and cleaned
if I'm not mistaken."

"Well, maybe I did dust and straighten up a little." She
paused, and added, "And do a couple loads of laundry."

Her gave her a withering look.

"I swear. I feel fi—" She broke off. "I feel great."

"Good. Let's keep it that way," Reese replied.

"Does that mean you'd kiss me in front of the fire again
if I asked you to?"

Reese laughed against her lips. "I thought you'd never ask."

"You can ask me, too, you know."

"Cool. Wanna make out?"

She swatted his arm as she laughed at him. "You can do better than that."

"Hmm. Let's see. How about this? It feels like I've been waiting for you my whole life. Now that I've finally found you, I can't get enough of you. I love the feel of you in my arms, the softness of your mouth, your passion, your intelligence, your humor. Would you do me the great honor of consenting to make passionate love with me?"

Making love? Well, then. "Wow. That's, umm, much better."

"Are you swept off your feet?" he asked hopefully.

She laughed up at his ridiculous expression. "Blown away."

"And?"

"And what?"

"Do you accept my offer?"

"Oh. That." She pretended to think about it for a few seconds. Then she said all in a rush, "Yes, you romantic man. Of course, I accept."

He wasted no time lowering his mouth to hers, capturing her lips for a lingering, cinnamon-and-apple-flavored kiss.

"You taste good," she murmured against his mouth.

"So do you."

"Remind me to keep an apple pie in the house at all times," she replied.

He kissed his way down the column of her neck and back up. "I could go for chocolate cake, or maybe brownies, too. You'd taste good flavored chocolate. The creaminess of your skin and the tartness of your tongue would pair perfectly with that."

She gazed up at him as she reclined in his arms, more relaxed and at ease that she could ever remember being with any guy. "Oatmeal cookies," she announced.

"I beg your pardon?"

"You'd taste great with oatmeal cookies. Not a bland one. A really good one with lots of spices and flavor. It would have to be a cookie because you're practically a walking milk commercial, and you remind me of whiskey or maybe rum. The raisins and spices in an oatmeal cookie would go perfectly with that."

"And here I was, thinking I was pure vanilla."

Her lips curved wickedly, "I certainly hope not. Personally, I prefer a little spice in my life."

His eyes smoldered with interest. "Do tell."

"I'm a show, don't tell, kind of woman."

"My kind of woman." He stood up, setting her on her feet in the flickering light of the fire. He ran his hands across her shoulders and down her arms to her hands, which he grasped lightly and brought up to his mouth for a kiss.

When he released them, she laid her palms on his chest, measuring the width of his shoulders and the bulk of his pectorals as her hands slid down his ribs to his waist.

"You're so beautiful," he breathed. "All woman." He trailed his fingers through her hair, pulling long strands forward over her shoulders. "Your hair feels like silk."

She touched his jaw with her fingertips. "Yours feels like sandpaper."

"Do you want me to go shave?"

"No. I like you this way. A little scruffy, very masculine. I like you best when you're not all buttoned down, polished and starched. Relaxed, off-duty you is the man I fell for first."

"Are you admitting you've fallen for my cop self, too?" he asked with a little smile.

"Maybe."

He tilted his head to one side, studying her quizzically, and she relented, saying, "Okay. Fine. I've fallen for that side of you, too. I like everything about you."

He let out a long, slow breath as her words sank into him, becoming part of him. His gaze went dark and serious. "I like everything about you, too."

"Everything you know, maybe. There's still a lot about me you don't know."

"I'd like to learn, Yvie."

Very slowly, she rose on her tiptoes, never breaking eye contact with him. She paused when her mouth was only a few inches from his and whispered, "I'd like that, too."

He closed the gap between them, kissing her slowly at first, reverently, even. It was so easy to sink into him, so natural. She loved losing herself in a kiss like this, with him. She felt absolutely safe with him, but she loved the edge of danger that clung to him, a promise of more passion than met the eye, of an alpha male to be unleashed.

She deepened the kiss, opening her mouth, doing everything in her power to draw out the dark and dangerous side of this man. She rubbed her chest lightly against his, relishing the way her nipples had tightened and become so sensitized that she gasped a little at the brushing contact.

The only light in the cabin was the flickering glow of the fire, and the darkness was sultry and mysterious around them. Reese reached for the hem of her sweater and paused in the act of starting to lift it over her head.

"Ground rules for tonight," he said quietly. "If you get a headache at any time, you'll tell me immediately. Yes?"

"But if I do that, you'll stop. And maybe I won't want you to stop, umm, whatever you're doing."

"Which brings us to the second ground rule. The doctor said no vigorous activity. You are to sit back and enjoy and not exert yourself. At all."

"Well, that sounds like no fun."

"Have a little faith. I believe you can have fun without overdoing."

"Challenge accepted," she said jauntily.

He shook his head. "You have to learn to turn down a dare now and then."

"I'm a Colton. We don't know how."

His eyes glinted. "Fair enough." He gently lifted the sweater over her head carefully avoiding her bandages. The laceration on the side of her head was healing nicely but she appreciated his caution with the wound.

She ran her fingers across the fine cotton of his dress shirt, reveling in the hard muscles beneath it as she reached for the small buttons and one by one pushed them through the starched fabric. The fabric peeled back to expose the base of his neck, a few dark chest hairs poking up, hinting at more below. She continued to unbutton the shirt, shoving it aside as she went, loving the feel of his smooth skin and crisp chest hair beneath the pads of her fingers. His heat and hardness drew her in and excited her deep in her core in a feminine place that responded powerfully to him.

She unbuckled his belt and slowly pulled it from around his lean waist. When it came free, she dropped it to the floor.

He lifted her cotton turtleneck over her head next, and her face popped free all at once,

"Is your head okay?" he asked in quick concern.

"I would tell you it's fine, but you would get mad. It doesn't hurt, and as far as I can tell, I'm not bleeding."

"Promise you'll tell me if anything hurts your head at all," he murmured.

"Will do."

"And tell me if you don't like anything we do."

"All right already. Any other rules of engagement, Officer?"

"My badge is in the kitchen. I'm not a cop in here."

"Just the way I like it best. No work between us and you fully in the moment with me."

"I'm right here. All yours."

She reached up to cup his face in her hands. "Same. I'm here, and yours."

He started at her right ear, kissing his way slowly down her neck, across her shoulder and down into the warm valley between her breasts. He reached the lace of her bra and dropped to his knees, then resumed kissing a path down her stomach to the top of her jeans.

He paused there, unbuttoning her waistband and unzipping the denim pants. He tucked his fingers into each side of her jeans and slowly shoved them down, skimming his hands over her hips and down her thighs.

She planted a hand on his shoulder for balance as he guided her feet clear of her pants legs. And then he kissed his way back up the outside of her right thigh to her hipbone, and then back up her stomach.

He stood and unzipped his own trousers, stepping out of the pooled wool at his feet. As she'd suspected, he was lean and hard all over his body. His abs were ridged with muscle, his thighs more powerful than they appeared at a first glance, wrapped in long slabs of muscle.

His skin retained a faint golden cast left over from what must have been a dark summer tan. Unlike her. She'd inherited Lilly's porcelain skin that burned at even the slightest exposure to sun, and hence she lived in hats and sunscreen nearly year round.

"You look like a statue of a Greek goddess," he murmured.

"Yep. That's me. Stone cold and hard as rocks."

His mouth curved up into a smile against her shoulder. "I meant your skin is alabaster and perfectly smooth. Also, I meant that you're an image of female perfection."

"Me? Not hardly."

He sighed, a gust of warm breath against the base of her neck. "When will you stop putting yourself down? Do you realize that every time you insult yourself, you're also insulting my taste in women? I chose you. Out of all the women I could have fallen for, I fell for you. If you can't honor yourself, at least honor that."

It was her turn to sigh. "I'm sorry. I make jokes when I'm uncomfortable."

His head jerked up and he stared down at her. "Why are you uncomfortable? Are we moving too fast for you?"

"Goodness, no. If anything, we're moving too slow! I'm impatient as heck to get naked and horizontal with you. I'm uncomfortable because I'm self-conscious about…how I look," she finished lamely.

He smiled a little. "Every woman I've ever known is self-conscious about how they look. But here's the thing. You're going to have to take it on faith that I find you beautiful. Beautiful and sexy and desirable above all other women."

Wow. That was nice to hear.

He continued to skim his hands across her skin lightly as he spoke. "If I wanted to be with another woman, I would have pursued this hypothetical other woman and not you. But the fact is, I've been waiting for you my whole life. And now that you're here, I have no interest in any other woman. None."

"You make it all sound so easy."

He laughed aloud. "Honey, you've been anything but easy. You've thrown up every roadblock in the book at me, and I've had to find a way around every last one. You've been a challenge like no other." He added, leaning in to drop a light kiss on the end of her nose, "Totally worth it."

She didn't bother arguing the point. He was right. "And you still want me?" she asked in a small voice. "You're sure?"

"Positive."

He took her face gently in both of his big callused hands, cupping her cheeks as if they were the most delicate crystal. He kissed her sweetly to prove the point, ever so slowly deepening the kiss until her head slanted to one side, his to the other, and their tongues swirled together in a sexy tangle of wet, hot need.

Without breaking the contact of their mouths, he bent down slightly, reached one arm behind her thighs and scooped her up into his arms. It was one of the best advantages of being petite. Big strong men like him could pick her up and literally sweep her off her feet.

"Protection?" he murmured.

She answered briskly, appreciating his concern for their health and safety, "I'm on the pill and haven't had sex with anyone since I came back to Braxville. I am so STD-free it's depressing."

"Ditto. I haven't been in a relationship in…longer than I care to stop and count, now. I'm happy to use a condom if you want, though."

"Fair. And thank you."

"I'm a safety guy."

"We'll see about that before I'm done with you. I plan to shake up all that caution and rule following of yours."

He laughed. "I look forward to it."

He strode swiftly down the hall to his bedroom and lowered her carefully onto the mattress. Unwilling to break the yummy contact with him, she kept her arms looped around his neck and urged him down with her. He stretched out beside her, supporting his weight on an elbow as he leaned over her to continue kissing her.

She loved the feeling of him pressing her down deep into the thick comforter and plush mattress, and she wanted more of it. She twined her legs with his and rolled more fully onto her back, dragging him with her.

He laughed a little against her mouth. "Impatient much?"

"Extremely."

"Good thing I like to take my time and savor the journey, or else this would already be over if you had your way."

She growled a little in the back of her throat.

"Oho, so the kitten has claws, does she?"

She pushed him onto his back and pressed up onto her elbows on his chest to mock glare down at him. "I'm no kitten, mister. I'm a wildcat, thank you very much."

"A very tiny, ferocious one," he teased, rolling her over and reversing their positions. She was aware that he'd made a cage of his arms around her when he'd very carefully rolled her over, protecting her the whole time from taking any of his weight.

"I appreciate your concern for my health, Reese, but I promise, I really am fine. My cut has a nice scab and has fully closed, and my brain is no longer scrambled. At least no more than it was before I got jumped."

He smiled against her collarbone, his mouth warm and

firm. As his kissed his way across it, he ended up in the hollow of her throat, licking and then nipping at the sensitive skin there.

"Come up here and kiss me, you tasty cookie of a man."

The heat of his mouth left a trail of devastation in its wake as he kissed his way up to her mouth. Tingles raced down her spine, ending in the vicinity of her toes, which curled in tight delight.

She turned into him and buried her nose in his neck. She couldn't get enough of his scent, mingled with a clean, citrus aftershave. It was the same delicious, masculine scent that rose off his pillowcases and had comforted her through her worst pain this past week. He smelled like safety to her. Warmth. Sun-drenched beaches and lazy waves rolling ashore and hissing back out to sea.

Her bra straps fell loose as he unhooked it in the back and pushed the narrow straps off her shoulders. She shrugged out of it and tossed it aside, sighing with pleasure as his warm hand cupped her breast, his thumb rubbing lightly across the pebbled nipple.

"Cold?" he murmured.

"Turned on."

"Yes," he said under his breath in satisfaction. Then, louder, "You're perfect."

"Keep telling me that. Maybe someday I'll believe you," she replied a little breathlessly, arching her back into the drugging pleasure of his thumb rolling back and forth across that sensitized peak.

He leaned down and his mouth replaced his thumb, making her gasp aloud as electric shocks radiated through her whole body. She reached for him, sliding his briefs off his hips. He kicked them the rest of the way off. The flat plane of his stomach was irresistible, and she ran her palms across it. She followed the well-defined V of muscles lower to the hard shaft of his erection. It filled her fist as she grasped its burning heat. He was rock hard—no need to ask him if he was turned on or not.

His flesh bucked in her hand as she ran her hand up its length to smooth her thumb over the satin tip. Hah. She'd get him to hurry things along, yet.

"Still determined to take all night getting around to making love to me?" she asked archly.

"Tease," he muttered against her breast. His free hand slid lower, following the inward curve of her waist and the upward curve of her hip, then plunging down to cup her core.

She felt her pulse pounding through the swollen, hungry flesh there as his fingertips stroked her once, twice.

"You're not the only one in a hurry," he murmured.

"Ahh, but I make no secret of wanting you right now."

"Your wish is my command."

He pushed lightly against her shoulder and she rolled onto her back, her thighs opening to welcome his explorations. His finger stroked her folds, finding the swollen bud within, so sensitive and slick she nearly came up off the bed when his fingertip rubbed across it.

"Please, Reese. Can we get this show rolling? I'm dying, here."

He laughed, burying his face against her neck for a moment. "We really are yin and yang."

"Well, if your yang doesn't get busy soon, my yin is going to throw you on your back and have its wicked way with you."

"As fun as that sounds, I want you to take it easy tonight."

"Easy? I don't want easy! I want it hot and wild and hard, and that's just the beginning." She tightened her hand around his cock, tugging it toward her in open demand.

He groaned in the back of his throat, and rolled away from her. She opened her mouth to protest until she realized he was fishing a condom out of his bed stand.

Finally, blessedly, he rolled over her, lowering his weight carefully between her legs. Impatient, she wrapped her legs around his hips and pulled him down to her. He resisted for a moment, reaching between them to position himself, and then he was pressing forward, a slow, careful glide of slick, hungry flesh coming together.

"You okay?" he asked.

"Better than okay. Amazing."

He filled her deliciously. He started to withdraw, and her legs tightened convulsively around his hips. He chuckled a little. "I'm not going anywhere." As promised, he surged forward a little more forcefully this time.

"Oh, that's nice," she sighed.

"Honey, you're a lot of things, but merely nice is not one of them. You're spectacular."

She smiled up at his shadowed face and he smiled down at her. "How did I get so lucky to find you?" she asked.

"Maybe I found you. Lord knows, I've been looking for you for a long time."

"Really?"

"Swear to God. I was beginning to despair of ever finding the kind of woman I want. But I just couldn't bring myself to lower my standards."

She brushed her fingertips along his jaw lightly. "Exactly. And then…you."

Their smiles mingled in a kiss of wonder and shared joy at the minor miracle of having arrived at this moment with each other. It wasn't one to be rushed through, but rather savored, treasured and remembered for always.

He began to move within her, and she rose to meet him, catching his rhythm quickly. He kept the pace maddeningly slow, but she had to admit it felt great. Beyond great. Her body had time to build layer upon layer of pleasure toward a towering climax unlike anything she'd ever experienced.

And still he moved within her, stroking her even higher. Huh. Had all of this always been possible and her previous lovers simply been too hasty and too selfish to take her here?

On and on their lovemaking rolled through the night, by turns leisurely and tense, but always tender and intimate. He never looked away from her, never hid the pleasure transforming his features into pure joy. And she smiled back at him, hoping he could see at least a little of the brilliance of her joy.

When she'd had at least three orgasms and was building toward number four, he finally sped up the pace a little. Her breath came in sharp, shallow gasps as pleasure clawed its way through her entire body in search of release.

"Harder," she gasped.

"Don't want…to hurt you…"

"My head is fi—in no pain." She added in desperation, "Please. I want you."

She gripped him tightly with her legs, urging his hips forward, and wrapped her arms around his neck, hanging on for all she was worth. She tugged his head down for a kiss and sucked his tongue, urging him to plunge it into the dark recesses of her mouth in a matching rhythm to their lovemaking.

He groaned and she felt his entire body tensing. She arched up against him as well, straining with him toward ecstasy.

All at once, her orgasm exploded throughout her being, scattering her in a million directions. She cried out in pleasure and Reese's entire body shuddered against hers.

They rode the wave together, crashing toward a far shore, flinging themselves onto it together, exhausted and sated.

He collapsed against her, but even then, he sagged on his propped up elbows, careful not to crush her.

"Head check?" he panted.

"Whatever's better than fine."

He rolled to one side, gently gathering her onto her right side against him.

"You've killed me," he sighed.

"I gather that means we've passed the compatibility-in-bed test?"

"There was a test?"

"Well, it was possible that we would have no chemistry at all in this way."

He laughed a little. "We've had chemistry from the first moment we met. It was just extremely flammable chemistry."

"Explosive," she agreed.

They lay together in silence, their hearts beating in unison as the wind whispered through the pines outside and rattled together the branches of the deciduous trees. The peace of the moment was complete. She'd never in her life felt so right with another person. This was exactly where she was meant to be. She grew drowsy and limp against Reese's equally relaxed body.

He murmured sleepily, "How long until I can reasonably ask you to marry me without creeping you out?"

That jolted her wide awake. "Uhh, I don't know. Certainly not yet."

Reese didn't respond. She waited a moment and then gave him a light poke in the side. He let out a light snore. Had he even been awake when he'd asked the question? She fell back to the pillow, blown away. He was think-

ing about proposing, was he? Even if only at a semicon-
scious level?

Wow. Double wow.

She was equal parts thrilled and terrified at the prospect. She'd avoided long-term commitments literally her
entire life. Was she ready to commit the rest of her life to
one man—to this man?

Did he propose to all the ladies in his sleep immediately after great sex? Or was she special? Worse, did he
actually mean it? Or was it merely the random ramble of
a dreaming mind?

An urge to slide out from under his arm, creep out of
the room and flee the scene roared through her.

Chapter 15

Reese woke up lazily, more relaxed than he'd felt in months. It took a second for his brain to kick in and remember why he felt so freaking great this morning. Yvie. Sweet, sexy Yvie. He'd guessed she would be a generous, enthusiastic lover, and she hadn't disappointed him. In fact, he suspected she'd held back pretty hard last night on account of her head wound. She had an adventurous streak that was sheer self-confidence and enthusiastic enjoyment of sex. He couldn't wait to make love with her when she was fully healed.

He reached out for her and encountered cold sheets. An empty pillow. He sat upright quickly, alarmed. He swung his feet out of bed and grabbed a pair of jeans, slinging them on fast. Padding through the cold cabin barefoot, he headed for the kitchen and his truck keys. She hadn't pulled a runner, had she?

He rounded the corner into the kitchen and screeched

to a halt. Yvette stood at the stove, turning over strips of bacon frying merrily in a pan. She wore his dress shirt from last night, and her slender, gorgeous legs were bare in all their sexy glory. His man parts stirred with interest.

"Hey, beautiful," he murmured, stepping up behind her to wrap his arms around her waist. "You should have stayed in bed and let me cook breakfast for you."

"I thought you had a big meeting this morning."

"Ugh. Work. Yeah, I do. Jordana and I are going to make one more run at Mary Dexter. Surely, she knows something about her husband that she's not telling us."

"Past something like knowing he was sleeping around, or current something like where Markus is hiding out?"

"Either. Both." He snitched a piece of already-fried bacon from the paper covered plate, and Yvette swatted at his hand.

"You like your eggs over hard, right?" she asked as he turned away to pull orange juice out of the refrigerator and get a pot of coffee brewing.

"Good memory."

"You're not the only person around here who pays attention to details," she replied. "Although, I have to admit I was impressed that you knew what my missing purse looked like. It's not a guy thing to register cute purses."

He shrugged modestly and set the table efficiently.

"I assume my purse hasn't been found?" she asked.

"Nope."

She sighed. "I had to cancel all my credit cards and order new ones. What a pain."

"It's better than the alternative. If that was Dexter who attacked you, he's fully capable of murder."

"Who else would it be?" she asked, carrying the frying pan over to the table. She lifted his eggs out onto his plate and two sunny-side-up eggs onto hers.

He held her chair for her, seating her with a quick kiss to the side of her neck. "I approve of your attire, Ms. Colton."

She looked over her shoulder at him, her eyes glinting appreciatively. "And I approve of yours. You can come to breakfast with no shirt on any time you like."

He sat down and reached out. Their fingers touched in sweet reassurance and affection. How was he going to last for hours without touching her again?

Unfortunately, he couldn't linger over the meal or make love to her before he had to take off for work. He took a quick shower and rolled his eyes when he discovered that Yvette had already showered before him and managed to get every towel in the bathroom soaking wet.

He grabbed a dry towel from the linen closet, totally willing to put up with wet towels if it meant having Yvette Colton in his life. He dressed and stepped out into the living room—and stopped in shock. Yvette was fully dressed and even wearing a coat. She stood expectantly by the back door of the kitchen and had a determined look on her face.

"I'm going to lose my mind if I have to stay home another day. I promise not to work too long, and my car is still at the department. I can drive myself home."

His stomach dropped like a lead brick, thudding to the vicinity of his feet. "But I want to keep an eye on you until your attacker is caught. I like having you here with me."

"I like being here, too. But you must be sick of me by now—"

"I want to spend the rest of my life with you. Of course, I'm not sick of you. If you want to stay at your place, that's fine. I'll grab a few things and meet you there tonight." He added, "If you want me there. I get it if you'd like some time to yourself—"

She interrupted, rushing forward to throw her arms

around him. "Of course, I want you with me. I just wasn't sure you'd want to be seen at my place."

He threw her a withering look. "We're in a relationship, now." He added for emphasis, kissing her between each word, "You. Are. My. Woman."

"Which makes you my Neanderthal," she quipped. "I'm nobody's property."

He rolled his eyes. "That's not what I meant, and you know it."

She laughed up at him. "I know. But you'd hate it if I didn't keep you on your toes."

"Truth." He followed her out to his garage, shaking his head and smiling privately to himself. That woman was surely going to lead him on a merry chase over the next seventy years or so. He made a mental note to ask Jordana what kind of jewelry Yvette liked. Would she be a traditional diamond engagement ring kind of woman, or would she prefer some other stone? A nice sapphire, perhaps, or maybe an emerald.

They arrived at the police department and parted ways after he gave her a quick warning not to freak out when she saw the shape her lab was in. She promised not to have a fit, they snuck a quick kiss in the stairwell and he hustled off to his interview with Mary Dexter.

The woman was punctual to the second, which didn't surprise him given how neat a house she kept. Bit of a control freak. Which worked to his and Jordana's advantage. They'd agreed in advance to play softball with the woman and try to trick her into revealing something rather than coming at her hard. To date, Mary had been exceedingly stubborn when confronted directly for information about her missing spouse.

He poured her a cup of tea with a splash of cream and two lumps of sugar, the same way she'd taken it the last time she'd been here. Instead of taking her into an inter-rogation room like before, Jordana showed her to his desk and then pulled up a second chair to make a cozy little cir-cle of the three of them. His job was to talk. Jordana would sit back and observe body language. Or more accurately, look for tells of lying.

"Thanks for coming in this morning, Mrs. Dexter," he said warmly. "I really appreciate it. We wanted to let you know there was a break-in at your house a few nights ago."

"Was anything stolen?" she asked rather too calmly for a woman who seemed obsessed with the tidiness of said home.

"We were hoping you could help us with that. Maybe you can go home, take a look around. Check for any miss-ing valuables. The robber did drop one item on his way out." He pushed a picture of the puzzle box across his desk to show her.

"That old thing?" she said scornfully.

"What is it, if you don't mind my asking?" he mur-mured innocently.

"It's one of those Chinese puzzle boxes with hidden panels. Markus kept it on his desk. Called it his golden parachute."

"Is there gold on it or in it?" Reese asked, trying to sound as dim-witted as possible.

"I have no idea. I doubt he even knew how to open the thing. It was bulky. Ugly. I kept trying to get him to throw it out and put something tasteful on his desk, but he always laughed at me and refused."

"Huh. Did it have some sort of special sentimental value to him?" he followed up.

"Not that I know of." Mary's voice took on a note of caution.

Dang, she was sharp. Time to shift subjects.

He leaned back casually. "At any rate, I've got permission for you to return to your house. We don't believe your husband is planning to return to it any time soon."

"My, my. That's so generous of you," she snapped.

"I'm sorry for the inconvenience," he murmured.

His contrite tone seemed to disarm her indignation a bit.

"Also, I wanted to let you know that your husband is now being classed as a missing person." Missing and wanted for murder, but he conveniently omitted the last bit. "To that end, we'll be turning our resources in the future to helping you find him. We're concerned at his continued absence and hope that no foul play has befallen him."

Myriad emotions flitted across Mary's face, foremost among them confusion. Interesting. She didn't know what to make of the downgrade from murder suspect to possible victim.

He leaned forward and lowered his voice. "If I could speak off the record for a moment?"

She nodded her haughty assent.

"I'm worried about the quality of the security system in your home, ma'am. If you're going to be staying there alone, I would personally recommend an upgrade. Motion detectors, sensors that will let you know when a window or door opens, that sort of thing. If anything should happen to you, I'd never forgive myself."

A normal human being who'd just found out that their home, their personal sanctum and refuge, had been violated, would show at least a modicum of nerves about being home alone.

But Mary literally snorted down her nose at him before declaring scornfully, "My current security system is perfectly fine."

She wasn't the least bit worried about the intruder, huh? Interesting. That lent credence to his theory that it had been Markus himself who broke into the Dexter house to search for that puzzle box. And furthermore, Mary knew it had been her husband.

"At a minimum, ma'am, you should change the security code. We believe the intruder obtained the code, somehow, and disabled your home alarm."

"Fine. Whatever."

"If you would like patrols to continue coming by your home for a few weeks, please let us know."

She waved a dismissive hand at that suggestion.

Oh, yeah. Markus had totally been the intruder who'd run over Yvette.

"If you'll wait here a moment, I'll go fetch your house keys from the evidence locker. Can I get you another cup of tea? It'll take a few minutes to do the paperwork to get your keys."

He stood up, leaving Jordana to take over chitchatting with Mary. His partner had known the woman most of her life. If anyone could coax information out of Mary Dexter, it was Jordana.

He signed out the house keys quickly and then loitered by the evidence locker until Jordana texted him an okay.

Mary left the building quickly, and he turned with interest to his partner. "Well?"

"She's been in Kansas City the past few weeks. Claims to have been visiting a friend but couldn't produce the friend's name."

"You think she was visiting Markus?"

"Possible. Mary gave me the name of the hotel she stayed at. I'll make a call to confirm her alibi and find out if she had male company."

He nodded and looked up quickly as a familiar form caught his attention across the room. Yvette's trim silhouette.

"What're you grinning like a fool for?" Jordana snapped.

"Yvette's here," he murmured.

"Dang, you've got it bad for her, don't you?"

"I'm going to marry that girl."

"What?"

"She doesn't know it, yet, so don't say anything." He looked up, saw the stunned look on Jordana's face and blurted, "Don't you punch me, too." That was all he had time to say before Yvette reached their desks.

"Hey, guys. I've got something you need to see. Do you want the old news or the recent news first?"

"Old," he and Jordana said simultaneously.

"Right. So, I got the DNA results back from a strand of hair I collected off Markus Dexter's hairbrush. I'll have to get a sample from him to confirm that it was actually his hair, and I'd like you guys to get a warrant for that when we find him."

Jordana frowned. "I don't understand. Why does it matter if it was his hair or not?"

Reese knew that look in Yvette's eyes. She was bursting with excitement over something. "Because the owner of that hair is Gwen Harrison's father."

All of a sudden, a bunch of pieces fell into place. He blurted, "Markus Dexter is Gwen Harrison's father?"

"If that hair is Markus's, yes."

Jordana jumped in excitedly. "That's our motive! Olivia Harrison was having an affair with Markus Dexter and it went sour. He killed her over it."

Yvette beat him to the punch, correcting, "We know he had sex with Olivia at least once to have fathered her daughter. That doesn't necessarily mean they were having an affair. And Gwen was several years old when her mother died, so he didn't kill her right away. My guess is she had the baby and started pressing him to leave his wife. That would be why he killed Olivia. Either way, it's a heck of a motive."

Reese spoke up. "What's the new news?"

"I got a hit on the key from the puzzle box."

He lurched upright in his desk chair. "Do tell."

"It's from the Kansas City Freeport."

His jaw sagged. "The freeport?"

Jordana chimed in with "What's a freeport?"

Reese explained. "They're bonded warehouses that accept cargo and shipments from other countries. A freeport can hold cargo indefinitely without ever sending it through customs. The stuff basically sits in lockers, in limbo between countries, as long as it's inside the freeport building."

Jordana frowned. "Why on earth would Markus Dexter have a locker inside a freeport?"

Yvette answered soberly, "He's hiding something. It's valuable, and he doesn't want any US authority knowing it exists. He's either avoiding paying taxes on it or it's illegal."

"How do we get a warrant to search it?" Jordana asked.

Reese winced. "That could be difficult. The contents of the freeport are in transit between countries. It would have to be a federal warrant."

Jordana groaned. "Great. I guess I'm spending the rest of the day doing paperwork, aren't I?"

"Sorry, sis," Yvette murmured.

Reese commented, "I wonder if Mary Dexter knows her husband has a daughter."

Jordana met his gaze sharply. "Could be interesting to find out. But you're going to have to tread lightly around her. Disarm her."

Yvette snorted. "That woman always scared me."

Jordana snorted back. "I don't know why. You were always the only one of us kids she could stand."

"Really?" Reese asked quickly.

"Oh, yeah. Yvette was a quiet, mousy little thing who dressed in girly clothes and was always neat and clean. Mary thought she was the perfect child."

He'd seen Yvette tussled and hectic after they made love, and frankly, it was his favorite way to see her. "Come with me to drop the bomb on Mary?" he asked her.

"Umm, sure. What do you need me to do?"

"Go get Markus's hairbrush, and I'll meet you out front," he answered.

When Yvette slid into his truck a few minutes later, she lifted the center console and slid all the way across the bench seat to plaster herself against his side. "I've missed being with you," she murmured.

"It has only been a few hours," he replied humorously.

"I know. A lifetime."

He laughed under his breath. "God, I love you."

She froze against him.

Oh, crap. Should he retract the statement, or would that make it even more weird? Should he let it stand as nothing more than a casual remark? Pretend he'd never said it? Paralyzed with uncertainty, he ended up doing nothing. The moment passed. Yvette eventually relaxed against his side, and she didn't make any grand or awkward statement in response.

Mary Dexter answered the front door of her mansion and promptly gave him an earful about cops tromping around her house in muddy boots and ruining her rugs. He finally got a word in edgewise to apologize humbly and ask to speak with her.

In a huff, Mary led him and Yvette into the living room. It was as stuffy a space as its owner and he perched on the edge of a deeply uncomfortable Victorian sofa. Mary and Yvette sat on the matching one across a coffee table.

Yvette opened her purse and pulled out a sealed, plastic evidence bag. She said softly, "Miss Mary, I'm hoping you can help me with something. Do you recognize this hairbrush?"

"Turn it over," Mary demanded.

Yvette turned the bag, and the elaborate monogram on the back became visible, a large *D* with an *M* and a *J* on each side of it.

"Where did you get that? I gave that to my Markus for his birthday years ago."

"You're sure it's his?"

"I can't imagine there's anyone else in Braxville with an imported boar's-hair brush with the initials MJD engraved on it."

Yvette nodded. "If you look closely, you can see some hairs in the bristles. Do those look like Uncle Markus's?"

"Why, yes, dear. You can see the gray roots and that stupid hair dye he uses to cover the gray in his hair."

Nice touch, calling him Uncle Markus. Yvette was putting Mary more at ease than he'd ever seen the woman.

"Why are you asking me all of this?" Mary asked, pinning him with a suspicious look.

He answered gently, "Ahh. That. Well, we ran a DNA analysis of several of the hairs from this brush. Turns out the hairs come from Gwen Harrison's genetic father."

"Markus? He's the Harrison girl's father? He and Olivia—" She broke off, visibly pale and stunned.

Yvette reached forward and took Mary's hand, patting it sympathetically. "Is it possible anyone else used that brush? Any male guests to your home who might've gone upstairs and borrowed it?"

"Guests—no—I don't like other people in my home…
I think I feel faint…"

Yvette stood quickly and help her lie back. He grabbed
a few pillows and passed them to Yvette to put behind
Mary, while he pulled a crocheted blanket off the back of
the sofa and laid it over her. "Rest, ma'am."

"Thank you, young man."

She wasn't that old. But if she wanted to play the frail
old lady, he would go along to gain her trust.

"Oh, Aunt Mary, I'm so sorry," Yvette murmured.
"You've been so brave over the years, looking the other
way all that time. It's not fair that he did this to you."

"All those women," she moaned. "And I never said a
word. Never confronted him. I kept the peace. I was a du-
tiful wife."

"And to have him betray you like this," Yvette tsked.
"It's disgraceful."

"How could he?" Mary wailed.

Reese mentally grinned. Here it came. The righteous
fury.

"I could kill him," she declared. "And to think, he
wanted me to protect his sorry neck."

Yvette glanced at him over Mary's head and he nodded fractionally.

Yvette said sympathetically, "He doesn't deserve you.
You've always been too good for him."

"I'm the one who came from the good family, you know.
I had money. He used my trust fund to buy into your father's company. And then this! Why, I'll take all the money
out of the bank accounts. It should all be mine, anyway.
He wouldn't have a dime if it weren't for me agreeing to
marry him and finance his business ventures. I'm the one
who told him to invest in Colton Construction in the first

place. Your daddy always had a good eye for real estate. I told Markus to take advantage of that."

"And then to run away like this and leave you holding the bag," Yvette made an indignant noise. "I can't imagine how you'll face his daughter. Ohmigosh, and all your friends when they find out…"

Mary groaned, and her diamond-clad fingers fluttered to her forehead. "I'll have to leave, too."

"You won't join him, will you?" Yvette asked in horror.

"Goodness, no. Kansas City won't be nearly far enough away to hide from the shame. But I have no interest in leaving the country, either. Oh, dear. What shall I do? I have people on the West Coast. My sister. We never got along, but maybe I could spend some time with her."

"I'm sure she'll understand," Yvette soothed.

Reese pulled out his cell phone and texted Jordana quickly. Dexter is in Kansas City. Planning to leave the country. Send alerts to customs and TSA to detain him on sight.

"How soon is Uncle Markus planning to leave the country? Maybe if he goes quickly enough you won't have to leave Braxville and all your friends."

"Oh, in just a few days."

"Do you know the details of his trip?" Yvette asked casually.

"No, no. He was going to go alone. He wanted to send for me later, but I hadn't made up my mind if I was going or not. I'm plenty sick of his shenanigans after all these years and all those women."

Yvette sat down on the edge of the sofa beside the older woman. She lowered her voice and asked conspiratorially, "Did you know the Harrison woman? Olivia, I think her name was?"

"Beautiful girl. I'm not surprised she caught his eye.

She had a friend in town who she used to come visit. They came to church together. That's where we met her—" Mary's voice became a hiss of fury. "He picked her up at *church*."

Yvette made an appropriate sound of shock.

"I hope he burns in hell," Mary spat.

"Aunt Mary, I found something strange in a piece of evidence that came into the lab a few days ago. It was a puzzle box with a key inside it. Do you know anything about that key?"

Mary frowned. "What was it a key to?"

"I was hoping you might know."

"He always was secretive." Mary's voice lowered to a hushed murmur. "Once, I found a whole bunch of money in the back of his desk drawer and a fake driver's license. It was his picture but it had a different name on it."

"What ever would he need something like that for?" Yvette responded on cue.

"He said it was a joke. But I never believed him. I figured he used it to get hotel rooms for him and his sluts."

"Do you remember the name on it?" Yvette asked, sounding suitably shocked.

"James McDowell. As if anyone couldn't see right through that to realize it was his initials scrambled. And his middle name is James for goodness' sake. It's not even a good fake name."

Yvette laughed a little. "You're so much more clever than he ever realized."

Mary responded archly, "All men think they're so smart. But we women…we always know what they're up to."

Reese suppressed a smile. He was happy to be the stupid detective who'd brought along the one person on earth Mary would spill her guts to. Yep. He was quite the moron.

He made a hand signal over Mary's head to Yvette to

wrap things up, and she asked Mary if she could call a friend to come sit with her. Someone agreed to come over, and he and Yvette made their excuses and left.

They drove away from the Dexter house, and a few blocks away, he pulled over to the curb. "Come here, you amazing woman." He pulled her into his arms and gave her a resounding kiss. "You were magnificent. She sang like a bird."

Yvette threw her leg over his leg and straddled his hips, grinning down at him. "I like interrogating people."

"If you'd like more training in how to do it, I'd be glad to arrange it."

"It's so…bloodthirsty. No wonder you love your job."

He laughed at her enthusiasm and kissed her again, loving her excitement.

"Can I convince you to christen this truck?" she asked hopefully.

"Soon, darlin'. Right now, I want to drive you home and put you to bed."

"Oooh, sounds fun. You'll join me?"

"You need your rest," he tried.

"What I need is you."

He sighed. "You are possibly the worst patient I've ever been around."

"I know. Isn't it great?"

He smiled up at her ruefully and set her off his lap. And it was, indeed, great stripping her naked, laying her down in his bed and making slow, sweet love to her.

But eventually, real life called. Or rather, texted. Jordana had verbal approval on the warrant for Markus Dexter's locker in the freeport. They needed only to drive to Kansas City to pick up the signed warrant and then they could find out what Markus was hiding.

Chapter 16

Yvette woke up with the setting sun pouring in through the window in crimson glory. "Reese!" she called. "Are you home?"

No answer. He'd undoubtedly gone back to work and left her to sleep the afternoon away. Which she, in fact, had. She showered and dressed, and noticed her phone had several text messages when she picked it up in the kitchen.

The first message was from Reese. Gone to Kansas City. Will call you when we arrest Markus.

Perfect. She still had a bunch of emails and paperwork to go through from being out of the office for several days. She'd just settled down in front of a fledgling fire with her laptop when she heard the sound of a vehicle coming up the drive.

Odd. She didn't see its headlights. Nor did she recognize the sound of its engine. That definitely wasn't Reese's truck. One of her siblings, maybe. It would be like Lilly to send one of them out to check on her.

A firm knock at the front door drew her out of her seat to open it, a greeting on her lips.

"Hi—" she started. She stopped. Stared. Blurted, "What are *you* doing here?"

"Come with me. Right now," Markus Dexter snarled.

"What? No. I'm not going anywhere."

His hand lifted away from his side. "Wanna bet?"

She stared in shock at the handgun pointed at her belly. "Are you kidding me?"

"I assure you, I'm not. Let's go. Now."

"I'm going to need shoes and my coat, Uncle Markus." She threw in the title to remind him of her lifelong relationship to him. He was sporting a scruffy beard and looked rather more unkempt than she was used to. He had a hard edge about him now, which was new.

"Make it fast."

She turned, thinking frantically. How to let someone know she was being kidnapped? He followed her into the bedroom where she made a production of fishing her boots out of the closet, strewing all of her shoes around the floor of the closet. She dumped several pairs of socks on the floor as she opened the drawer, too. She threw a huge log onto the fire as she passed by it, confident the thing would burn most of the night. She didn't close the steel mesh curtains in front of the fire and prayed she didn't burn Reese's house down. But he would know something was terribly wrong if she'd made a mess and hadn't made the fire safe before leaving.

She grabbed her coat off the rack by the door and surreptitiously dropped one of her mittens on her way out. It was the best she could do on short notice.

Markus herded her into the back seat of what looked

like a rental sedan, where he zip-tied her hands together in front of her. Sheesh. He didn't think much of her survival skills if that was all he did to her. But she wasn't about to complain.

He drove away from the house, and she sat quietly in the backseat, trying to figure out where he was headed. Cell phone coverage out here could be spotty. They went around the city center of Braxville on country roads and appeared to head generally east. She dared not wait any longer to call for help. She reached into her front jeans pocket surreptitiously and pulled out her phone.

It was hard to type while covering its lighted face with one zip-tied hand and trying to press letter keys with the other. It was painstaking work, but she finally typed out a message to Reese.

Kidnapped by Markus. Heading eastish in gray sedan. Not hurt.

Reese looked away from the window impatiently as his cell phone vibrated. "Take over watching the entrance," he told the Kansas City detective at the other window in the cramped office. They'd set up a surveillance hide on the freeport across the street from this warehouse's front offices. He didn't love the sharp angle to the front door from here, but this building had a second floor that lifted them above street traffic and parked cars.

Darkness was falling and streetlights threw dull pools of light on the slushy pavement. The lights were off in the office, of course, so he stepped back from his window perch to pull out his cell phone.

Shielding it with his hand, he opened the text from Yvette, smiling already.

And then he read her message.

Had he not had so many years of experience on the force, he'd have dropped the phone in his panic. As it was, he yelled, "Come here, Pat! Oh, my God. Call the SWAT task force commander. And the FBI while you're at it."

"What the hell?" the other cop said.

It was easier to shove the cell phone at the guy than try to explain.

"Oh, shit," the other cop responded. "I'll call the hostage-negotiation guys, too."

Ohgod ohgod ohgod. Reese paced the office they'd commandeered for this operation as frantically as a caged tiger.

Belatedly, it dawned on him that he should text her back. Let her know he'd received her message. But what if an incoming text made noise? Got her in trouble? Worse, what if Markus turned off her phone?

Pat poked his head into the room. "Come with me. We're shifting this operation to the SWAT command center, now that we know where Dexter is. What's the woman's phone number so we can get a GPS location on it and track it?"

He rattled off Yvette's phone number quickly as he all but ran from the building. He jumped into the unmarked car with the Kansas City cop, who blessedly drove like Yvette's life depended on it across town to police head-quarters.

Thankfully, it took about two minutes to bring the SWAT operators on call up to full speed. This was not their first rodeo. They called in a full SWAT team and began preparing a briefing for them.

In about two more minutes, a red blip popped up on a large wall monitor. Someone superimposed a road map of Kansas on the screen, and it became clear quickly that Markus and Yvette were headed this way.

Unable to wait any longer for the process to unfold, he

asked the SWAT team commander, "Now that we've got positive ID on the vehicle, can I text her back? Let her know we're on our way?"

He waited through a brief, agonizing conference among the tactical experts.

One of them turned to Reese. "She's a cop, is she?"

"Forensic scientist for a police department."

"Close enough. She the type to panic?"

"Not at all," he answered firmly.

"Okay. Tell her we're tracking her and then ask her to delete the text conversation."

"Got it."

He texted quickly, We're tracking you and need you to delete all my texts after you read them. He hesitated for a moment and then typed quickly, I love you. I promise you'll be safe. ALL the law enforcement types are here. Hang tough and keep him as calm as possible.

He waited three minutes or so for a response but got none. He hoped she'd gotten his message and merely wasn't in a position to respond right now. And then he prayed. He'd found her so recently. He couldn't lose her, now. In what universe would that be fair or right?

When he was sure Yvette wasn't going to respond immediately, he placed a quick phone call to Jordana.

"Hey, Reese. What's up?"

"We've got a situation. Markus has surfaced. He apparently went to my cabin and kidnapped Yvette. She's texting me from a car he's driving toward Kansas City, as we speak."

Jordana swore colorfully, which was wildly unlike her. "What can I do?" she demanded urgently.

"Pray. If they're headed for the freeport they'll arrive in about an hour and a half. I'll update you as I can. SWAT's gearing up, and the FBI's on scene. She'll be okay. I promise."

Jordana said soberly, "You can't promise that, and you know it. But if anyone can make sure she comes through this safely, it'll be you. Take care of my baby sister, Reese."

"You know I'd give my life for her."

"Yeah. I do. How are you holding up?"

"I'm on the ragged edge," he confessed. "This is way too much like the last time."

"You mean when Christine was taken hostage?"

"Yes." He shuddered at the memory of his partner's lifeless, bullet-riddled body lying in a pool of blood beside the corpse of the man who'd killed her. An image of Yvette dead the same way flashed through his head and he nearly lost it. His breathing sped up until he felt lightheaded and nauseated.

"I can hear you hyperventilating, Reese. Breathe, buddy. Yvette's smart, levelheaded and resourceful. She won't do anything stupid and heroic like Christine tried to do."

Jordana knew the details of his first partner's death at the hands of a deranged criminal with a bag full of weapons and ammo. The man had been trying to achieve suicide by cop, and had taken Christine Crocker hostage to draw as many police as possible to his home. When he'd tried to shoot at the police outside the home he'd holed up in with her, she'd leaped at him to stop him. He'd panicked and shot her. By the time police dropped the shooter, entered the home and found Christine, she'd bled out.

Reese snorted. "You know as well as I do that Yvette would do something stupid and heroic."

"All right. Fine. She can be impulsive. But she has you to live for now."

"Is that enough?" he asked desperately.

"It has to be. Believe in her, Reese. This time will be different. This will end well."

"From your mouth to God's ear," he said fervently.

Jordana said lightly, "By the way, you two are doing a terrible job of keeping your relationship secret. It's all over your faces any time you're in the same room together. You two look freaking radiant, for crying out loud."

"Uhh, I don't know what to say."

"You'll need to go public sooner rather than later that you two are in love."

"I'm totally in love with her. But I don't know how she feels about me. I mean I know she likes me. But does she love me?"

"Oh, she's a goner. I've never seen her look at another man the way she looks at you. She's head over heels, my dude."

How was it possible to be so elated and so panicked in the same breath? She had to be okay. She *had* to.

Yvette's composure threatened to crack when the text from Reese finally came in. She read it quickly and then deleted it like he'd asked. The car was currently traveling a dark stretch of highway, and she was afraid the glow of her cell phone screen would be visible to Markus from the front seat, so she didn't dare try to respond to Reese, right now.

She wasn't surprised that Reese had called out every law enforcement agency in this part of the country the moment he got that text. She took his advice and decided to attempt to strike up a conversation with Markus. Although frankly, she was more interested in throwing him mentally off-balance than in keeping him calm. The calm ship seemed to have sailed a while ago where her father's ex-partner was concerned.

"So, Uncle Markus. I found out today that Gwen Harrison is your biological daughter."

The car swerved sharply and then righted itself. "What the hell arc you talking about?"

"I ran a DNA test on some of your hair. You and Olivia Harrison are Gwen's biological parents. Did you know Olivia had your baby?" She was tempted to add, *When you killed her*, but there was no need to antagonize him *that* much.

"I didn't even know the Harrison woman, let alone have a child with her."

Riiight. Because DNA lied all the time. Not.

"Aunt Mary's plenty pissed off about it."

That made him squawk, *"What?"*

"She threatened to empty out all of your bank accounts. In fact, she might have already done it this afternoon, she was so mad."

Markus snorted. "That bitch always thought she had me by the short hairs because of her family's money. But she never knew I put back money for myself. Squirreled it away in accounts she didn't even know existed. Bit by bit, I've wiped out that old hag."

Hag, huh? "So, Aunt Mary isn't the quiet, docile wife she acts like in public?"

That got Markus going but good. He ranted about his wife for most of the next hour. Long enough for her to start seeing signs for the suburbs of Kansas City.

Under the cover of his tirade about how Mary Dexter had everybody fooled, she sent another text to Reese. Approaching Kansas City. And I love you, too.

He texted her back immediately with the question that had been agreed upon would be asked the next time she contacted him. Are you in imminent danger?

Her response was fast. No.

Thank God. His legs actually felt weak with relief. He replied with, Police following you in unmarked cars. SWAT and FBI mobilized here in KC. Sit tight and don't provoke him. Don't be a hero.

She didn't respond right away. A sinking feeling that she wasn't willing to agree to that settled heavily in his gut. He tried again. Keep your head down, stay quiet, don't do anything unpredictable. Let the professionals take care of you.

She responded right away with a single word that made him smile reluctantly. Fine.

If she was cracking jokes right now, she must not feel as if her life was in danger at the moment. That was reassuring. But still. She was the prisoner of an armed and angry man who'd killed before and could kill again.

"Did you know they arrested Fitz for the whole arsenic scandal?" she said conversationally. "And they're questioning him about the Harrison and Crane murders. Do you think he killed those two?"

"Definitely."

"Why, I wonder?" she asked.

"He was the one having an affair with the Harrison girl. Hell, I'll bet he's that Gwen girl's father. You should test his DNA."

Denial, much? She already had her father's DNA profile in her database, and it hadn't been the one that popped up as a perfect parental match to Gwen Harrison's. But she was happy to play along with the lie if it kept Markus talking.

"Where are we headed, Uncle Markus?"

"To the Kansas City Freeport. You're going to get my

golden parachute out of storage for me, little girl. And then, I'm out of here."

"What is this freeport place?" she asked innocently.

"Don't play dumb with me, Yvette. You're a cop. You know darned good and well what a freeport is."

"I'm not a police officer—"

"Cut the crap. You swiped my puzzle box."

"I did not! You're the one who fished it out of your attic and then dropped it on the way out the door."

"So," he commented. "That was you in the attic. I thought I recognized you."

"I knew I recognized you," she retorted.

"You found the key, didn't you?" he accused. "I figure it took you cops about two minutes to figure out it belongs to a safe-deposit box. But I fooled you all. It's a freeport and not even technically US territory. You can't touch my stuff in there."

Far be it from her to explain to him that federal laws still applied to any facility located on US soil.

"How am I going to help you get into this freeport place?" she asked.

"Shut up. I'll tell you what to do when we get there."

"Sure. No problem," she replied evenly.

As they approached the outskirts of Kansas City, she risked texting, Going to freeport. She expected Reese and company would already have anticipated that, but it didn't hurt for them to have confirmation of Markus's destination.

It wasn't too much longer until they pulled up in front of a long, low building that stretched away into the darkness in both directions.

"You're going to go inside in front of me," he directed, "and show them the warrant I have."

"What warrant?"

"I know a guy. He forged one for me."

"What guy?"

"Quit interrupting. You're gonna show the warrant and your police ID."

"I don't have my police ID—"

"I have it." He held up her cute pink purse with the butterflies from the night of the mugging.

"You knocked me down in the parking lot and took my purse?" she exclaimed.

"Shut up. And don't make me tell you to be quiet, again." He shoved her purse at her. "Show your ID to the guy at the front desk along with the warrant. Make him unlock my storage unit for you. I couldn't find my key in your cursed police department. Turned the place upside down, but there was no sign of it. Where'd you put it, anyway?" he asked truculently.

"It's locked in a safe where all valuable evidence is stored."

He swore in frustration.

He resumed giving her orders. "When the guard leaves, you'll put everything on the table into this bag." He lifted a large duffel bag from the front seat of the car.

The bag was clearly empty. Thank goodness. She'd been worried when she glimpsed it as she'd climbed into the car that it might have weapons inside it.

"When I have my stash, you and I will walk out of the freeport. Nice and quiet. Got it?"

"Yes. I like the nice-and-quiet part."

"If you do anything, try anything, I'll kill you. Understood?"

"Uncle Markus. I would never do anything to hurt you, and I can't believe you'd do anything to hurt me," she said in as innocent a voice as she could muster.

She climbed out of the car and waited patiently while

he draped her coat over her zip-tied wrists. He grabbed her elbow and yanked her along beside him, growling, "Don't mess this up. I'll shoot you, and I'll shoot the guard. His life is in your hands, Yvette."

She refrained from looking around the parking lot. It wasn't necessary, anyway. She could feel Reese nearby, his gaze upon her. She figured there was probably a whole SWAT team out here somewhere, too, if she knew Reese. Which meant there would be snipers covering every angle. They wouldn't shoot until Markus did something to threaten her or the security guard inside the lobby of the freeport, or until the commander on scene gave an order to take the shot.

Her guess was they would let this play out as long as she wasn't in immediate danger. It would help the prosecution if he took personal possession of whatever he'd stashed in the freeport. He wouldn't be able to claim it had been planted or that it wasn't his. Not to mention, he would need to remove whatever was in his storage unit for it technically to be on US soil.

The security guard looked up from behind a high front counter. His eyes were hard and even. She would lay odds he was an FBI agent.

Markus nudged her with his elbow. Right. She was up. An attack of nerves startled her as she opened her mouth to speak. Until now, she'd been mostly calm, feeling relatively confident that Reese would take care of her and everything would be fine.

But now, with the hard bore of Markus's pistol jammed against her side and the security guard looking up at her intently, the reality of her danger slammed into her full force.

"May I help you?" the guard asked.

"Umm, yes. I'm, umm, from the Braxville Police Department, and I've got a warrant to search one of your lockers."

Markus took her ID card from her purse and passed it over to the guard, along with the forged search warrant.

The guard looked at it for a while and passed it back to her. She started to reach for it with her tied hands, but Markus snatched it off the counter quickly.

"Do you have the key?" the guard asked.

"No, we don't," Markus responded for her.

"I'll send a guy with you, then, to unlock it." A second guard, big and fit looking and also reeking of being a federal agent, stepped out of a door behind the first guard.

"Come with me," the second guard said.

Frantically, she tried to figure out how to signal this guard, who looked plenty big enough to take down Markus, that her captor had a gun hidden under his coat. But, with Markus's pistol literally pressed against her side, her options were limited. Maybe when they got to the storage unit she would get an opening.

The guard walked in front of them down a wide hallway lined with doors spaced at even intervals. Other than the concrete floor and walls and dim sconce lighting, this could be a regular office building.

"Here we are," the guard said. "Do you want to go in alone, or shall I accompany you?"

"Alone," Markus said quickly. "You first, Yvette."

The guard threw open the door, and complete darkness was all she saw. Markus jabbed her side with the pistol and gestured with his head for her to reach for, presumably, a light switch.

Everything happened all at once.

She reached with both hands for the wall, Markus shoved her inside and then the guard jumped for Markus. She stumbled and fell as the door slammed shut behind her, landing on her knees and then pitching forward. She rolled and hit the floor with her right shoulder, disoriented.

Markus swore violently in the complete darkness, and she rolled away from the sound of his voice hastily. The light switched on, and she was in a small room, perhaps six feet wide and maybe ten feet long. A single table stood in the center of the room and she lay curled up next to one of its legs. Markus was pointing his pistol at the door with both hands.

She grabbed the table leg in both hands and hoisted herself to her feet. She stared at the contents of the table. It was covered in tall stacks of cash, bundled into rubber-banded packets of twenties and hundreds. She guessed at a glance that at least a couple of million dollars was stacked there. One corner of the table held two passports with New Zealand covers, and an assortment of jewelry—a couple of diamond rings, a gaudy gold watch, a necklace with an impressive emerald in it and a tangle of other pieces.

Markus tossed the duffel bag at her. "Put everything in that."

She commenced awkwardly shoveling the cash off the table into the big bag as Markus pressed his ear to the door. He swore aloud at whatever he heard.

"Okay. Here's how this is going to go down. You and I are walking out to the parking lot together and getting in my car. You're driving me to the airport, where I'm going to get on a charter plane that's waiting for me. If you don't mess this up, maybe you get to live. Otherwise, I'll blow your head off."

Not while she was driving the car, he wouldn't. If she was incapacitated, she would crash the car, he wouldn't get to the airport and he might get hurt. Once they reached the airport, though, that was another story.

Shoving her in front of him, he forced her to crack open

the unit's door a few millimeters. "I'm coming out!" he shouted. "Any funny business, and the girl is dead!"

"Understood," a familiar voice called out.

Reese? He was out there? A wash of warmth went through her trembling body.

"Open the door wider," Markus ordered, pressing his pistol to the back of her head. The barrel was hard and cold against her skull.

Nervously, she did so, praying there wasn't a hair trigger on his weapon. One slip of his finger, and she would be dead. Of course, it was also possible the snipers outside would accidentally take her out in the course of trying to stop Markus from leaving.

"I'm coming out first," she called. Her ad-lib ticked off Markus, who jabbed her neck painfully with the weapon.

"Let's go," he snapped, shoving her forward.

The hallway was lined with men in full tactical gear. Kansas City SWAT, if she had to guess. All of their weapons were trained in her and Markus's direction, and it was the scariest sight she'd ever seen. All those hard, emotionless faces pressed against eye sights, staring back at her. As she'd suspected, Reese had called in *all* the law enforcement in this part of the country.

"All of you, stay in front of me," Markus ordered.

It was a slow procession, waiting for the various tactical officers to move ahead of them toward the exit in an ever-increasing crowd of black uniforms and weapons. The parade spilled outside, and Markus's car had been repositioned at the side door.

She slid across the passenger seat with Markus's pistol pressed to her neck, just below her right ear. She crawled awkwardly over the center console, and lowered herself carefully into the driver's seat of Markus's car while he climbed in after her, never taking the pistol's aim off her.

He seemed to know that the second he gave all those cops outside even the slightest opening, one of them would take him down. He slouched down below the level of the windows as she started the car, his shoulder against her side and his pistol still maddeningly aimed at her head, now pointing up at her jaw from underneath. She knew all too well that would be a lethal angle from which to take a bullet.

An escort of police patrol cars led her out of the parking lot slowly and drove toward an airport. Their lights flashed, but blessedly, their sirens were silenced. She counted four police cruisers in front of her and a dozen or more trailing behind in a slow-motion parade of flashing lights. She didn't see the big SWAT vans, but she suspected they'd gone another route to the airport, racing to get there and get set up before she arrived. The cop cars in front of her drove well under the speed limit, lending credence to the idea of giving the tactical folks time to get into place.

Markus was agitated beside her, and the more nervous he got, the more nervous she got.

They were escorted directly out onto the tarmac and up to a low, sleek business jet. This was it. If Markus was going to kill her, now was the time. He could just as easily use the pilots as his hostages. Her usefulness to him would be done the moment he set foot on that airplane.

"You good, Detective Carpenter?" the SWAT officer asked him after tugging Reece's shirt collar up a little higher.

"Yep. Let's do this."

He jumped out of the tactical van and stepped around it. The Learjet Markus had chartered was parked on the tarmac with its front hatch open and steps folded down. A pair of FBI agents sat in the cockpit, dressed as pilots.

The gray sedan pulled to a stop in front of the jet, and he spied the petite form seated at the wheel. Surely, Markus would use her as a human shield and not shoot her until he got inside that plane. The guy was smart enough to know the cops would take him out the moment he killed Yvette.

Yvette's door opened. From his vantage point, Reese saw Markus practically lying on her lap. Very slowly, she climbed out of the car, her hands clasped behind her neck.

Reese stepped forward and she spotted him.

Their gazes locked, and for a moment, everything around them fell away. There was no crisis, no madman with a gun pointed at her, no SWAT team. Just the two of them. Here and now. In love.

And apparently in sync, for she shook her head slightly in the negative, as if to tell him not to do what he was about to.

He'd had to argue and ultimately beg to be the guy to make the close approach to Yvette and Markus. Through sheer cussed stubbornness, though, he'd prevailed and convinced the crisis team leader to let him do this.

He walked forward slowly, his hands held well away from his sides.

"Stop right there!" Markus shouted at him. "Don't come any closer. I'll shoot!"

"Hey, Mr. Dexter. How are you doing, sir? I'm sure you remember me—I'm Reese Carpenter of the Braxville Police Department."

"What are you doing here?" Dexter demanded.

"Well, you're from my town. I thought you might be more comfortable talking to somebody you've met before than to a total stranger."

"What do you want?"

This was a good sign. The man was rational enough to follow the conversation and ask logical questions.

"Well, I'd like to make a trade with you, Mr. Dexter. Myself for Miss Colton."

"No!" she cried.

He smiled ruefully at her and continued, speaking over her protests. "I'll be your hostage in her place. Let her go and you can have me. She's a civilian and has no part in all of this."

"Like hell she doesn't," Dexter sneered. "She's the one who kept turning up evidence that closed the net around me. First that damned arsenic thing, and then those bodies. Nobody was ever supposed to find those. But Fitz. He wouldn't listen, would he? Had to renovate. Couldn't be satisfied with the building he had. Always wanted things to be bigger and better. The man's ambition knows no limits."

Reese made a sympathetic sound. "I have to admit, it was really satisfying to arrest Fitz Colton and take him down a peg. Did you happen to see that on TV?"

Dexter devolved into a rant about how overdue the arrest had been, and Reese let him vent to his heart's content. And while Markus monologued, Reese eased closer and closer until he was practically within arm's length of Yvette.

He saw the pistol against the back of her neck, jerking and sliding around as Markus raged. Terror tore through him that Markus's finger would slip and pull that trigger, ending the life of the woman he loved.

No more time to wait.

No, she mouthed.

Trust me, he mouthed back. Dammit, her life depended on her letting him help her in this moment. She had to let go. Just once in her life. Let him take care of her.

"Yvette, step to your right so I can take your place," he said easily.

"No!" Markus yelled.

Reese made eye contact with her, silently begging her not to question him. To trust him. To do exactly what he asked of her.

She nodded very faintly.

He said merely, "Drop."

Yvette relaxed all her leg muscles at once and let gravity take over. She plunged toward the ground, falling without warning. Time slowed as the tarmac rushed up at her, and all she could think was that with her body out of the way, Markus would have a clear shot at Reese.

A scream started in the back of her throat, and by the time her body slammed into the ground, it burst out of her in a piercing shriek.

A gunshot exploded above her head at extremely close range deafening her and vibrating through her almost as if it had hit her. Reese grunted in front of her, staggering back. A blackened hole in his white shirt, directly in the center of his chest told the tale. Markus Dexter had shot him at point-blank range.

"Nooo!" She screamed. Rolling to her hands and knees, she launched herself forward at Markus's knees as hard as she could spring.

She slammed into his legs, knocking him backward just as the pistol fired again. Markus fell backward hard, slamming down to the tarmac with her sprawled across his legs. She scrambled to push up, but something big flashed past her, moving fast.

Reese. He landed on top of Markus, both of his hands gripping Markus's wrist just below the butt of the pistol. The two men wrestled for control of the gun, and she rolled to one side to get out of Reese's way. On her knees, she looked for an opening to help, and when Markus rolled away from her with Reese still plastered to his front, she slammed her fist forward as hard as she could at the spot just over Markus's kidney.

He groaned, and she punched him again. He jerked his hands down and the pistol disappeared between Markus's and Reese's torsos. It exploded once more, this time the report of the gunshot muffled.

Both men collapsed with Markus on top of Reese.

"Nononononono…" She moaned as she lunged forward, grabbing at Markus's shoulder and yanking at him with all her strength. Reese couldn't be dead.

She'd just found him. He couldn't be dead.

They hadn't had enough time together. He couldn't be dead.

She wanted so much more with him. He couldn't be dead.

She would die without him. She was already dead…

Chapter 17

Pain.

As if someone was splitting his chest open.

Unable to breathe. Unable to speak. Unable to move.

And then there were hands. So many hands, lifting away the massive weight from his chest. Picking him up. Standing him on his feet. Tearing open his shirt.

A SWAT guy saying jovially, "Good thing you had a vest on, man. That bullet would have gone right through your heart. Reese looked down, and a flattened disk of lead was half embedded in his Kevlar vest.

"That must hurt like hell," the SWAT guy continued casually. "Close-range shot like that. You're lucky it wasn't any bigger caliber of pistol or a shot like that could've busted a few ribs. As it is, I'll bet you get a wicked bruise on your chest."

"Yeah. No doubt," he managed to gasp past the pain.

And then something new barreled into him, warm and soft and fierce.

Yvette.

"Hey, babe," he managed before she half choked him to death with her arms wrapped around his neck too tightly for him to breathe.

"A little air," he gasped.

Her arms loosened. But not much.

There was a flurry of activity as the SWAT guys climbed off Markus, handcuffed him and hauled him away, escorted by a bunch of armed police.

"Don't you ever scare me again like that," Yvette declared against the side of his neck.

He turned his head and captured her mouth with his. Ignoring the pain in his chest, he wrapped his arms around her and held her so tight he actually lifted her off the ground.

"I died when you told me to drop," she confessed. "You were going to sacrifice yourself for me."

"Yes, but I knew I was wearing a vest and you weren't."

"But what if he'd shot you in the head?"

"Yvie, Markus Dexter is a lot of things, but a good shot is not one of them. During one of his interviews with the district attorney, Fitz griped at length about what a crappy hunter Markus was and how he scared away all the wildlife because he was such a lousy shot."

"Still—"

He cut her off gently. "I'm fine."

"You are *not* fine! You just got shot and are going to be seriously bruised!"

He grinned down at her as he let her slide down his torso until her feet touched the ground. "Now you know how I feel when you tell me you're fine."

"All right. We're agreed that neither of us will ever be fine again, then?"

"Deal," he replied, laughing.

The next few days were a whirlwind of activity for Yvie. She had to give a statement to the police, a statement to the FBI and more statements than she could count to the press.

Markus was arrested and being held by federal authorities. After Mary testified that it was her husband's intent to flee the country, a judge declined to set bail for him, so he was cooling his heels in a prison cell in Kansas City.

He was forced to give a new DNA sample, and when confronted with the confirmed DNA evidence that Gwen Harrison was, in fact, his daughter, he finally confessed to having had an affair with Olivia Harrison.

Yvie was able to use Markus's own datebooks to show assignations with Olivia over the span of three years. He claimed that Olivia insisted on getting married, but that Mary wouldn't grant him a divorce.

Mary, no longer interested in protecting her husband, confirmed that Markus had, indeed, asked for a divorce right around the time Olivia Harrison was murdered.

As for Olivia's and Crane's bodies ending up hidden in walls, Yvette and Reese went through Dexter's files again and found orders for fake construction delays in Markus's own handwriting. Those delays would have emptied the job site and allowed him to sneak the bodies into the building and hide them in the walls.

When confronted all the evidence, Markus finally broke down and confessed to killing Olivia Harrison and hiding her body in the wall of the Colton warehouse.

Given that Fenton Crane's cause of death was identical to Olivia Harrison's, it wasn't difficult to get Markus to admit to killing the private investigator, too.

On top of all of that, Markus was formally charged with attempted murder in the shooting of Tyler Colton. Seemingly broken by the earlier confessions, he admitted to shooting Ty immediately when asked about it.

Practically the first chance Yvette had to be alone with Reese was when he picked her up in his truck two weeks after the kidnapping to drive to Kansas City, where they attended a touching memorial service for Olivia Harrison. Yvette's brother Brooks made a moving eulogy about Olivia and the wonderful daughter she'd given the world.

After the service, Yvette noticed Brooks having an earnest conversation with Gwen's grandmother, Rita. At the end of it, the two exchanged a warm hug. Yvette murmured to Reese, whose arm she hadn't let go of since they got out of his truck, "I'll bet Brooks just got approval to propose to Gwen from her grandmother."

"Good for him," Reese replied warmly. "I was annoyed with him when he kept butting into the murder investigation of Gwen's mother, but I get it now. The man was drowning in love and so dumb with it he couldn't help himself."

"Is that why you decided to take a bullet for me?" she asked tartly. "You were dumb in love?"

He grinned unrepentantly. "Guilty as charged."

No surprise, at the conclusion of the gathering, Brooks got down on one knee and proposed to Gwen—who tearfully and joyfully accepted. Everyone applauded, and it was a happy note to end a somber event on. Yvette was delighted for the two of them. After everything Gwen had been through, she'd surely earned a happy-ever-after. And Brooks couldn't quit beaming. She'd never seen her brother happier.

The congratulations and socializing wound down, and while Gwen and Brooks elected to spend the night at her grandmother's house to start the more joyful project of planning their wedding, the rest of the Colton clan headed back to Braxville for a family supper.

It would be their last time together for a while, since Jordana and Clint were about to head out for Chicago. Yvette sat back and enjoyed the noisy meal, letting the conversation flow around her full of laughter and warmth. This was the sound of family. And she loved it.

Reese reached under the table for her hand, and she smiled at him as their fingers twined together. He knew how much it meant to her to be part of all of this. He squeezed her hand, and the brand-new engagement ring on her left finger bit into her flesh. She was still getting used to it being there, but it wasn't coming off again for the rest of her life. They hadn't set a wedding date yet, but she was thinking about something small, maybe next summer.

Luke and Bridgette spent much of the meal picking Tyler's and Ashley's brains about the best places to eat and shop in Wichita, but near the end of supper, Bridgette called for everyone's attention. Yvette frowned slightly. Was her sister actually blushing?

Bridgette continued, "Luke and I have an announcement to make. You know when he had to go on that buying trip to Las Vegas a few weeks back? I, umm, went with him, and well, we got married while we were in Vegas."

Yvette squealed along with the other women at the table, and everyone congratulated them warmly.

Luke grinned, abashed, and said, "Now that your family knows we eloped, does this mean I can wear my wedding ring, now?"

Bridgette laughed. "Why? Are you getting tired of sweet old ladies throwing themselves at you?"

"Yes. Yes I am," he replied fervently.

"While we're making announcements," Neil piped up,

"Elise and I have a little news. We found out yesterday that we're expecting twins."

Yvette's face hurt from smiling so much, and she and Reese congratulated them warmly. Of course, being Coltons, the clan did razz Neil and Elise thoroughly over who was going to change the most diapers in their household.

Brooks asked from the other end of the table, "Any more announcements while we're at it?"

Lilly spoke up from the head of the table. "Umm, yes, actually."

Everyone fell silent and stared at her, startled that she, of all people, apparently had news.

Yvette was even more surprised when Uncle Shep got out of his seat at the foot of the table and walked down its length to stand beside her. But Yvette about fell out of her chair when Lilly reached up and took Shep's hand in hers and laid her cheek fondly on the back of his hand.

Lily said simply, "Shepherd and I are getting married."

Dead silence fell over the table.

Yvette stared in slowly dawning joy.

Reese was the first to break the shocked silence. "That's fantastic. Congratulations to both of you. Here's to many happy years. You both deserve it." He raised his beer glass in their direction.

There seemed to be a collective blink and deep breath around the table, and then everyone was talking at once, congratulating Shep and Lilly, and laughing in surprise… and not surprise.

There always had been a certain something between the two of them. Now that Yvette thought back over the years, Lilly had leaned on Shep many times when Fitz had let her down. The same way Yvette, herself, had.

Shep said quietly, "We have one more announcement to

make. By rights, we should do this in private first. But as I've come to learn, not much of anything stays private in this family for long. You all seem to operate on the theory of one for all and all for one. With that in mind, I'd like to ask all of you to give Yvette your unqualified support."

Yvette froze. Everyone was looking at her, glancing back and forth between her and Shep. Reese's hand tightened reassuringly around her fingers, and she was grateful for his silent comfort.

"What's up?" she croaked.

Lilly said quietly, "Honey, Shepherd and I have something to show you." She passed a folded piece of paper to Jordana on her left, who passed it to Clint, who passed it to her. Frowning, Yvette unfolded it.

It was a DNA test. A paternity match. She saw the heading on the sheet of paper. Paternity results for Yvette Elizabeth Colton.

What on earth?

She glanced farther down the sheet and stared. Her jaw fell open. She read the sheet again.

Tears filled her eyes as she shoved the sheet of paper blindly at Reese. She stumbled to her feet and headed toward her mother—

—and her father.

She flung her arms around Uncle Shep's waist and squeezed for all she was worth. "Is it true?" she asked against his chest. "Are you really my father?"

She vaguely heard a collective gasp behind her.

"Yes, sweetie, it is. I've suspected for years. But when you were in the hospital after the mugging, I asked your mother for permission to run a DNA test to prove it. Are you okay with this?"

"I'm more than okay with it!" she exclaimed. "I've always secretly wished you were my real daddy." In quick remorse, she looked down at her mother, whose face was streaked with tears. "I mean, Fitz wasn't an awful parent. It's just that whenever I really needed a father, Uncle Shep was always there for me."

"I know, darling," Lilly said through her tears. "He was always there for me when I needed him most, too. And now he's going to be part of the family, officially."

Lilly looked down the table at the other children. "I hope all of you can forgive me. But Shepherd and I felt that Yvette was owed the truth. Your father and I had a complicated marriage, and I was far from perfect, too. I hope you can be happy for Shepherd and me and that you won't hold this against Yvette. If you want to be angry, be angry at me."

Jordana was the closest to Lilly and leaped to her feet to wrap Lilly in a tight hug. "I love you, Mom. As long as you're happy, I'm happy for you."

The other children rushed forward, and before long, Yvette was smothered in a massive group hug that included a great deal of tears and laughing.

Eventually, she started to feel claustrophobic, and using her small stature to her advantage, wiggled free of the whole gang. Reese was standing right in front of her when she popped clear and he opened his arms in invitation.

Relieved, she stepped into the circle of safety and trust and let him wrap her up in his love.

"Are you okay?" he whispered against her temple.

"More than okay. I might even be that F-word."

"Just this once, I'm okay if you use it," he replied humorously.

She gazed up at him in adoration. Her life was truly complete, now, all the voids filled. She had the father she'd always dreamed of, and she had the man she'd always dreamed of. Her family was whole and happy. The Coltons had weathered the storm of the past year and come out stronger and happier than ever. Love had seen them all through crisis and disaster, fear and loss.

"Oh, Reese, I'm fine. Perfectly, wonderfully fine."

* * * * *

Be sure to read the other books in
The Coltons of Kansas series:

Exposing Colton Secrets *by Marie Ferrarella*
Colton's Amnesia Target *by Kimberly Van Meter*
Colton's Secret History *by Jennifer D. Bokal*
Colton Storm Warning *by Justine Davis*
Colton Christmas Conspiracy *by Lisa Childs*

Also don't miss other thrilling stories by Cindy Dees:

Navy SEAL's Deadly Secret
Special Forces: The Recruit
Special Forces: The Spy
Special Forces: The Operator
Her Mission with a SEAL
Navy SEAL Cop

Available at Harlequin Romantic Suspense!

#2119 COLTON 911: THE SECRET NETWORK
Colton 911: Chicago
by Marie Ferrarella

When a child is found at a crime scene, social worker January Colton's main goal is to protect the girl now in her care. Detective Sean Stafford is no stranger to protecting children, but he needs to know what she saw. As January and Sean work together to keep Maya safe, they find their opposite personalities create a spark they never expected.

#2120 COLTON'S DANGEROUS LIAISON
The Coltons of Grave Gulch
by Regan Black

Struggling to resolve a baffling betrayal within her department, police chief Melissa Colton must team up with Antonio Ruiz, a handsome hotel owner with a tragic past. Can she keep her heart protected in the process?

#2121 THE WIDOW'S BODYGUARD
by Karen Whiddon

Jesse Wyman is charged with protecting a high-profile widow from the men who killed her husband. He may have fallen in love with Eva Rowson while previously undercover in her father's motorcycle gang, and his secrets could ruin any chance they might have at a future.

#2122 HIGH-STAKES BOUNTY HUNTER
by Melinda Di Lorenzo

For six years, Elle Charger has managed to keep Katie away from the girl's father, but now the vicious man has caught up to them and has kidnapped Katie. Elle's only hope is Noah Loblaw, a bounty hunter who has his own haunted history.

"Get down," he shouted. "It's a drone."

Eva had seen enough movies to know what drones could do. Jumping aside, she dropped to the floor and crawled toward the door, glad of her dark room. If the thing was armed, she wanted to make herself the smallest target possible. Luckily, her window was closed. She figured if it crashed into the glass, the drone would come apart.

By the time she reached her closed bedroom door, the thing hovered right outside her window, its bright light illuminating most of her room. She dived for the door just as the drone tapped against the glass, lightly and precisely enough to tell her whoever controlled it was very good at the job.

She'd just turned the knob when the drone exploded, blowing out her window and sending shards of glass like deadly weapons into her room.

"Eva!" Jesse's voice, yelling out her name. She focused on that, despite the stabbing pain in her leg. Somehow, she managed to pull the door open and half fell into the hallway, one hand against her leg.

Heart pounding, she scrambled away from her doorway, dimly registering the trail of blood she left in her wake.

"Are you all right?" Reaching her, Jesse scooped her up in his muscular arms and hauled her farther down the hall. Outside, she could hear men yelling. One of the voices sounded like her father's.

"Is everyone else okay?" she asked, concerned.

"As far as I know," Jesse answered. "Though I haven't been outside yet to assess the situation. What happened?"

"It was a drone rigged with explosives." Briefly she closed her eyes. When she reopened them, she found his face mere inches from hers. "Someone aimed it right at my window."

Fury warred with concern in his dark eyes. He focused intently on her. "There's a lot of blood. Where are you hurt?"

Hurt. Odd how being with him made everything else fade into insignificance. In his arms, she finally felt safe.

Don't miss
The Widow's Bodyguard
by Karen Whiddon, available January 2021
wherever Harlequin Romantic Suspense books
and ebooks are sold.

Harlequin.com

Get 4 FREE REWARDS!

We'll send you 2 FREE Books plus 2 FREE Mystery Gifts.

Harlequin Romantic Suspense books are heart-racing page-turners with unexpected plot twists and irresistible chemistry that will keep you guessing to the very end.

FREE Value Over $20

YES! Please send me 2 FREE Harlequin Romantic Suspense novels and my 2 FREE gifts (gifts are worth about $10 retail). After receiving them, if I don't wish to receive any more books, I can return the shipping statement marked "cancel." If I don't cancel, I will receive 4 brand-new novels every month and be billed just $4.99 per book in the U.S. or $5.74 per book in Canada. That's a savings of at least 13% off the cover price! It's quite a bargain! Shipping and handling is just 50¢ per book in the U.S. and $1.25 per book in Canada.* I understand that accepting the 2 free books and gifts places me under no obligation to buy anything. I can always return a shipment and cancel at any time. The free books and gifts are mine to keep no matter what I decide.

240/340 HDN GNMZ

Name (please print)

Address   Apt. #

City   State/Province   Zip/Postal Code

Email: Please check this box ☐ if you would like to receive newsletters and promotional emails from Harlequin Enterprises ULC and its affiliates. You can unsubscribe anytime.

Mail to the Reader Service:
IN U.S.A.: P.O. Box 1341, Buffalo, NY 14240-8531
IN CANADA: P.O. Box 603, Fort Erie, Ontario L2A 5X3

Want to try 2 free books from another series! Call 1-800-873-8635 or visit www.ReaderService.com.

---

*Terms and prices subject to change without notice. Prices do not include sales taxes, which will be charged (if applicable) based on your state or country of residence. Canadian residents will be charged applicable taxes. Offer not valid in Quebec. This offer is limited to one order per household. Books received may not be as shown. Not valid for current subscribers to Harlequin Romantic Suspense books. All orders subject to approval. Credit or debit balances in a customer's account(s) may be offset by any other outstanding balance owed by or to the customer. Please allow 4 to 6 weeks for delivery. Offer available while quantities last.

Your Privacy—Your information is being collected by Harlequin Enterprises ULC, operating as Reader Service. For a complete summary of the information we collect, how we use this information and to whom it is disclosed, please visit our privacy notice located at corporate.harlequin.com/privacy-notice. From time to time we may also exchange your personal information with reputable third parties. If you wish to opt out of this sharing of your personal information, please visit readerservice.com/consumerschoice or call 1-800-873-8635. **Notice to California Residents**—Under California law, you have specific rights to control and access your data. For more information on these rights and how to exercise them, visit corporate.harlequin.com/california-privacy.

HRS20R2

Love Harlequin romance?

DISCOVER.

Be the first to find out about promotions, news and exclusive content!

 Facebook.com/HarlequinBooks

 Twitter.com/HarlequinBooks

 Instagram.com/HarlequinBooks

 Pinterest.com/HarlequinBooks

ReaderService.com

EXPLORE.

Sign up for the Harlequin e-newsletter and download a free book from any series at **TryHarlequin.com**

CONNECT.

Join our Harlequin community to share your thoughts and connect with other romance readers!
Facebook.com/groups/HarlequinConnection